BOOKS BY
ALEX TEMBLADOR

NOVELS
Secrets of the Casa Rosada
Half Outlaw

ANTHOLOGIES
Living beyond Borders: Growing Up Mexican in America
Speculative Fiction for Dreamers: A Latinx Anthology

ALEX TEMBLADOR

**BLACK
STONE**
PUBLISHING

Printed in the United States of America

First edition: 2022
ISBN 978-1-7999-3210-9
Fiction / Women

Version 1

CIP data for this book is available
from the Library of Congress

Blackstone Publishing
31 Mistletoe Rd.
Ashland, OR 97520

www.BlackstonePublishing.com

For Mixed kids . . . This story is for you.

1

The shiny black-and-silver motorcycle growled at me. It guarded the front porch of a trailer home floating in a sea of knee-high yellow grass. Ms. Cook pulled on my hand to hurry as she walked up the front steps. She didn't hear the small growl that came from the beast's belly right before it lunged at me and tried to bite off my leg. I scrambled up the steps and away from its steely jaws.

Ms. Cook knocked on the door, looked down at me, and squeezed my hand. "Your uncle will be so happy to see you." Her palm was sweaty, and she smelled too strongly of peppermint. Behind us, the motorcycle continued to growl, but I was too scared to look. I scooted closer to Ms. Cook.

A skinny white man with black hair and a bushy black beard answered the door. He wore a black sleeveless top with arm holes that were rough around the edges and blue jeans that had a mustard stain on the right leg. The smell of acrid smoke and sweat floated off him in waves. His lips pulled back in a slight grimace revealing yellow teeth. He didn't seem happy to see me at all.

"What?" His voice was gruffy and when he spoke spit flew from his lip toward Ms. Cook. She winced. I stepped back, pulling Ms. Cook's hand in mine. This couldn't be Mama's brother. He didn't look like her, didn't smile like her. Ms. Cook tsked me and turned back to the man.

"Hello, Mr. Warren. I'm Ms. Cook with the State of Texas Department of Child Services, and I—"

"This her?" His black eyes bore into mine with complete disappointment. I stepped back again. This time, Ms. Cook jerked me forward and I stumbled.

Cheerily, she replied, "Yes, this is Raquel. Raquel, say hi to your Uncle Dodge."

I swallowed, my throat dry. I didn't open my mouth and I didn't say hi. Dodge and I stared at each other until finally, he turned around and walked into the house, leaving the door open. Ms. Cook hesitated then pulled me in, feet dragging and all.

My uncle's home had brown shaggy carpet and wood-paneled walls. The room was sparsely furnished with a couch, coffee table, and a small square TV with knobs that sat on the floor. A chair with a leather jacket haphazardly thrown upon it stood next to the door. On the wall to our left was a tattered American flag that hung limply by tacks. Beside it was a black flag with words I didn't understand lining the top and bottom. Between the words was a motorcycle, with a skull in its center. A tongue whipped out of the skull's mouth, tasting my fear.

Ms. Cook sat down on the brown couch and pulled out a stack of papers from her leather bag. I stood next to her, while my uncle sat a foot away. He placed his elbows on his splayed-out knees. The couch wasn't like the one in my home—my old home. That one was gray with tiny pink lines stitched into it; this one was brown with dark-stained blotches. As I stared at the stains, they expanded and reached for one another with tiny blotchy arms, attempting to unite and take over all the clean spots. Ms. Cook must have noticed the stains too because she sat lightly on the edge of the couch and kept looking at the bottom of her purple dress.

Dodge watched me as Ms. Cook sputtered on. He only looked away to sign something, and occasionally grunted in acknowledgment. This close, his stench mixed with the beer and used cigarettes on the coffee table. Out of the corner of my eye, I watched charred cigarette butts crawl across the glass top like squirmy white maggots in search of food. They had to move around shot glasses with droplets of foul drink, two loose bullets, tiny gold and silver pins with logos, and patches with colorful embroidered symbols.

"How old are you?" Dodge asked me. I couldn't stop staring at his hands, which opened and closed one of the blades of a Swiss Army knife. A grimy and greasy substance blackened his knuckles to his fingernails.

When I didn't answer, Ms. Cook said, "She's four." She handed Dodge another stack of paperwork and said, "These forms officially change Raquel's last name from Gonzalez to Warren." Dodge signed my name away as indifferently as he had every other piece of paper.

At one point in the process, Dodge interrupted Ms. Cook to say, "You sure that's Jean's daughter?"

I became still, but Ms. Cook's mouth opened wide in surprise and her hands flew to her face and then back to her lap. "Sir, I assure you, Raquel is your niece. I mean—I can't—" Her voice had reached high-pitch levels.

Dodge stared at me harder, his eyes wrinkling along the edges. "She don't look like my sister."

This upset Ms. Cook even more. "Sir, I'm sure you are aware that your sister was married to a,"—her voice lowered to a whisper—"a Mexican."

Dodge growled low in disgust and stared at me for a second longer. I pursed my lips together and looked away, unable to hold his gaze. He put the Swiss Army knife in his pocket and pulled out a cigarette and a lighter. He lit the cigarette, inhaled, then blew the smoke out without pulling the cigarette from his lips. Ms. Cook waved the fumes away.

"Sir, I'm allergic to smoke—"

"This is my house," he said. "You got any other goddamn papers to sign or are we done?" Like with the Swiss Army knife, he opened and closed the silver top of the rectangular lighter repeatedly. The clicks echoed in the quiet room. Ms. Cook frowned and looked at me sideways and then back at Dodge.

I'd once heard Dad cuss. He'd been chopping a carrot and accidentally cut his finger. As soon as he said the bad word, he turned to me and told me never to repeat it or I'd be in trouble. No one told me not to repeat Dodge's bad word.

Ms. Cook gathered her papers and walked to the front door. I followed her and grabbed the side of her purple dress, which didn't slow her down. Once she reached the door, she stopped and lowered herself to my eye level, patting my shoulder two times.

"Raquel, you are going to have a great life here in Escondido with your uncle. It's so close to Hollywood—isn't that something?"

I think she wanted me to say yes or smile, but I couldn't. I tried to make my eyes communicate what I couldn't say in front of my uncle and hoped she would understand.

Her smile faltered, and she patted me once more on the shoulder. "I must go now. Bye-bye."

I shook my head and whispered, "Don't leave me." I grabbed for her collar, but she averted her eyes and quickly stood up, so my hand grasped at air. I watched Ms. Cook as she got into her small, white car and drove away, never once looking back.

"Close the damn door. You're letting in the heat," my uncle said behind me.

I closed the door slowly, hoping that at any minute she would return. Every ounce of heat followed Ms. Cook out the door, so when I shut it, I saw my breath crystallize in the air before dropping to the ground and breaking apart in tiny little pieces. I turned slowly and leaned my back against the door, shivering slightly in my tank top and shorts. Dodge and I resumed our staring match as he finished his cigarette. Eventually, he put the butt out on the coffee table, before throwing it among the graveyard of used cigarettes that wiggled and welcomed a new friend.

"You sure you're Jean's daughter?"

I nodded.

"You don't speak? Or do you only speak Mexican?"

I looked down. "Yeah." It didn't exactly answer his question, but it seemed good enough for Dodge.

"What kind of name is Raquel?"

I shrugged. No one called me Raquel. Mama and Dad called me Raqi. It sounded like 'rocky' but was spelled differently. I didn't want to tell him that.

He shook his head as he stood up. "Don't make me regret this." He walked into a room down the hall and closed the door.

As soon as the door shut, the shivers consumed my body. I sat down, curled my arms around my legs, and put my head on my knees hoping to keep out the icy air that wanted to get inside me. I hugged myself as tight as I could because I didn't think that Mama's brother would ever do that for me.

2

I dreamed about the Red River, just north of Wichita Falls, Texas. The muddy brown water with a slight red tinge separated Texas and Oklahoma like a mother holding her two children apart.

In the dream, my mother and I sat on a picnic blanket on the shore of the river. Her pale skin burned bright red from a sunburn. It contrasted with her yellow bikini. My father wore a black hat and swim trunks. Unlike his wife, his tan skin darkened under the Texas sun.

My mother pointed to the middle of the river and said, "Tom, go get that for me."

My father replied, "Okay, Jean," and walked into the fast-moving current.

I barely remembered our time at the river, hardly remembered my parents at all, but I knew this wasn't what had happened that day. I wanted to cry out for my father to stop, but I couldn't. Nothing would come out. He walked farther into the river until finally, the dirty red water covered his head and he disappeared. My mother stood up and said, "Raquel, I'm going to help your father," and then followed him in.

Panic built in my chest as I stood up and took a few steps forward. The muddy water nearly covered the top of my mother's sandy blond hair when I caught a whiff of cigarette smoke. It pulled my attention.

That smell . . . it didn't belong here. I looked behind me at the scraggly Mesquite trees surrounded by brush. I was alone. Turning back to the Red River, I realized my mother had disappeared without a witness.

The shrill sound of the phone ringing woke me from my sleep.

"Hello?" Trevor had picked up the phone.

I put the pillow over my head, pissed off at being woken up in the middle of the night. I hated when anything interrupted my sleep—sex included.

"Raqi, it's for you."

I groaned into the mattress. Not another legal emergency. I moved the pillow beneath my head, catching my long brown hair for one second before I yanked it out, then grabbed the phone from him. Trevor fell back onto his pillow and rubbed his eyes, pushing the curled cord away from his face but to no avail.

"What?" I said sharply into the receiver.

"It's me," a deep, scratchy voice said.

I now wished for a legal emergency, any other emergency beyond the one Billy was about to lay on me.

"Billy, I already told you I'm not doing shit for you anymore. Whoever he is, he can rot in jail for all I care—"

"You'll do whatever the fuck—" Billy snapped.

"The hell I will—"

"Raqi, shut up. I'm calling about something else."

Billy only called to have me bail out one of his Lawless. I couldn't do it anymore. People were beginning to label me as *that lawyer* with *those criminals.* I didn't put in so many years of hard work to be associated with the drug-dealing motorcycle club I had tried so hard to escape. The one thing I'd kept from my time with them was my foul mouth— but that fit right in with the cutthroat world of Los Angeles law. That and my tattoo . . . But I had plans to get rid of it soon.

There was only one other reason Billy might call.

"I won't do shit for Dodge either," I said.

"You won't have to."

"Meaning?"

"He's dead."

I had expected this call, in fact, years ago. Heroin, meth, coke—name it, he did it all.

"Drugs?" I asked.

"Heart attack."

Surprising . . . though drugs could cause heart attacks, too.

"So, you're calling me because . . . ?"

"We ride out on Friday. Meet me and the club at Dodge's that morning."

"You're a dumb son of a bitch if you think—"

"Goddamn it, Raqi!" Billy yelled. I pulled the phone away, my ear ringing with the volume of his voice. A crash echoed in the background. He'd probably kicked a chair.

"Be there at nine in the morning, or goddamn it, I'll drive up to that gated community of rich slickers, kick your little Black boy's ass, and drag you on this ride. Do you hear me?"

I squeezed the plastic phone, itching to slam it against the bed frame. "Racist asshole," I muttered.

Trevor sat up in bed and mouthed, "What's going on?" I was sure he'd heard Billy. My stomach clenched in embarrassment.

I gave my head a hard shake. He tried to touch my arm, but I jerked away. Trevor knew better than to try it again, so he crossed his sinewy arms and laid back on the bed. If he interrogated me after, he'd lose. He wasn't half as ruthless of a lawyer as I was.

"You can't bully me into coming," I told Billy through gritted teeth.

"No, but I'll give you something you want if you do."

What did he have? My mind raced, and I stopped breathing. Billy waited, drawing out the silence like a long, stringy piece of cheese that stretched between a bite of pizza and its slice.

Finally, he said, "Go on this ride and I'll give you an address."

What was Billy talking about? "Whose address?"

"Your grandfather's."

Another punch. "Which—?"

"Your dad's."

My hand gripped the receiver so tightly I could hear the strain of the plastic trying to stay together. My grandfather. My Mexican grandfather. I had no idea he was alive. I thought Dodge was the only family I had left after my parents died in a car crash. I'd always believed that if there was anyone else, *anyone*, I would have been sent to them and not Dodge. How did Billy get this information?

"Well?" Billy asked.

As I thought about his offer, the spiral cord of the phone wrapped around my neck and squeezed slowly, leaving behind deep impressions of rubbery waves. The world had played a horrible trick giving a little brown girl to a racist white man with a substance abuse problem. Now, Billy was telling me that there was someone else, someone from my Mexican side, my dad's side, someone who might look like me, might even be a decent human being. It became harder and harder to breathe as the cord cut off my breathing supply. I couldn't say no to this offer, or else I'd suffocate.

"Fine," I choked out, loosening my grip on the phone as the cord loosened its grip on me. "If I go, you give me the address *and* I'm out for good. No more legal assistance for you or the Lawless, no more calls. No contact—ever."

Billy remained silent. I held my breath.

"Deal," he said.

I inhaled deeply, not quite believing it had worked.

"Friday then, and don't forget to cut your hair," he added.

"I'm not cutting my hair. That's a ridiculous tradition."

"That's your uncle and you'll do it, damn it," Billy replied.

My body had started to relax into the mattress, craving to go back to sleep, and yet my mind reeled with this news. "Whatever," I said, hoping that would be enough to get him off the phone.

Billy sighed heavily, and the smell of the three glasses of whiskey he had consumed wafted through the phone. Dodge's passing weighed hard on his black soul.

"They'll be glad to see you," Billy said.

"I bet they'll throw me a ball."

"Fuck you," he said, then hung up.

I gave the phone to Trevor, and he placed it on the receiver.

"The Lawless?" he asked.

"No, it was bloody fucking Christ." I turned away and onto my side, glancing at the tattoo on my upper arm. The one I tried so hard to hide. The one where tiny droplets of blood now rose from the faded black Gothic lettering, fresh ink to darken it after years of neglect. It wanted to look its best when it returned home.

Trevor wrapped his arms around me, cupping my left breast. He pulled me close to nibble on my ear. I pulled away and closed my eyes. Neither of us moved for a few seconds, but then I felt his arms squeeze me a little tighter. He kissed my neck and whispered, "I love you." Although I was annoyed and frustrated by Billy's call, Trevor's kisses felt good.

What the hell? I was already wide-the-fuck-awake.

3

"Raquel, remember when you said, 'I'm only half outlaw?'" Dodge's face lay plastered to the toilet which lacked a seat. "Remember, Raquel? Because you're half Mexican?" His slurred speech came out like "Messy-can." He wore only underwear and from the smell of it, he'd pissed himself at some point.

"Raqi?"

I might have responded except he passed out on the toilet just then. I hit the door frame with the side of my fist.

"Fuck." I hit the door again, the sound echoing in the sea green–tiled bathroom.

"Are you kidding me, Dodge?" I said to his seemingly lifeless form.

I kicked the sink with the toe of my boot. Something rattled inside then fell hundreds of feet down the long line of piping. I hadn't been home from college in three months and the place looked worse than ever. Bits of trash crawled across the living room leaving behind trails of rotting stink. Mountain ranges of clothes covered in a soft layer of white dust spread across the house and tripped me when I walked. Dark mold-like substances plagued the counters and infected the white grout of the tiled floor. My room seemed to be the only place untouched by the apocalyptic madness of dirt and filth.

I turned around and placed my back against the wall, sliding down until my butt hit the floor. I kept my knees pulled in tight and ran my hands through my long hair. I didn't want to deal with this again, couldn't deal with his shit anymore. Fifteen years of drugs and alcohol and filth and bullying. The real world wasn't like this.

"Why?" I yelled, knowing Dodge wouldn't respond. He'd probably be out of it for an hour, but I needed to say something. I hadn't said anything before. "You asshole. Why would you go cold turkey again? You're not fooling me. I'm not like your dumb hoes."

I scream-grunted and tightened my fists for a few seconds. All I wanted was to come home for break and go on a ride with the club. This motherfucker thought he could stop using, get better before I returned home, and then everything would be right as fucking rain.

"You fucking dumbass!" I screamed at him.

Even though my breath came out in fast puffs of steam and blood pounded in my ears, I swore I heard him reply. My body stilled and I leaned toward him and whispered, "What did you say?"

Dodge moved his face so that his left cheek rested on the toilet and his bloodshot eyes met mine. "Bitch, don't you fucking talk to me like that."

"Bitch?" I stood up quickly. "I'm not a bitch, you motherfucking addict!"

Suddenly, with the speed and strength he shouldn't have had, Dodge stood up and ran toward me. I couldn't get to the door in time. His hand grabbed my throat and squeezed. The blood vessels in his eyes burst at once, drowning the white around his pupils in a fiery red.

"You don't talk to me like that. Get out, Mexican bitch!" he yelled and pushed me by my throat to the doorway. I grabbed at his arm as black-and-blue spots sprinkled across my vision. With one more shove, he released my neck and slammed the door in my face.

"Thankless, worthless whore!" he screamed, banging a few times for emphasis. I bent over, holding my neck, gasping for air. Dodge had never hurt me like that. Swats, shoves, pinches, and the occasional grabbing of my collar or hair, but he'd never choked me before. I felt tears coming to my eyes, but like always, I clenched my jaw and halted them in their tracks.

He quieted, and I heard him slide to the ground. I stood up and put my ear to the door, but there was no sound. Maybe he had passed out again. I waited two more seconds, then turned and went to my room. I grabbed my bag from the bed and walked to the front door. When my hand touched the knob, I paused, then touched my neck.

Fuck him.

I put my bag down and went to work. Dodge kept all of Billy's drugs he needed to sell in his house. I rounded them up. Under the couch cushions—LSD. In the freezer—heroin. His nightstand—marijuana. His shoe—Quaaludes. I tore apart the house until I had a small pile that I threw in a trash bag.

It was dark outside, but I didn't need to see. I went to the back, past the garage, and to the charred spot in the clearing next to the trees. With a match, I lit the bag and watched as the fire grew and licked up pills with a forked tongue. The fire pushed its muzzle into the bag in search of other drugs like a dog mad with hunger for something it was never meant to taste. As it twisted its red-and-orange body in search of more delicious finds, it occasionally coughed sparks that jumped beyond the bag in search of something else to consume.

I smoked a cigarette and watched the fire digest the bag into a black ooze that seeped into the charred ground. Billy would flip his shit and Dodge would pay. When the fire died down, I threw dirt on the melted bag to prevent the flames from rising again.

I went to the garage for my bike. Dodge had convinced me to leave it the last time I'd been home to do some maintenance and add some rad custom pieces Ross had created at the auto shop that Dodge occasionally worked at.

Although it had hurt to part with my bike, without it, I'd had my first taste of normalcy. No one called me "that biker girl" or made jokes about my sexuality. I didn't have to deal with dickheads who thought they knew more about bikes than I did. Without the bike, I felt separate from the club. Sure, they were family, but I'd begun to grow tired of the drugs and violence over the years and wanted to be normal . . . free of it all.

When I pushed open the door to the garage, I saw my Ironhead uncovered. The seat looked wrong and jiggled a bit when I touched it. I grabbed a screwdriver from the wall and unscrewed the seat. When I turned it over, I paused. There. A small opening in the side of the leather cover. I ripped the seam open with the screwdriver and stuck my hand in and dug around.

I froze when I felt plastic and the outline of a small round pill. Drugs . . . in my bike, the one Dodge and I had spent weeks building together. Had he been using my bike to move drugs? Had he broken our one unspoken rule that my bike was separate from that world?

Hot sweat appeared on the back of my neck, and something rose inside of me that I had held in for so long. I slowly pulled my hand out of the seat and stood still for two beats. I flung the seat across the shed, where it barely missed Dodge's two bikes before hitting the wall and clattering to the floor.

Grabbing a tire iron from the wall, I destroyed the precious bike that Dodge and I had built together. I felt the blow to the handlebars fracture my forearms and every hit to the wheels break the bones in my legs. The force of the tire iron against the main frame ripped my ribs away and ruptured the organs they were meant to protect. By the time I was done, the bike was nothing more than scrap metal, and I was left in pieces.

4

The next morning, Trevor asked what Billy had wanted.

I took a long sip of my coffee before answering. "Dodge died." Trevor had been standing at the counter reading the newspaper, but he paused and looked up at me, struggling to keep his face together. If I was a normal person, he'd have run over to give me a hug. But I wasn't touchy-feely. Plus, he knew my feelings about Dodge well enough to know that I wasn't exactly sad about the news.

"Drugs?" he asked.

I sipped more coffee. "Heart attack, apparently."

Trevor snorted. He was thinking what I had been thinking—the drugs had caused a heart attack. I liked that Trevor and I thought similarly. It was one of the things that had drawn me to him.

This morning, Trevor wore his tailored gray suit which fit his lean frame perfectly. His hair was clipped short, and he was freshly shaven. Trevor had to look his best, be the smartest, work the hardest, because he was an African American lawyer, and no matter how liberal Los Angeles was becoming, there were still people that would not believe he was as smart or capable as his white colleagues. Though our experiences were different, Trevor and I could relate in some ways. There were still too few women of color with successful careers in law. Those of us who made it had to scrape and claw our way through the male-dominated

spaces of law school, firms, and courts. We had the broken nails and
scarred arms to prove it.

"Funeral?" Trevor asked.

"Sort of." I didn't like to have large conversations in the morning and
Trevor knew that. His head cocked to the side in question, but I chose
not to answer. I didn't have the strength or the mental aptitude to explain
Billy's offer. It was too early, and I hadn't had time to process it myself.

Trevor had a thirty-minute commute, forty with traffic, and mine
was ten. Before he left, he said, "Don't forget. Dinner at seven." Right.
Dinner with one of his bosses and his wife. Trevor and I had to go to
dinners like this often. It was hard enough for any lawyer to make partner, but harder if you weren't a rich WASP—hence the schmoozefest
dinner. I'd made partner but Trevor hadn't, despite how much work and
time he'd put into his firm and how many wins he'd gotten in court.
Trevor suspected it was because he was Black, and I couldn't argue. He
didn't work at the most liberal law firm. The firm's clients were mostly
Orange County residents, conservative types who voted for George H.
W. Bush in the last election and upon meeting Trevor, assumed he was
a paralegal or an assistant and asked him for a coffee. I told Trevor to
find another firm, but he was as determined as I was to break through
any resistance just to prove he was as good as anyone else.

I don't like social gatherings, but dinners like this were important.
Trevor and I backed each other up when it came to our jobs. I may not
want to grab a drink with the neighbors or visit his family for Christmas, but I'd help Trevor make partner.

I nodded once and Trevor replied with a slight grin. He put his
coffee cup in the dishwasher.

"Love you."

I raised my coffee mug in reply. We'd already talked too much for
my comfort this morning.

I stood in the kitchen alone thinking. I didn't want to go on a
Grieving Ride, especially not for Dodge. A Grieving Ride was a Lawless
tradition. When a member died, their specific chapter conducted a ride to
take the member's ashes to his final resting place. Lawless weren't allowed

to be buried. *For you are dust and to dust shall return.* Non-churchgoing Billy always quoted that saying.

What did Dodge want? A simple ride or some inconvenient, elaborate trip? I thought when Dodge died, Billy wouldn't have any hold on me, but I'd been wrong. He'd been holding my grandfather in his hands like it was his winning card, and I guess it was because I'd agreed.

My grandfather. I took another sip of my coffee, which was starting to get cold. My dad's dad. How surreal. I thought I'd been alone all this time—sans Dodge—but now, I had family. Brown family. I knew my dad was from Mexico and had moved to the US as a young adult. Was my grandfather's address in Mexico?

I'd never had a chance to learn about that side of my family. Heck, I didn't even know much about my mom's side. Dodge wasn't exactly the sharing type. How old was my grandfather? Where was my grandmother? I tried to imagine my grandfather by imagining my dad's face, which was futile since I didn't have any photographs of my dad and my memories of him weren't complete. Sometimes it was his laugh, or a silly dance he did, or the black hair on his neck that he'd missed while shaving.

I placed my coffee mug in the sink and grabbed my briefcase. I couldn't stand here thinking about this all day. There was work to do.

My assistant Lisa greeted me with a coffee and a doughnut at the front door of the firm.

"Busy day, Raq."

I took a bite of the doughnut and relished the sweet sugar coating. Dental visits twice a year made me feel less guilty about my sweet tooth.

Lisa had already started going over the day's plan. Court in an hour, briefs, meetings, phone calls. She kept everything factual, brief, and to the point. She was the best goddamn assistant I could find, and as the only two women in the firm, and the only two people who weren't white—Lisa was Black—I was thankful she was there.

Lisa was going to night school to be a lawyer so I did everything

I could to ensure her work during the day didn't affect her studies at night. I'd be damned if she wouldn't have a spot in the firm when she passed the bar exam in a few months.

I pulled off a chunk of the doughnut and handed it to her. She grabbed it, plopped it in her mouth, and kept talking. Lisa would only take one bite, even though I was willing to buy her a billion doughnuts or whatever else she wanted to show her my ever-growing gratitude. Like most days, she had her hair relaxed and her bangs swooped to the side. She always wore neutral colors, and today that presented itself in a black skirt that reached her knees, black tights, black pumps, and a white blouse. Her gold earrings were the only hint of color in her ensemble.

Lisa was one of the few people I could call my friend. Our friendship grew from many late nights at the firm going over cases with cheap wine and takeout. We occasionally grabbed drinks together at bars, did step aerobics Tuesday and Friday mornings, and I let her drag me to a Paula Abdul concert last year, even though I'm not a fan of pop music. I didn't like most people, but I liked Lisa. I could be myself around her.

When we arrived at my office, she asked, "Anything else you want to go over?"

I paused, opened my mouth, then closed it.

"What?" she asked.

"Tomorrow . . ." I drew out the word.

One of Lisa's perfectly manicured eyebrows rose. She placed my calendar on her desk. "You have a meeting with the Brown family tomorrow. They want him out on bail."

"We both know that judge isn't going to go lower than a million. I've told them that." I sighed. "I have to go out of town."

Lisa's eyebrow threatened to touch her hairline. I placed my briefcase on the desk and sat down.

"Vacation? You never take off."

I groaned. "Not vacation. My—" I ran my hands through my hair to calm myself. "My uncle died. It's a funeral thing."

Lisa's forehead scrunched and her lip snarled a bit. "Don't we hate him?"

God, I loved her.

"We do." I chuckled. "But—I do this and it's over. No more Lawless, no more representing them in court."

She crossed her arms and looked out my window for a second and then back at me. "That's a good enough reason to me, but David isn't going to like it."

"I know." I moved some papers around on my desk, looking for the file I was going to have to take into court in forty-five minutes. "Maybe no more pro bono Lawless M. C. cases will make him happy enough?"

Lisa held out the file I was looking for.

"Thanks," I said before grabbing it.

"You're about to tell him now and then run off to court, aren't you?"

I smirked. "Now, that's not something a responsible partner would do, is it?" She laughed.

I was about to walk out the door when she asked, "Move everything back a day then? You'll be back on Monday?"

"No later than Sunday." Dodge wasn't the sentimental type. If I knew him, and I did, his Grieving Ride would involve getting drunk at some bar in the middle of nowhere and scattering his ashes on the side of the road.

I added, "Be sure to reschedule that tattoo removal appointment too." I glanced at my arm. I'd soon be free of Dodge and everything he left behind.

David, my main partner at the firm, was not happy. He threw a cigarette butt into the ash tray on his desk just as his face turned red and he sputtered, unable to form words. For a man who was never thrown off balance in court, he always seemed a little unsure outside of it. When he finally got his tongue in check, he berated me about the Brown case, four other cases, and my responsibilities, until I interrupted him.

"David!"

He stopped talking, but his mouth formed a thin line and the vein in his forehead pulsed incessantly.

"It's happening. As your partner, I will not let this ruin our firm, and when I return on Sunday—"

David said, "At the latest—"

"—I'll be done with the Lawless for good and we'll continue on our road of success."

He huffed a few times and lit another cigarette to calm down. At forty-three years old, David's stress levels threatened to put him in the ground from a heart attack. That wouldn't make his wife and two kids happy.

"Fine. Get Smith and Clay to cover your cases until you return."

I smiled.

"They better not fuck up this Brown case," he said.

I slapped the folder onto his desk. "Or we'll have their asses."

He nodded hard and lightly tapped his cigarette on the rim of his ash tray. I left for court to argue with someone else.

My hour in court went well. I shot down the DA's argument with some stellar evidence that Lisa and I had gathered on behalf of my client. The rest of the day was full of meetings, two bites of a sandwich for lunch, calls with a few clients, and an hour and a half call with the Browns, assuring them that Clay and Smith would get their son's bond down to $800,000. That was as low as the judge would go. I knew because I'd called him earlier trying to butter him up before Clay and Smith talked to him in court the next day. The judge couldn't give me a definite answer, but it seemed promising.

By the time I made it home after work, Trevor was already dressed, and I had thirty minutes to rinse off and change into a more relaxed power suit. I did not wear dresses no matter how much Trevor begged. There wasn't enough time to wash my hair, so I pulled it back into a low ponytail. I looked posh in the mirror with a fresh layer of makeup. I twisted the ends of my ponytail in my fingers.

Billy wanted my long hair gone tomorrow. It was another one of his weird traditions. He made the entire chapter and the deceased's direct family members cut their hair when a member died as a symbol of mourning. I didn't think I could do it, especially not for Dodge.

I let go of my ponytail, adjusted the collar on my suit, and looked myself over in the mirror one last time. The suit was high-end and the white button-up I wore underneath it hid my full breasts. Diamond earrings graced my ears, and my makeup was light, not too packed on. I didn't need much. My skin had always been an even tone of golden brown and combined with my small round nose, almond eyes, and big lips, I looked twenty-one, not thirty-one.

After my once-over, I stared into the eyes of my reflection. It was unnerving to see the gold flakes in the brown ring that surrounded her black pupil, but I didn't want to look away. She was telling me something. Her eyes flickered to my ponytail for just one second. I understood her now.

Her lips moved, releasing the faint smell of stale smoke, telling me to accept the decision I'd already made.

5

Two days after Ms. Cook and the State of Texas dropped me off with Dodge, he took me to a Lawless barbecue. We drove there in his white pickup truck that lacked seat belts and had rusted polka dots on the exterior. The leather booth had faded long ago and was torn around the seams. With each bump in the road, I sank farther into the seat where the metal coils poked me in fun. Dodge drank a beer as he drove. He smelled sour and hadn't been nice to me so far. I sat as far away from him as I could.

When we parked, Dodge opened his door and hopped out, but I didn't move. I didn't want to get out, didn't want to be around people I didn't know. At four, I was old enough to know that I no longer lived in Texas, my parents were dead, and I lived with a strange man who wasn't fond of how I looked or even glad that I existed. I couldn't imagine the people we were meeting would make that better.

Dodge turned back and looked at me. "Get out. I ain't going to wait on you all day."

With a pit in my stomach, I opened the door and jumped down. I followed Dodge past the gray trailer home to the backyard, dragging my feet in the knee-high yellow grass that scratched me from the top of my thighs to my ankles, leaving behind long scrapes. Big motorcycles and old trucks like the one Dodge drove filled the front yard. They leaned toward me menacingly, baring their grills and bucking at me once or twice so that I picked up my feet and walked faster.

We rounded the corner to the sight of a crowd of burly men with round paunches, emaciated men with long beards, curvy women with back rolls protruding from bras, thin women with visible rib cages, and kids dirty from play. The adults sat in a colorful selection of lawn chairs by the back porch. They had drinks in their hands—a few had two. Some of the women sat on the laps of the men and laughed too loudly.

"Dodge!" a woman with red, curly hair yelled. She jumped off a skinny guy with big black square sunglasses and ran to my uncle. She kissed Dodge on the mouth and grabbed his hand and pulled him to the others. Someone threw him a beer. He caught it and took a drink before flopping down in an empty lawn chair. The redhead sat on his lap and twirled his long beard hair in her finger. His hand wrapped around her waist, but he didn't smile.

I stopped. I didn't know where to go. It didn't feel right to follow Dodge, so I stood near the fence, watching. The kids played on the other end of the yard. The boys wrestled one second, then screamed and chased each other the next, their hands placed together to form pretend guns. A few girls tried to join in but were pushed away. There were a handful of other girls playing with dolls in the dirt.

"Hey! Kid!"

I turned to the adults and discovered their eyes fixed on me. It was Dodge who had yelled. The red-headed woman's lips pursed in annoyance that I had Dodge's attention.

"What the hell you standing there for? Go play."

I didn't move. Dodge took a drink. "Don't make me say it again."

The way he said it—sharper than the way Mama or Dad had ever spoken to me, sent chills across the skin of my arms. I moved toward the kids, even though I didn't want to.

I walked over to where the girls were playing in the dirt. When I got close enough that I thought Dodge wouldn't yell at me again, I stopped and watched them. Their dolls had missing limbs and shorn-off hair or were cheap rag dolls with buttons for eyes. When the dolls waved their chewed and frayed hands at me, I wondered where my old toys were now.

The girls never took notice of me, but before long, a group of six boys walked up. I stepped back as they approached. These boys didn't look like the ones from my old school. They had dirt on their faces and holes in their shirts. Many had cut-off jean shorts and two didn't even wear shirts.

The tallest, a boy with a white-blond buzz cut, skinny arms, and one large front tooth said, "Who are you?"

I looked at the others before replying, "Raqi."

The boys laughed. "That's not a name," One-Tooth Boy said.

I put my hands in my pockets and looked at the ground. "Is too."

One-Tooth Boy crossed his arms and looked me up and down. He twisted his lips to the side, as if thinking hard. Finally, he asked, "You a beaner?"

His friends laughed again. One boy whispered in his neighbor's ear.

I shrugged, not knowing if I was or wasn't.

One-Tooth Boy moved closer to me and poked my shoulder. "Hey, I'm talking to you. You a beaner?"

I stepped back. "I don't know."

A boy with red hair that hung over his eyes in curly tangles spoke up. "You know, a Mexican!"

I shrugged. Ms. Cook had told Dodge my dad was Mexican, but I didn't know if that meant I was.

"That ain't an answer," One-Tooth Boy said. "Why you so dark?" He smelled like sweat and mud and I fought not to scrunch my nose.

"My dad had dark skin."

"Who's your daddy? I ain't ever seen you before," the boy said.

My stomach clenched. "Dodge is my uncle."

The boy looked over at the adults. "No, he ain't. He's white."

"Is too," I said and crossed my arms.

One-Tooth Boy turned and looked at his friends. "She a lying beaner. You too dark to be kin to him."

I didn't like how he used that word, and I didn't think my parents would like it either. I couldn't say why I said, "stop," but I did.

The boy faced me; his friends laughed. "Stop what? Stop calling you a beaner? My daddy said Mexicans are stupid, poor beaners that should go back to where they came from." He shoved my shoulder lightly. "Go back to Mexico."

I hadn't ever been in a fight, so I was as surprised as he was when I pushed him and he stumbled backward, mouth open in shock. He regained his balance and ran at me, pushing me to the ground. The air was knocked out of my chest as he landed on top of me. I fought to breathe. My lungs and chest ached with each inhale.

One-Tooth Boy's balled fist hit my right cheek. I tried to fight back, but his heavy frame made it difficult, and I only struck his arms. Someone yelled, "Fight!" I struggled to push the boy off. We pushed and shoved until we were rolling in the dirt.

Just as he'd finally managed to get on top of me again, a hand pulled the boy away, and I was dragged up by my shirt collar, which burned a ring into the skin around my neck.

"Goddamn it, girl!" Dodge pulled my shirt so tightly that it choked me. My cheek throbbed as I fought to keep my balance and stay on my feet.

"What the hell are you doing?" He let go of my shirt, and I fell to the ground, my knee hitting something hard.

"He started it," I mumbled. My knee throbbed as I stood up.

Dodge leaned down. "What did you say? Speak up, damn it."

My eyes burned with hot tears, but I knew it wasn't the right time. It would make Dodge angrier. I blinked back my tears and gritted my teeth.

"He called me"—I didn't want to say the word—"something bad." I muttered the last part.

Dodge turned sideways and tugged his beard. My bottom lip trembled, as I did everything I could to hold back my tears. I balled my hands into tiny fists and pushed my fingernails into my palms. If I looked above Dodge's head and not at him, I wouldn't cry. I wouldn't.

Dodge turned back to me. "That it?"

I shook my head.

"What else?"

I looked over at the boys. A stocky man spoke to One-Tooth Boy, but he didn't look mad like Dodge did. I caught the end of the man's words, "—big mouth, boy." He ruffled the boy's hair and pushed him toward his friends. They began a game of tag, like nothing had happened.

I turned to Dodge. "He said you weren't my uncle."

Dodge shook his head and without looking at me, said, "If only," and walked away.

I didn't move. If I moved, I would cry or run or die. I stared at the yellow grass and rocky dirt and willed myself to not feel anything. I wanted to go home. I wanted my mom and dad, to be sitting between them on the couch in the living room of our redbrick home in Texas.

I thought of that home, how it was the last place where I felt safe. Without moving an inch, I reached for the safety of that house across space and time. I returned with a pile of bricks and laid them in a circle around my feet. I added another row of on top of them, and another and another and another, until I'd built an impenetrable brick tower that came together over my head. The tower would keep in the sea of tears and anger and keep out this new life full of bad words and people. It would protect me now that no one else would.

An hour passed before I saw something move between the cracks of my brick tower. It was a small girl with white-blond hair that hung in strands around her face. She had lots of freckles on her nose and wore a pink dress with an orange stain near the collar. Her feet were bare. She stood on her tiptoes and peeked through a crack between two bricks.

"I'll play with you," she said so softly that I couldn't be sure if I heard her right.

I didn't respond, so she moved closer. "I said I'll play with you," she said.

"Why?" I asked.

She shrugged and twirled a piece of hair around her pointer finger. "I don't care if you're a Mexican."

"Why—"

"I'm Bethie."

6

1990, thirty-one years old

I looked at the clock on the wall. Six thirty in the morning. I had a few hours. To go or not to go. Why was I even considering this? Sure, Billy said that he had my grandfather's address, but could I trust that? How long had he had it? Did my grandfather even know about me? Why hadn't he found me? I had so many questions, but I knew that only Billy had the answers.

If I went on the Grieving Ride, I'd be done with the Lawless for good. No more Dodge, no more Lawless Motorcycle Club. I wouldn't have to interact with them. Billy was generally good about keeping his word. I put my coffee mug down, went to my closet, and threw a few outfits in a duffle bag.

Before Trevor had left for work, I'd told him I would probably go on the ride.

"Probably?" he asked.

I nodded, not wanting to meet his eyes.

"When will you be back?" He walked up to me and put his arms on my shoulders. I didn't like sentimentality, so I pulled away and walked to other side of the kitchen island.

I shrugged. "Maybe a day or two." I had told David I'd be back by Sunday, and I meant that, but my goal was to return by Saturday.

"Want me to come with you?" Trevor asked.

"God no." I didn't quite shout it, but the volume was louder than I intended, and Trevor noticed. His eyebrows furrowed.

"Sorry," I muttered. "It's just . . . you're not going to help the situation."

"I think you're exaggerating. It's the nineties and you haven't seen them in a while. They probably aren't as bad as you remember."

I shook my head. Racism was embedded in the Lawless DNA, and I didn't want Trevor to experience that from the people who had raised me. Besides, Trevor could have been as white as a pearl, and they'd still hate him. He didn't ride bikes, was an educated lawyer, and for lack of a better term, was a bit "soft." Or at least that's what the Lawless would think. He didn't work with his hands, hadn't been in the military, and knew nothing about mechanics. To them, Trevor wasn't a real man, and they'd eat him and me alive for it.

"I'm going alone," I said.

"But what if—"

"Alone," I repeated, my voice lowering an octave. I was not in the mood to argue.

"Fine." His frustrated sigh told me it wasn't fine.

He placed his coffee cup in the sink and grabbed his briefcase. I waited for him to try to kiss me or say goodbye, but he didn't. He walked out the door without looking my way.

I groaned loudly. Had I been too cold to Trevor? I could be that way sometimes. Trevor was warm and kind, not like me. He liked hugs, kissing, holding hands, and needed more attention than I wanted to give. I always toed the line, making sure not to push him too far away so that he wouldn't come back to me.

Growing up in Dodge's household, I quickly learned that kindness was weakness and love was doled out when it benefited the person giving it. We never hugged or showed affection, and that had fucked me up in a lot of ways. Maybe finding my grandfather could help me become less guarded with Trevor.

This went through my mind as I packed my toothbrush and toothpaste and looked for the name-brand black leather boots that Trevor got me last Christmas. I grabbed a black leather jacket and threw it on the bed. I stood with my hands on my hips. Was I really doing this?

That question turned into why am I getting in my car? Why am I sitting in traffic biting my nails at the thought of seeing everyone? Why am I pulling into a hair salon that I spied off the highway? Why did I tell the stylist to "Give me one of those boy-looking haircuts that Linda Evangelista has. I don't know what it's called. But make sure you leave me some bangs or something. I have a big forehead." Until finally, I wondered, why was I sitting at the stop sign down the street from Dodge's and not moving?

I heard the roar of the bikes before I saw them. They were calling me home with the growling of their engines and I was heeding the call. It made my stomach clench and my heart flutter, made me want to grit my teeth and smile. Memory after memory washed over me. I could smell the oil, feel the rumble of the engine between my thighs, taste the exhaust on the back of my tongue.

I pulled into the dirt driveway and parked on the grass, my tiny Mercedes, probably filthy now, rattling with every natural dip in the ground. There were a few other cars in the front lawn. They probably belonged to families saying farewell to their men; members of Billy's chapter—the first Lawless chapter—didn't miss a ride unless they were in prison, dead, or needed to stay behind to keep the business running smoothly.

I turned off the car and looked in the rearview mirror to find everyone's eyes on me. The crowd of men and women wore dark jeans, ragged headbands, and tattoos that snaked up arms and around necks. The men's leather vests sported Lawless M. C. patches. They had scraggly beards of varying lengths, and many were peppered with white or gray. I couldn't help but envy the women, many of whom had their hair pulled back in braids or ponytails. I rubbed the short stubble on the lower back of my head.

"Fuck." I hit the steering wheel.

A sense of foreboding washed over me, telling me danger was ahead. During my childhood, I'd trusted that tiny voice inside me. It had kept me safe. I couldn't do that now. I had to walk into the danger if I was going to come out with my grandfather in hand.

I took three deep breaths. Raqi. Relax. You're a lawyer, not a kid anymore. These people don't have any kind of hold on you. You have a new life, a successful career, a boyfriend, a house. You're doing this entirely for one reason, one address, and with that will come some good changes in your life.

I jumped at a knock on my window.

A man with a brown-and-white scraggly beard and a shiny bald head smiled wide, revealing short teeth that were an odd shade of greenish-gray. Eddie. He had been like an uncle to me—better, in fact, than the one I had. Eddie showed me how to shoot guns and tequila, made me Sunday breakfast, and surprised me at school with hamburgers for lunch. Even though he was a large man with broad shoulders and a round gut that protruded over his jeans, and had arms covered in tattoos of an American flag, a skeleton on a flaming motorcycle, and one that read, "Drunk Bitches Get Stitches," he could always make me smile.

I opened the door and he moved back to let me out.

"It's about time you showed up," he said.

I rolled my eyes and smirked. "You should have left without me." Eddie wrapped me in a hug, and I couldn't help but soften. He smelled like leather and sweat.

"As if Billy would let us. Thought we were going to have to drag you from your house and strap you to a bike."

The hug ended, and we pulled apart. "Glad you guys haven't lost your sense of subtlety."

"Never." He laughed. "Got a bag?" I nodded and pulled the duffel that I had packed from my front seat.

"Am I riding with you?"

Eddie's mouth opened wide in mock shock. "Am I hearing this right? Raqi is willing to ride bitch?"

I covered my face with my hand and shook my head. Honestly, I hadn't even thought about my question.

"Was a time when Raqi would have kicked and screamed when

she was made to ride bitch." He laughed. "What's that you said, 'Bessie Stringfield didn't ride bitch; neither am I!'"

I dropped my hand. Bessie Stringfield was a badass Black rider who became the first woman to ride across the US solo and even served in WWII as a bike dispatch. She had been a hero to me as a kid.

"It's—I—Whatever, man. Shit, I don't have a damn bike which is why . . ." I trailed off, unsure how to get out of my mess-up and inwardly cringing at how my voice and dialect had quickly changed as soon as I started talking to Eddie. Even though I never lost my penchant for cussing, my diction had become posher when I became a lawyer. Legalese was a second language, but now my tongue was quickly loosening to that old Lawless speak.

Eddie laughed at me and stroked his beard. "Guess Billy didn't tell you. He's got your Ironhead."

My bike. My Ironhead. The one I had destroyed and left in pieces. Dodge must have fixed it.

"Great," I said with little enthusiasm, though secretly, thrilled. I had thought it was lost forever at my own hands. Sometimes I dreamed about it, could feel the hot metal burning my fingers and the smell of rubber on the road . . . but mostly I tried not to think about it, because I had destroyed it and that felt fucked up.

Eddie turned and walked to the other Lawless, expecting me to follow. Like everyone else, he flew colors over his plaid button-up shirt. When Dodge left me at home at the age of ten to go to a bar, I snuck into his room to try on his black leather vest. I fingered the three-piece rocker, gray-on-white patches that read "Lawless M. C." and "Escondido." I took careful time pouring over the center patch—a motorcycle with a skull in the middle, tongue out in a salacious jeer. Rubbing my fingers over the skull awakened it from slumber. Its empty sockets looked around wildly until it saw me and calmed. The skull whipped its tongue inside its mouth for just a second, then flicked it out and licked my hand from the bottom of my palm to the tip of my fingertips. Its tongue was rough like worn tires embedded with metal nails, glass, and dirt. It marked me as one of its own until I died.

Now, seeing Eddie's colors, the skin on my hand itched and I felt nauseous.

The voices of the men lowered as they watched me approach. There were a few smiles, mostly from the older members who knew me from back in the "Dodge raising Raqi on drugs" days. They didn't look much different beyond a few more tattoos, gray or white hair, and missing teeth.

The Mamas and the Sheeps didn't smile, which didn't bother me. Sheeps were women that were passed around the club for sex; Mamas were the same, usually older, tended to ride bikes, and had stuck around in the hope of being chosen as an Old Lady. Mamas and Sheeps were women who came for the party, the booze, the danger, but only a few stayed around for good. It wasn't worth learning their names or caring what they thought.

However, the coarse looks of the Old Ladies were unnerving. These were the serious girlfriends and the wives of the club members. They rocked Property patches with pride, were committed to only their men, and were treated with more respect. Some had college degrees and ran their own businesses, others raised families, but no matter their background, they knew their place in the hierarchy of the club, and they were fine with it—fulfilled even. They'd been harvested by the Old Ladies before them to learn to submit and show respect to their men and the club.

There were Old Ladies I didn't recognize, but it was hard to ignore the disapproving looks of the ones whose kids I'd grown up with. Some had fed me when Dodge was on a bender, others gave me secondhand clothes, many had watched me when Dodge was out on a run. But I wasn't a Property, an Old Lady. I had tits and didn't submit, and everyone knew that I didn't respect the club, what it did, what it meant. It may have been tolerated or ignored when I was a kid, but now that I was a grown woman—it was less so, especially to the Old Ladies who had crafted roles and rules that I couldn't give two shits about. I was a threat to the club's ecosystem; of course, they didn't like me.

I noticed John, Stephen, Liam, and Mason were now Lawless. We'd grown up together, riding bikes, shooting the shit, getting drunk on beer at parties. They were covered in Harley tattoos and the words, "666," "Hells on Wheels," and "Lawless M. C." Scars from military service or bar fights graced their faces, and greasy hair hid beneath bandannas. The ink in my tattoo pulsed and burned under my long-sleeved black shirt, like it knew it had returned home.

All the men had short hair now, and like me, a few rubbed the backs of their heads as if trying to figure out where it had gone. Eddie broke away from me to speak to a few Prospects. I continued walking toward the Harleys closest to me. Billy stood at the other end of the bikes with longtime Lawless members like Ford, Bob E., Grim, and Gray. Whew, Gray had gotten old. His hair was solid white, and he had lost at least thirty pounds. He looked like a skeleton in a skin bag.

Harris stood nearby speaking to a woman in her fifties or sixties. I didn't recognize her as an Old Lady from back in the day, but I hadn't been around in thirteen years. She stared hard at me, her lips set in a straight line. Her brown curly hair, cut right below her ears, had a few gray streaks. She had large thighs and watermelon-sized boobs that stretched her black shirt tight and would never allow her leather vest to zip up. She wore a lot of silver rings on both hands and a chunky turquoise necklace that matched her eyes—green one second, blue the next. Her unfriendly look felt personal, like she knew me. I fought not to sneer back.

I hoped to lay low, but Billy noticed me. At the same time, I saw my Ironhead. God, it looked sharp. I walked up to it slowly. A strong lemon scent told me it had been recently cleaned. The chrome glistened, the boat tail had been buffed, and the handlebars softened in color in the early morning light. I ran my hand over the seat and my Ironhead leaned in for more, growling in its belly like a pet being scratched behind the ears.

Dodge and I had built my Ironhead between my junior and senior year, and I went everywhere with it when it was done. We painted it the darkest black I could find, because that's what most of the Lawless rode and I couldn't look any different. Granted, I had a sissy bar to attach my backpack to when I was in high school, but it wasn't too tall, and we'd managed to customize it to include chrome skulls.

If I looked around, I knew that my Ironhead would be one of the oldest out here. Hell, we finished it in 1976 and now that it was 1990, the bikes had become bigger and faster. But I didn't care. This was my Ironhead, and she had always been good to me. I touched the left handlebar for a second, my throat becoming tight, then let go.

"It's clean, if that's what you were thinking," said a woman's voice behind me. I turned around to find the woman with the turquoise eyes.

By clean, she meant, clear of drugs. "Fan-fucking-tastic," I replied.

The wrinkles stretching out from her thick-eyeliner eyes deepened. "You know he worked on it for years. Cleaned it every day. Replaced the parts each year, too."

"What's it to you?" I scrunched the left side of my lip in annoyance. Who was this woman?

Billy walked up behind her. "This here's Lenora. She was Dodge's Old Lady."

"Is that right? Who would have guessed Dodge was the marrying type?"

The woman's mouth opened slightly as if I'd offended her, and she looked down for a second before her turquoise eyes shot back up at me.

"We weren't married," she grunted out, clearly annoyed that she had to explain it.

I shrugged in response. I had never known Dodge to have a serious relationship. I'd seen him with women, sure, but he spoke about them like they were a VHS he got from Blockbuster—called it "just renting."

Lenora put her hands on her hips, not impressed with my nonchalance at her standing and significance to Dodge. She shifted the weight between her feet and chewed the inside of her cheek. "He called you a lot, you know. Tried to fix things with you."

The tits on this bitch. I cocked my head to the left. "Lenora, is it? It's early. Shoo, Mama." I batted my right hand back a few times to signal for her to go away. I knew calling her a Mama and not an Old Lady would send her over the roof, and that sent a thrill through me. In the club, it was all about power and lording it over someone else. I wanted her to know that I held the power.

She stepped forward, her finger pointed at me, but Billy cut her off and motioned to her to get going. Lenora narrowed her eyes. She cracked her neck, then trudged off. I had a feeling that she was going to make this ride a lot longer than it was already going to be.

"Aren't you a fucking delight, making enemies on your first day back," Billy said dryly.

I ignored him and placed my hands in mock prayer before me. "Tell me Dodge wants his ashes spread in the middle of the desert two hours away. I need to be back by tomorrow night."

Billy looked weird with short hair. Not that I hadn't seen him cut his hair before, but the picture of Billy that I had in my mind never changed—taller than most, his broad shoulders and thick upper body added to his domineering personality. And the picture always came together with his peppered hair pulled back in a leather-banded pony-tail and his large white-and-black mustache connecting with his beard. At least, he still had the mustache-beard thing going on.

"You'd like that, wouldn't you?" He pulled a cigarette from his back pocket.

"Fine. Where are we doing this?" I leaned against my Ironhead. It felt natural, like I had done it for the last thirteen years of my life. But I hadn't and that made my stomach churn.

"Kentucky." He lit the cigarette, took a drag, and exhaled.

I jumped away from my bike. "What the hell?" A few heads turned our way.

He nodded while taking another drag, the cigarette glowing bright orange. "Apparently, your family comes from Kentucky. And there's some mountain where he wants to be laid to rest."

I raised my hand to pull on my hair. Shit. I didn't have any hair. My mouth went dry, and I felt hot.

"Kentucky? Like, Kentucky?" I repeated.

"That's what I said, Raqi. You gone deaf?"

"Kentucky," I repeated under my breath. Kentucky had to be like a six-day ride or more. After the ceremony, I could jump on a plane in some godforsaken cowtown in—*fucking Kentucky*—and return to my life in LA. Maybe I could ship my bike back or leave it there—who cared. I'd have to schedule some other time to see my grandfather. David would go batshit if I didn't return right away.

"Like, six days then?"

"Well . . ." Billy squinted at everyone through the haze of his smoke. "More like eight or ten."

"No, no, no, no. No way." I put my hands on my hips. "Why would it take us ten days to get to—" I choked on the word again. "Kentucky?"

Billy flicked ash off the cigarette. "Seems like Dodge wanted us, well, wanted you, to go on his main route. Meet some people."

Wait . . . "When you say route, you mean, like, his *route-route*?"

Billy threw his cigarette down. "Don't act like you're too good to ride the routes anymore. Yes, *the route*."

I threw my palms in the air. "I can't go on a route, Billy. I'm a lawyer for God's sake. Shit like that can get you disbarred."

"Honey, what do you want me to do? And don't act like you represent saints."

I lowered my voice. "We both know that hasn't always been my choice."

Billy huffed. "I don't care what you want. This is about Dodge, so take a piss, grab a drink. We leave in thirty." He started to walk away but called over his shoulder, "And try not to piss off my people."

Ten days. Ten days. I had brought clothes for a few days. I had so much work to do. And there was my firm and Trevor and cases and appointments. My chest felt tight and my head woozy. I inhaled deeply, realizing I had momentarily stopped breathing.

I looked at everyone milling about and felt naked, surrounded by people who did and said things that I stood against. It was lonely and chilling and I wasn't sure what to do. Ten days with the Lawless. I wasn't sure I could handle it. That was ten days surrounded by people who were unpredictably violent, reckless criminals. I would have no control over what went on, and the thought of that made my anxiety rise.

But I had to do this. Something was missing inside of me, and my grandfather might be the only answer. So, I swallowed my anxiety down and took a few more calming breaths.

To get my mind off what I was about to do, I headed toward Dodge's house. The Lawless and their women and children were walking in and out, probably using the bathroom before we left. Not that any of the children would be coming. I was the only one that ever did. The little mascot. The half outlaw. My hand went to my upper arm tattoo, the one I always hid, the one I was putting down big-ass checks to get rid of through some new technology that could make it disappear. Here, I didn't have to hide my tattoo, but to show it off, to let it breathe among its brethren, felt like a chance I couldn't take.

I walked up the creaky wooden steps I'd not set foot on in a decade and opened the screen door. The dimly lit room offered enough light to see that the bare-bones place I had known no longer existed. Lenora had apparently moved in.

The blue floral couch was new, as was the cream carpet. Somewhere in the house, a radio played "Sweet Child O' Mine" by Guns N' Roses. A large box-shaped TV sat in the middle of a wooden entertainment stand, and not on the floor where it had always been for as long as I could remember. There were gemstones and small wooden angel figurines on the shelves of the TV stand. A few pictures graced the walls which were now covered in white wallpaper with tiny blue flowers. I walked up to look at one of the photos. Dodge sat at the front of his bike and Lenora, with long hair, sat behind him rocking a black headband and leather vest.

Dodge looked different—fuller, with more fat around his neck and a belly that protruded slightly over his belt. His long, straight black hair framed a face that had more wrinkles than I had ever known it to have. He looked ahead at something in the distance, while Lenora stared at Dodge like God had personally gifted him to Earth.

Still an ugly old fuck if you asked me.

I left the living room and moved into the hallway to my old room. The door handle stuck for a second then loosened with a deep exhale.

Nothing had changed since I had left—minus a few duffel bags and cardboard boxes piled in the corner. My posters of Led Zeppelin and Black Sabbath were curling around the tacks; the brown quilt on the twin bed had held up over the years. Pictures from high school had been taken off the mirror of the bureau and placed in a pile on the corner next to a milk crate with my old records. The room was musty, but if I stayed long enough, I knew it'd soon smell familiar and bring about memories that had long passed.

I closed the door. It wasn't really my room. Hadn't been for a long time. As I turned around, the bathroom door opened and out walked a woman with heavy black eye makeup and wispy, long blond hair that draped past her shoulders. Her thin frame looked sickly against a bright blue tube top and dark jeans. She paused, and we regarded each other for a second. God, she looked like a Sheep.

I tried to speak but the words stuck in my mouth. I cleared my throat again and tried once more. "Hey, Bethie."

She swallowed hard and bit her lip. Her fingers rose slowly to grab a strand of hair as she looked away, toward the living room.

"It's Beth now." Her voice was raspier, like she hadn't stopped smoking.

She glanced at me for a second, then walked away.

Bethie—Beth—had left the bathroom door open, revealing the ghost of Dodge's limp body lying on a seatless toilet.

7

Three days after the barbecue where I fought with One-Tooth Boy, some-one pounded on Dodge's front door. I sat up on the couch and let the thin blanket fall off me. They knocked on the door harder. I flinched.

Mama and Dad said never to open the door to strangers, but Mama and Dad weren't here, and Dodge was in his room with some woman. They had made weird noises earlier and I had to plug my ears with my fingers and whisper to myself all the things I wished I still had—Mama, Dad, a bed, my dolls, friends—until it stopped. Dodge and the woman had been quiet for a while now.

"Dodge!" A man with a deep voice yelled through the door. He pounded again and the door shook.

"Wake up, man!" said a different voice.

I wasn't sure what to do. If they kept knocking, Dodge would wake up and he'd be mad, and he might get angry with me. He told me earlier to be quiet and go to sleep, and not to bother him.

My bottom lip trembled, but I couldn't cry. I had to be brave, like Dad said when the storms rattled the windows and made the trees hit the side of the house, and I thought a tornado would blow us all away. I stood up and bit my lip hard. Tangy copper blood coated my tongue, but the pain kept the tears back.

I padded barefoot to the door, which bulged inward from the

pounding. Reaching up, I turned the knob. The light blinded me for a second, and I closed my eyes. When I opened them, there stood two tall men. One had a bald head and a brown beard and the other was even taller with black hair and a mustache that had a little bit of white mixed in. They wore clothes like Dodge did—jeans and T-shirts with leather vests. Even though their eyes were hidden by sunglasses, I could tell they were surprised I had opened the door.

We stood there, all three of us, not moving or speaking. Finally, the bald one smiled and knelt. I stepped back.

"Hey," he said softly. "You must be . . . ?" He took off his sunglasses. He had green eyes and a goggle tan line that contrasted with his sunburnt nose and cheeks. He looked like a raccoon.

"Raqi," I whispered.

"Raqi," he repeated. "I like that name. My name's Eddie. And this is Billy." I looked up at the taller man. His nose wrinkled. He didn't like me, but not the way Dodge didn't like me. This was different.

"Where's Dodge?" Billy's voice was rough and reminded me of a bad guy in a cartoon.

I pointed toward the hallway, then walked into the living room. The men followed, their boots making the floorboards under the carpet shake. I headed to the couch and stood next to it, one hand in my shorts pocket and the other on the armrest.

Billy closed the door and looked around the living room. Beer cans, my cup of water, and a plate of stale chips covered the table. Mama never let me eat in the living room, but Dodge didn't care since he didn't have a dining room table. The cigarette butts crawled around the table, moving out of the heart shape I'd guided them into earlier that day. They were my only friends now.

Eddie shook his head when he saw my pillow and blanket on the couch.

"Raqi, is this where you sleep?"

I nodded.

"Every night?"

I nodded again, took my hand out of my pocket, and twirled my hair. It felt sticky and didn't pull apart like it did after Mama washed it in the bath. He sighed and looked over his shoulder at Billy, who'd taken off his sunglasses and placed them on top of his head. His eyes were as black as his vest and if I looked at them too long, I knew my eyes would blacken and die, too.

"Where's Dodge?" Billy asked.

I pointed down the hallway.

"Stay with her," Billy said before walking to Dodge's door. The skull on the back of his vest smiled wide and winked at me.

I stepped forward and Eddie held out his hand to stop me.

"He shouldn't go in there," I said to Eddie. "Dodge will be real mad. He doesn't want to be bothered."

Eddie smiled. His teeth weren't white like Dad's, but he smelled like trees, and he was nice, so I didn't think it mattered.

"Don't worry. Dodge won't get mad at Billy or you."

Billy opened Dodge's door and walked in. "Dodge!" Billy barked. "Get the fuck up, now!"

I flinched. Eddie picked me up and set me on the couch. "It's okay, don't be scared." He grabbed the plate of chips and beer cans from the coffee table and took them to the kitchen.

Muffled voices from Dodge's room reached my ears, but I couldn't hear exactly what they said. I tried to peer down the hallway. The woman walked out. She wore jean shorts and was putting on her red shirt over her white bra when she rushed out the door.

Eddie kept cleaning, barely taking notice of the woman.

"You dumb piece of shit!" Billy yelled again. "You're fucking around while she's out there with dirt all on her shirt and a busted lip."

A crash echoed right after.

"You hit that little girl?"

"I didn't touch her!" Dodge's voice sounded funny, strained.

Another crash.

"You chose to bring her here," Billy said. "If you aren't going to take care of her, send her to foster care."

"No!" A thud, like the sound of a fist against wood, rang out. "I can't do that to my sister."

"Then get your ass—"

Eddie came up to me and held out his hand. I looked up. He smiled and I put my hand in his and let him guide me to kitchen.

"Help me dry the dishes?"

I nodded. He pulled a chair to the sink. I climbed up and he handed me a towel. Mama and I used to do this sometimes.

Eddie handed me the cups and plates and I dried them, then put them on the counter. He asked me things, too, like the last time I ate, if I'd had a shower, my favorite color and movie. Eddie was nice. I liked him, though I couldn't figure out why he was friends with Dodge. The yelling had stopped, and I wondered what Billy and Dodge were talking about.

Eddie was rinsing the last dish when I heard boots behind me. I turned around, expecting to see Dodge, but it was only Billy.

"Here, Raq." Eddie handed me the last wet plate. "Dry that for me while I talk to Billy."

I nodded and took the plate from him. As I dried the plate, I tried to listen.

"Said he didn't hit her—"

"But her lip is bleeding," Eddie said.

Billy grunted.

"Even if he's telling the truth, he hasn't done shit else. She's barely eaten, hasn't had a bath in a week, and all her clothes look dirty."

"I talked to him about it," Billy said.

"Will he actually step up?"

"He chose this. He has to." Billy huffed. "Don't need Social Services or anybody else sniffing around here."

I peeked over my shoulder as I twirled the plate in my towel-covered hands. They were looking at me. Eddie seemed sad, but I couldn't figure out why. Hadn't we been having a good time? He seemed so happy before. Billy looked grumpy with his arms folded across his chest.

"Let's eat," Billy said.

Eddie nodded and walked over to me. I set the plate on the counter.

"Good job, Raqi," he said as he lifted me off the chair. He leaned over and placed his hands on his knees. "Want to get something to eat?"

I smiled. "Yeah."

He reached out and touched a strand of my hair. "Let's get you cleaned up first. Just a little at least."

Getting cleaned up involved Eddie putting my head under the kitchen sink and rinsing it with dish soap. He had wanted me to take a bath, but when he looked inside the tub he grimaced and mumbled something about it being dirty. He was right. Green stuff crawled up the side of the tub and yellow stains covered the bottom.

Billy waited on the couch while Eddie wrapped my head in a towel, like Mama used to do. He went down the hallway and returned later with a large black shirt that read, "Veteran" on the front.

"Put this on," he said before turning around. Billy looked away and stared at the front door.

I took the towel off my head before taking off my shirt and shorts. I left my panties on, even though I'd worn them for two days. I didn't have any clean ones left.

"Done!"

Eddie turned around and laughed. "A little big for you, huh?"

I giggled and nodded. The bottom of the shirt hung to the floor and the sleeves went past my elbows. I pulled my hair out of my face. It was already starting to dry. My fingers caught on a knot, but I pushed them through and pulled out a few brown strands. I let them drop to the floor, which swallowed my hair in thanks.

"Put your shoes on and let's go get a burger."

We left Dodge at the house and when I asked Eddie why, he said Dodge would meet us there.

Billy led us outside to two large, black motorcycles bathing in the warmth of the sun. They turned their dark heads toward me and sniffed the air, trying to figure out if I was foe or friend. I stopped and pulled on Eddie's hand.

"It's okay, Raqi. You'll ride with me."

"But I'm scared." The motorcycles stretched their front tires and then their backs, loosening out their gears and sockets for the ride. Eddie squatted down, and as he did, Billy's motorcycle howled to life. I gasped and stepped back. The roar was loud at first, but it calmed to a growl that sounded like the low hum of my dad's lawnmower when it sat in one place. Billy looked at me, then away. His bike ached to run but didn't move, having been trained by its master to go only when commanded.

"I won't let anything happen to you. I promise," Eddie said, before picking me up and carrying me to his bike. He set me on the leather seat and pointed at the handlebars. "Hold on here." I couldn't hold them at the top because my arms weren't long enough. I had to hold the bottom part, a spot that was warm and soft. Eddie straddled the bike behind me and jumped. I yelped when the bike awakened, its metal muscles shaking beneath my legs with carnal power. Billy's bike howled and Eddie's bike dipped its head in respect to its leader.

Eddie sat down behind me and put his left arm around my waist, holding me close to his body.

"Tighten your legs around the bike, Raqi," he yelled over the noise. "When we get moving, mirror my body. If I lean right, you lean right. If i lean left, you lean left. Don't let go of those handlebars, okay?"

I nodded, my heart beating fast. I was so scared, but Eddie kept his grip firmly around me when we moved forward.

We followed Billy out of the driveway. I gripped the handlebars tighter and closed my eyes for a second before opening them again. Once we left Dodge's gravel driveway and rolled onto the main street, the bike didn't shake as much. The bikes stretched their legs and increased their speed, Billy leading the way. I whimpered. My eyes began to water.

"It's okay! I got you!" Eddie yelled.

My eyes watered more, so I risked one hand letting go of the handlebars to wipe them. I leaned my head down so the wind wouldn't hit my face. The road blurred below us. I felt the bike turn to the right, but Eddie sat up straight, then shifted slightly to the left. I remembered what he said and followed his movements just as he did them.

"Good job, Raqi!"

I smiled, happy that Eddie thought I was doing something good. Even though I was scared, I felt for the first time in a while that I might be okay.

8

After going to the bathroom, I went outside to find the Lawless gearing up to leave. The bikes and owners itched to move, to hit the road and ride. Even though we were there because Dodge had died, the opportunity for a long ride sent the skulls on the Lawless' three-piece rockers into a chorus rendition of AC/DC's "Highway to Hell." I made my way to my bike reluctantly as the skulls sang, *Hey Satan, paid my dues.* What a way to spend my first vacation away from the office.

Eddie walked up carrying something behind his back.

"What do you want?" I asked suspiciously.

"Since you ain't ridden in a while—"

"Who says I haven't?" Truly, I hadn't.

"—we wanted to make sure you don't hurt that pretty new hair of yours." He smiled mischievously and presented me with a black helmet.

I looked at the glossy facade and knocked it out of his hands. "Get that shit out of here."

Eddie let out a big laugh at the same time most of the Lawless started their bikes, a symphony of jarring engines that slashed through bone and meat and went straight to my heart. I hadn't heard so many bikes come together at once and it made my knees weak.

Eddie waggled his pointer finger at me. "She's still in there," he said, before walking to his bike.

I looked at the helmet lying in the dirt. Oh, I wanted to pick it up. It *had* been a long time since I'd ridden. California didn't have a helmet law, but even if they did, the Lawless would never wear them because it wasn't masculine or tough. Anytime the club rode by a motorcyclist wearing a helmet, they surrounded the rider and pulled up close to their wheels, to freak them out. I'd seen it happen, even watched a few riders swerve and crash. The Lawless always rode off laughing.

I left the helmet on the ground and grabbed my small bag. I pulled out a pair of sunglasses, then tied my bag to the skull-emblazoned sissy bar tail. I gave the kickstart a few kicks, then put the choke, gas, and ignition on, and opened the throttle. From there, I positioned my body on the right side above the kickstart. My stomach turned in knots and my face warmed. Kickstarts were hard as shit, and it'd been almost thirteen years. This was going to suck.

I set my left knee on the seat, planted my right foot on the pedal, and kicked. Nothing happened. The silence set the tops of my ears ablaze in embarrassment.

"Fuck, fuck, fuck," I whispered and tried again, failing. My Ironhead may have nuzzled my hand earlier, but she was letting me know she didn't like being abandoned for a decade. I was going to have to convince her I was worthy to ride.

I did not look up. If there were smirks or laughs, I could not handle that right now. On the third kick, the engine started, and I swung my leg over and kept my gaze slightly down, unable to see who had watched my shameful bitch-ass attempt at starting my bike. When I dared to glance up a minute later, no one was looking at me, and I breathed a sigh of relief.

The noise from the engine barely registered above the thirty or so other bikes, but the vibrations beneath my legs sent a tingly rush through my limbs. My heart beat faster, adjusted, and then matched the tune of the machine's rumblings. It was the only way to ride.

I relaxed and waited for the others to move out. Eight rows ahead of me, Lair helped his wife Melinda on the back of his seat. Among the Lawless, they were decent people. I had grown up with Melinda's daughter, Jordan. Melinda had once taken me to the doctor for a cold I'd had for two weeks because Dodge refused to, and Lair had paid for it. Melinda gave Lair a kiss on the cheek once she settled on the back of the bike, and he smiled in return. If I hadn't known that Lair had killed a man with a broken beer bottle for running his mouth in a bar and Melinda had helped him cover it up, I'd have thought they were a sweet, sixty-five-year-old couple who liked riding bikes together.

Suddenly, a creeping feeling spread across my shoulders, and I knew that someone was watching me. All the Lawless looked forward to Billy, who was finishing a cigarette before we rode. Some nonsensical super-stition of his—one more for the road, for luck.

I spied the one rider looking back at me. Tall and thinly built, his blond-white hair grew slightly longer in the front and had been shaved short in the back. He had on a black leather vest over a white sleeveless shirt, and black jeans and boots. Colorful tattoos that spoke of broth-erhoods and hate covered his arms. He took a long drag on a cigarette as he watched me. Beth walked up to him and climbed on the back of the bike. He threw his cigarette down, looked at me once more, and then turned forward.

It was Jackson, Beth's twin brother and my first boyfriend.

He had come a long way from being One-Tooth Boy.

Riding a motorcycle is not like riding a bike. People who say that aren't riding with thirty other bikes in formation on a California highway. My big-ass, 492-pound bike would crumple like a bag of chips if a small car sideswiped it. At least if I died, I wouldn't have to finish the ride.

As a kid, I quickly learned that it wasn't just the engine, sprockets, pistons, and wheels that made the machine move along the asphalt road. My body melded with metal and every shift of my weight, turning of my head, soft squeeze on the brake, affected the motorcycle that moved beneath me. Over time, I had developed a sixth sense, one that knew how to keep the bike upright. I didn't have to think about the mechanical aspects of riding. I was the bike, and the bike was me. But it'd been many years since I'd ridden, and that sixth sense felt covered in rust.

If I had been riding sweep, or last in formation, I might have felt a little better. Non-club members always rode near the back, with the sweep tailing behind to make sure no one got in trouble. As a kid, I used to ride in the front with Dodge, but I'd grown up and left and that had changed things. My spot was now toward the end. I could have asked to ride closer to the front for the Grieving Ride since I was family of the deceased, but I had no interest in riding in the center of the pack, walled in by other motorcycles nipping at my ankles. Besides, my presence here was rocky to begin with, and riding in the family's spot wasn't going to make it better. I wasn't an associate of the club, not even an independent. There wasn't a term for what I was to the club. Billy was already going out on a limb with the club by making me ride. No point in rocking the boat and pissing off his men. I'd keep my head down and well out of everyone's way.

Billy had put four people on the tail end, probably in fear that I would ride off to my warm, comforting home if no one prevented me from doing so. At the front was Billy, and near him were his seconds-in-command like Eddie, Gray, and Jackson's dad, John. Lenora would have usually been in the back as a solo Mama, but since this was Dodge's Grieving Ride, she was still his Old Lady, at least until the end. Plus, Lenora was riding Dodge's bike which meant she had temporarily moved up in the ranks to the middle.

I had to keep up with the riders in front of me or be the reason why the rest of us got cut off from the others. Did they notice my cautiousness, how often I touched the brakes? This trip wasn't just a nuisance; it was now humiliating.

We finally broke free of the city and set off on the open highway into the desert, taking the 10 toward Arizona. The car-infested roads of Southern California slowly drifted away, but that was a problem, too. We'd ridden too far from the ocean to have a breeze. The sun beat down on the asphalt and us, creating an invisible cloud of UV rays, exhaust, and heat which didn't mix well with the leather jacket and jeans I wore.

Sweat dripped down my back to my jeans and pooled between my boobs and in the crack of my ass.

Despite my sunglasses, my eyes stung from the eastern-facing sun. Then there were the bugs. God, it was the worst part of riding. I kept my mouth shut and tried not to think how ridiculous I probably looked with my bangs blowing straight off my head. My ass and legs hurt from balancing, my shoulders from holding the handlebars, my hands from white-knuckling the throttle. Goddamn you, Dodge. God-fucking-damn you. That small excitement in my stomach disappeared and was replaced by misery, heat, and hunger.

But then slowly something changed. I grew used to the dull ache in my shoulders, and comfortable with the watering of my eyes. My fear of hitting another rider slowly subsided even though we were clocking in speeds between seventy and a hundred mph. We had hit that point in the ride where the individual needs, wants, and fears of the Lawless were carried away in black Gothic lettering on the wind. *Jobs, marital problems, taxes, kids, sex, appointments, court dates* flitted past me in a long strip that would be deposited on their Escondido doorsteps to consult upon return. Rides were no place for everyday problems. It was only without them that the club could ride, use their single-mindedness to follow every order of their alpha male.

The tears in my eyes accumulated until it became too blurry to see, and when I wiped them away and my vision cleared, I finally took notice of the scene around us as we passed by. The desert was flat in some places, rocky and rolling in others. Riding by at eighty miles an hour, it became an impressionist painting of earthy reds, yellows, oranges, greens, and blues. The sky, almost too bright, stood out against clouds that never seemed to move.

My mind eventually wandered from the landscape to my court cases, to the call I'd have to make to Trevor to tell him the ride would be longer than I expected, and eventually settled on my grandfather. I tried recalling any mention of my grandparents, but I was four when my parents died, and no matter how hard I tried, I couldn't remember a lot of things about my time with them.

I wasn't sure what I would do when Billy gave me this address. If my grandfather lived in Mexico, would I go to Mexico? I didn't speak Spanish despite what a lot of people assumed. No matter where I went—a restaurant, bank, shop, grocery store—Latinos tried to speak to me in Spanish. Shame washed over me when I had to sputter back, "No hablo español."

I didn't like feeling uncomfortable, not knowing things, especially something that everyone else seemed to think I should know. It's not like I didn't want to understand and speak Spanish. I did. My lack of fluency was another reminder that I didn't know my heritage, myself.

The white necks of the riders in front of me turned red in the sun. It was a view I was used to. I'd grown up the only brown kid among white people. I never had friends who weren't white until I went to college and cut myself off from the Lawless. Even though I'd never liked the racist things the Lawless had said, I'd been conditioned to believe stereotypes about Black, Latino, and Asian people, and every other person who was "different." In college, I had to learn how to spot those ingrained assumptions, and sometimes they were only revealed at my own embarrassment.

Making friends with people in college who weren't white had been liberating and eye-opening. I discovered that we had similar experiences of being *other*ed. We were looked at with distrust in certain spaces, mistreated in others, told we had it easy because of affirmative action, and felt pulled between American culture and that of our racial and ethnic identities. I finally had people I could talk to, people who would understand how Dodge and the Lawless had made me feel like I was less than, unwanted, not good because my skin was darker than theirs.

I had considered minoring in Spanish thinking it'd help me meet Latino friends, but something held me back. The Latino students at UCLA talked about family celebrations full of food, sweets, and dancing into the night and joked about their aunts' obsessions with telenovelas. They spoke a language that I strained to understand and when I didn't, I felt like I wasn't Mexican enough and ridiculous for wanting to know it in the first place. Eventually, I gave up and accepted English as the only language I'd ever know. I didn't try to make Latino friends. I never sought out opportunities to get to know that side of me because I feared my own people would see me as a fraud who had never tasted traditional Mexican dishes or listened to Latino music, and didn't understand their pop-culture references.

Now, I was faced with the opportunity to meet my Mexican grandfather. Maybe this would be my chance to learn about that part of my identity. At the very least, I could learn more about my dad, maybe even my mom, too. I couldn't pass that up.

After an hour and forty-five minutes, Billy finally pulled over at a gas station, and I couldn't have been happier. I had to pee, my lips were chapped and sunburned, and my eyes felt like shriveled grapes in my head. We parked on the far side, near the large semis. I tried to move quickly off my Ironhead but discovered that my legs were tight and achy from unconsciously clenching the sides of the bike. By the time I made it into the girl's bathroom, the two stalls were full and a Mama with a bandanna and saggy breasts waited in front of the mirror for the next one.

Two minutes passed, and no one came out of a stall. I tapped my foot furiously, a sound that echoed in the bathroom. It drew whispers from a few of the other women in line behind me. Fuck them; I had to pee. After finally releasing my bladder, I bought a bottle of water, pain medication, a cheese sandwich, Chapstick, and sunscreen. I popped a few pain pills and started eating the sandwich before I walked out the door.

I hadn't taken two steps before I spotted Jackson touching my duffel bag with a cigarette in hand. He wasn't looking my way, so he didn't see me approaching.

"Never knew how to keep your hands to yourself, did you?"

Jackson turned around and looked me up and down, then smirked.

We had started dating in high school and lasted into my second semester of college. I had cut myself off from Dodge, but not the entire club yet. Things were changing though. Distance had crept between me and Bethie since I couldn't visit her much in Escondido where she worked at a bar and didn't have a car. I saw Jackson more often because he was willing to make the drive. I thought his commitment to visit me indicated we were in love and meant to be together. I ignored how he'd become possessive since I'd moved to UCLA, questioning me about my classmates, the parties I attended on the weekends, and encouraging me to drop out and move in with him.

One night, I surprised Jackson by showing up at an apartment where he lived with two classmates from our high school. The place reeked of beer and cigarettes. One roommate was making out with a girl on the couch. Moans and grunts came from Jackson's other roommate's bedroom down the hallway. I should have known what I'd find when I opened Jackson's door, but love can manipulate even the smartest of us.

Jackson sat in a chair next to his bed while a woman with a massive blond perm knelt between his legs and sucked him off. His eyes opened when I pushed open the door. He only had time to mutter, "Fuck," before I ran at them. I pulled the girl away and swung her against the wall. She was so surprised by the attack that she tripped on her bright purple heels and fell to the floor. I went after her, but Jackson pulled me back, which gave the girl enough time to crawl out of the room.

Jackson and I got in a huge yelling match. When he said that the blowjob didn't count as cheating and that it was my fault because I was never around, I swung and hit him on the side of his head with my fist. He reacted by shoving me. When I fell, my forehead hit his bedside table. I put my hand to the aching area, and it came away slicked in bright thin blood that flowed gently down my face.

"Stay down, Raqi." Jackson sneered at me and stomped out of the bedroom. I heard him grab the girl, her friend in the living room, and his roommate before they quickly left through the front door. I sat on the floor all night. My emotions oscillated between sadness and rage as the blood from the gash slowed and eventually stopped.

Jackson and the others never returned, so around five in the morning I grabbed whatever clothes and items I'd left in Jackson's apartment. When I got downstairs, I saw Jackson's bike in the parking lot. They must have taken his roommate's truck. I stole the bike and parked it by a dumpster in an alley behind a diner ten miles away. I went into the diner and bought myself breakfast. That's where I decided to cut myself off from everyone for good. Jackson, the Lawless, even Bethie. I was done with the violence, the hatred, the illegal activities, and the only way I'd be free was to remove them from my life entirely.

The Jackson who stood in front of me today looked slightly different from the one I knew so long ago. The five o'clock shadow around his jaw had darkened over the years. His biceps stretched the sleeves of his shirt, and his shoulders seemed broader if that was possible. He looked like he wanted to say something back to me, but instead he took a long drag of his cigarette, spreading out the silence like margarine on bread.

We stood for a few pauses eyeing one another until finally, Jackson's eyes flicked above my head. I fought not to punch the air in glee.

"Good to see you, Raqi," he finally said, his scratchy voice monotone.

I crossed my arms over my chest. "For you maybe."

He smiled that half smile, the same one he'd used when we were teenagers. He looked down at my thighs. They were big and muscular, and he'd worshipped them in a weird way when we dated. I shifted my weight and stood up straighter.

"Could you move?"

Jackson shrugged and stood up before heading to his bike, looking over his shoulder at me while he walked away. I shot him the bird, with both hands.

My body screamed not to get back on the bike, but after another thirty minutes, I settled back into a rhythm that I had long forgotten. I used the long stretches of time to watch the Lawless write their story on the highway. Their tires drew endless ribbons of black lines across the road, telling a story that would never be read or understood. Motorcycle clubs like the Lawless were chapters left out of books, so they wrote their own with rubber and asphalt.

If I hadn't been forced to go on a multiday motorcycle journey with a band of unlawful drug and gun dealing bikers for my uncle's funeral, I might say the ride was somewhat pleasant, almost relaxing in that it let the incessant chatter in my mind quiet down. We stopped every two hours for gas and bathroom breaks, which sucked because I wanted real food—not a boiled hot dog or a soggy sandwich.

Highway signs eventually showed we were getting closer to Phoenix. But before we made it to the city, we left the main interstate and turned north, taking smaller highways and back roads. When there were no cars in the oncoming traffic lane, the Lawless spread out across both lanes and then moved back over when a car appeared.

As a kid, Dodge had taken me on a few runs, though at first, I didn't know that's what they were. I thought we were on a vacation of sorts, the type of thing I saw on TV. And it felt like that, too, minus the creepy places we went like shacks, restaurants, or houses, where I stood outside, waiting for Dodge, who took a backpack in and told me not to talk to anyone. Afterward, he'd come out, sometimes hours later, sometimes drunk or high, and we'd ride toward the main highway, find a spot in the middle of nowhere, camp for the night, and take off to another seedy place the next day.

About the time I turned ten, I finally figured out what Dodge was doing. Beth had told me, in fact. She heard Jackson talking to his friends about how their dad planned to take him on a run to sell cocaine, and soon he would be making his own money to buy himself a Harley.

Around four o'clock, we pulled into a small town that had one stoplight and shack-like houses with peeling paint and structures that drooped toward the ground away from the blistering sun. We drove through the town slowly, our motors echoing off the houses and metal fences before reverberating through my chest. Some residents came out to watch us pass by in a Hollister-like procession—minus the revelry, drunkenness, and property damage.

We finally pulled up to a bar on the edge of town. It was the largest building I had seen so far—a two-story stone edifice with Greek-inspired columns that had probably been lovely thirty years ago before the town had fallen into ruin. On the outside, a white sign with black letters spelled, "Bones." The *n* had almost completely faded.

Billy parked and everyone else followed suit. I ended up a few bikes from Jackson and Beth, and I fought not to look their way. When I got off my bike, she sighed at our separation, but I patted her twice to let her know I'd be back. I stretched my arms over my head at the same time Billy walked up and thrust a bag into my chest. I let out an "oomph."

"Here," he said.

I fumbled to grab the bag before it fell to the ground, then opened the flap. "What the hell is this?"

"Your uncle. Among other things. You're going to keep it tonight." He lit a cigarette.

I held it back toward him. "Gross, I don't want to hold that." Billy eyed it for a second but made no move to take it from me.

"You're going to need it." He blew out smoke. "We're heading in for food and drink. Sleeping here tonight."

I unstrapped my duffel bag, threw it on my shoulder, and started to walk toward the front door of Bones like many of the Lawless were doing.

Billy reached out, his arm blocking my way forward. "You're not going in there with us."

"Wha—why?"

"Go 'round back. There's a house about a hundred yards into the desert. That's where you're staying." He pointed his head in the direction.

My stomach grumbled.

"Why?"

"Dodge's request."

I waited for a second, but he didn't seem keen to explain. "I don't want to go to a house in the middle of the desert. It's almost dark. Who knows what's out there?"

Billy chuckled. "Scared, Raqi?" He threw down his cigarette and rubbed the ash into the ground with the toe of his boot.

"Fuck no. I'm hungry and tired and want a damn beer."

Billy shrugged his shoulders. "Tough luck, kid. I'm sure she'll feed you."

He turned and walked to the front door of Bones.

"Who's 'she'?" I yelled out.

"Don't open that bag until you get to the house." He walked inside to join the others.

Well, fuck.

I held the bag with Dodge's ashes in my hands and listened to the club laughing and talking loudly inside Bones. My stomach growled again.

Where the hell was this house? And who was "she"? Would there be any food? A bed? A shower? If there wasn't anything to eat or drink at this desert house, I'd drop off the bags and head back to the bar.

I walked around Bones and trudged through tall grass that scratched and grabbed at my jeans. The thought of a slithering snake hidden in the brush crossed my mind and I quickened my pace. When I finally made my way around back, I saw the cabin in the distance. The shrubs and grass disappeared as I got closer to the cabin, replaced by red earth that spread infinitely toward cliffs and canyons.

Soon, I was able to make out the details of the house. It was a wooden cabin with stacks of firewood and a stone well on the right side. On the other end of the cabin sat a rusting car with no windows and a missing front right wheel. When I was about thirty feet away, the door opened, and a woman exited. I paused for a second. This must be the "she."

Each Grieving Ride differed, depending on the Lawless. Sometimes the dead wanted you to drive along their route, but I had been on a few rides where we had to stop to speak to someone, like family members, or engage in an activity like swimming in their favorite river. Was this Dodge's wish—to hang out with this woman? But why? Maybe I was overthinking it and she was a caretaker setting things up for me.

The woman had long black hair with silver streaks and could have been Native American or Mexican or both. Her skin tone was like mine. She moved slowly, but her wrinkle-free face made it hard to tell her exact age. Her hips bulged against a brown peasant skirt and her shoulders were petite and covered in a gray shawl over a cream top. The girth around her stomach added to an overall curvaceous figure that men would eye.

She walked over to the pile of wood and placed a few pieces in the crook of her arm. I was about to say hello when she spoke. "Grab a few logs." She stood up and, without glancing at me, walked to the front door.

I opened my mouth to say something in response, but she hurried inside, and I was left standing there with Dodge in my arms. I picked up a few logs, fumbling as I did. It wasn't easy to balance Dodge, the logs, and my bag, and it took a couple of seconds to steady everything in my arms before heading to the front door. My frustration levels rose when it took a few tries to turn the doorknob.

I finally got the door open, entered the house, and almost dropped the logs again, this time in surprise. For one, it felt like a boiling kettle. A fire had been built even though it was still in the high eighties outside. Yet, more curious were the bones.

The house was a small studio with no walls separating the living room, bedroom, and kitchen. A single door stood in the right corner which I assumed led to a bathroom.

Bones of different sizes filled every inch of the place—the tables, the chairs, the walls, the floor, and even the bed. Some were pearly white, others had a yellowish tint, and some were caked in varying shades of dirt and mud. Placed among the bones were large and small animal skulls, their incisors sharp and pointy, ready to feast carnally on anything that came too near.

"Are you going to stand there or bring me those logs?"

I turned toward the fire where the woman stood, poking it with a metal rod. I was usually quick to say something—a sarcastic retort— but what do you say when you see this many bones in a sauna in the middle of the desert? I walked over and placed the logs on the ground next to her. She grabbed them without looking at me and threw them into the fireplace.

I stepped back a few feet, the hair on my arms standing on end. I'd go to the bar. Tell Billy I'd sleep on the ground, outside—whatever. I mean, where would I sleep here? On bones?

As I turned to leave—she didn't seem to be paying any attention to me anyway—the woman spoke, "Hand me the bag."

I paused and turned back around. "It's, um, you see, all that's in here is—"

She stood up and smirked, and I noticed light-brown freckles covered her nose. "I know who's in there." She held out her hand and beckoned to me with her pointer and middle finger. I handed her the bag.

"Sit if you want," she said. I pushed a few large animal skulls toward the back of a dusty dining table chair before sitting down. I dropped my bag to the ground, half expecting to hear the crush of bones.

She pulled out Dodge's urn and looked it over. It wasn't particularly interesting, just smooth and black. The woman raised it and looked at the bottom and smiled. She moved it closer to her chest and began unscrewing the bottom lip. Something clicked, and she set the urn on its side on the table before pulling out a small packet with a black powdery substance, a clear packet of pills, and another bag with a few small bones.

"What the hell?"

She laughed and the sound made the bones scattered about the room turn toward her ever so slightly. "Dodge provided one last time."

"Since when does—I mean, bones?" I shook my head, unable to form sentences correctly.

She left the pills on the table and took the bag with the black powder to the kitchen. She slid the bones into a pocket in the side of her skirt.

"Who are you?" I asked.

"My name's Juana."

Her name didn't explain who she was. Juana grabbed a few mugs from a wooden shelf and filled them with steaming water from a kettle on the stove.

Her back faced me when she said, "I heard you didn't like Dodge."

"No one liked Dodge," I said.

She added a spoonful of black powder and stirred it in before bringing the mugs to the table. She handed one to me and held the other as she pulled up a chair and sat down.

The warm mug held a clear liquid with a slight green tinge. I sniffed but it was odorless.

Juana smiled. "It's tea."

"What kind?" It didn't look like any tea I'd ever seen and if it came from Dodge, it probably wasn't.

"Golden Assam. I'm sure you noticed on your way in that we don't have large supermarkets. Sometimes Dodge brought me things that are a little rare to find in the area."

I looked around her house. "Obviously."

She laughed again and the bones responded by turning again in her direction. She took a sip of tea as silence filled the room until it became uncomfortable.

"You don't look like Dodge's typical customer," I finally said.

"How's that?"

"You're a woman and you're not white. And you don't seem like a drug dealer."

"Maybe it's because I don't consider myself a drug dealer," she said.

I shrugged and took a sip of the tea, which was a little bitter and now lukewarm. She'd been drinking hers, so I figured it wasn't poison.

"Toh-may-toe, toh-mah-toe. Those are drugs in that little packet." She picked up the packet and raised it above her eyes.

"They are drugs, but I don't use them in the same way that I'm sure most of Dodge's customers do."

I shrugged. "If you say so." I took another sip of the tea and looked around the room.

"I use them to heal people, poor rural people."

My eyebrow rose. "You use drugs to heal people? That's not how it works, lady."

She chuckled. "You'd be surprised how 'bad' drugs can do a lot for cancer patients in pain who don't have insurance."

"Hmm." I shrugged. "Maybe." In my experience, Dodge didn't deal drugs to help people, and while some of the stuff she said made sense, I was a bit wary. Especially since she had a house full of bones.

Juana read my mind. "You're wondering about my bones."

"I don't even know where to start."

Juana smiled again and looked at the room, wistfully. She breathed in deeply and exhaled slowly, and though it was a simple movement, I couldn't look away. I leaned toward her like the bones around me did. Her eyes turned to me and the spell broke. I exhaled shakily.

"I'm a collector. Always have been." She grabbed a tiny rodent skull from the table next to her and studied it. It smiled and wriggled in her hand, honored to have this bone woman's attention.

"As a kid, I found the leg bone of a wolf. It was the most interesting thing I'd ever seen. I became obsessed with finding the rest of the skeleton." She smiled. "From there, my interest in bones expanded, but I've always had a soft spot in my heart for wolves."

"And the bones that Dodge gave you?"

She placed the skull back on the table. "Sometimes I can only find half the skeletal bones during my own digs, so I asked Dodge to find the rest."

I looked around the room. It was a weird hobby to say the least, but it didn't sound illegal. I couldn't quite imagine where Dodge would find bones or why he would even go to the trouble of helping her find them. If she paid, and paid well, I guess Dodge would do about anything.

Suddenly, Juana changed the conversation. "Would you like a shower? Something to eat?"

I nodded yes, and she got up and showed me the bathroom before letting me be. When I got out of the shower and walked back in the living room toweling my hair off, Juana balanced two plates and two tin cups in her hands as she walked to the front door.

"Meet me in the backyard," she said over her shoulder.

I hung the towel over the shower rod and put my boots on before heading to the back of the house. It was that hazy time between sunset and night, when the sun is gone but still sits close to the horizon, casting a beautiful glow across the sky.

Juana sat in a green lawn chair next to a small table. Another chair was placed on the opposite side. On the table were the plates and tin cups. The backyard was also filled with bones, but unlike inside where the bones were scattered about in an unfathomable pattern, the bones in the backyard were laid out in a formation. It took a second for my brain to grasp what I saw.

The skull was animalistic, almost wolflike, and placed at the top of a form with two legs, two arms, and a tail. It was almost as if the bones had been staged to look like a human splayed out on the ground, hands raised above the head. The hair on my arms tingled, but I ignored it and walked to the empty chair and sat down.

When I saw the plate of food, I remembered how hungry I was and pushed my questions to the back of my mind. Juana had prepared a meal of dried meat—deer, I soon discovered—cheddar cheese slices, nuts, and crackers. I would have preferred a burger, but it was enough to stave off the gnawing of my insides. The tin cups held whiskey on ice, or at least, mine did. It was filled to the top, and I tried not to let any drop spill as I took sips, allowing the liquid to burn my throat in all the right ways.

We sat silently and watched the hazy night turn a cobalt blue and the stars become more prolific in the night sky. The desert lost its shape and became filled with blue, purple, and black shadows that moved on their own accord. My food had all but disappeared when she turned on a small lantern that sat on the ground near our feet.

"Why are you here?" Juana asked.

I took a sip of whiskey. "Had to. You were on Dodge's list."

"But you didn't fight not to come here."

"I did, I mean—I didn't have a choice . . ." My words faded. Why was I explaining myself to her? I didn't owe her that. Besides, she didn't know about my grandfather, the golden ticket at the end of the ride.

"You had a choice, and you chose to be here."

I shook my head, which made me dizzy. "I don't want to be here, doing this ride for Dodge, but it's the last thing I can do to wash my hands of him and the club once and for all."

"And that's what you want?" Juana asked.

"Duh." God, did I say 'duh'? That was such a valley girl thing to say, and I had never sounded like a valley girl. The whiskey was starting to make me ramble. My chest warmed, and my head felt soft.

She smiled. "Dodge stopped at my bar one day for a drink. That's how I met him."

"Bones is yours?"

She nodded.

"Makes sense."

She looked away from me and into the night. "He arrived and asked for a beer, but it was clear he was sick. He couldn't stop shaking."

"Drugs will do that." I chuckled at my own joke.

Her lips twisted to the side in annoyance. "You talk a lot."

I took another sip of whiskey and felt the trapped heat of the desert earth rise through my feet and course through my limbs, leaving the smell of dry dirt in my nose and a swirl of wind in my head. I smiled and relaxed into the chair. Alcohol didn't usually make me this loose and happy.

"I had seen this kind of thing before," Juana continued. "He was trying to get clean, to heal, but he didn't have a goddamn clue how to do it correctly."

I laughed, not sure why I found that funny. The alcohol was starting to hit me good, and the long day of riding had settled in my bones and mind. I felt too comfortable in the hard-plastic chair. I laughed again.

"I told him that I could help him get clean for good."

I sat up in my chair—or tried to. My body swayed forward then back, and my vision slid sideways. "His Old Lady said he was clean. That true then?" She settled back in her seat and looked up at the sky. "I told him I would help him in exchange for two things. One, he'd have to bring me the bones I was looking for. And two, he would provide me with the pills I needed."

My lips tingled now, a sign I was tipsy. "What were the pills—"

"He agreed. He wanted to get clean for his niece."

I looked at the bones and took another drink from a glass that never seemed to go empty.

"So, I brought him here and I told him to lay down on the ground under the night sky and place his arms over his head."

"And den wha you do?" My words sounded slurred, even to me.

"I asked him if he was really ready."

"Fo wha?" I took another sip of the whiskey and looked in the cup. The drink threatened to spill over the top even though I'd been drinking it for a while now. I flicked my tongue out and lapped up a few drops. Laughing at myself, I took a full drink then toasted Juana mockingly.

"Ready for what?" I repeated.

She smirked, then walked over to the closest set of bones. I suddenly realized the skull resembled a large dog—or maybe even a wolf. As Juana got nearer, the skull looked up and smiled excitedly.

"I asked him if he was ready to let go of it all."

"Ha!" burst from my mouth followed by hysterical laughter. Dodge lying on the ground, with shivers and this Bone Lady asking him weird questions. I imagined Dodge saying, "What the fuck?"

Juana waited until I stopped laughing, then squatted down next to the bones and lightly ran her hands over them. They trembled with happiness under her touch, then in sadness when her fingertips left them for another.

"He was ready. You, not so much."

I put the tin cup on the table, but it was a bit too hard, and whiskey slopped over onto my hand. "What are you talking about?" I said, leaning back in the chair. The sky above me was full of millions of stars. I never liked stars. Looking at them for too long caused a lump to form in my throat and tears to come to my eyes. They made me feel . . . insignificant and hopeful at the same time. I reached up to wipe them away but only managed to clear the sky of a few before my arm felt too heavy and fell in my lap.

"I can help you when you're ready to accept it all and be free."

I wanted to say I was fine, I didn't need to be free of anything, but I couldn't make my mouth open and words come out. Or maybe I did because she laughed. Had I said something funny?

Juana continued laughing, her mouth growing wider and wider and her teeth becoming sharper like the large incisors of the skulls that littered her home. Tears flowed from her eyes and into the ground creating a river that circled the bones but never washed them away. Her energy pulled the colors of red, orange, and pink from the desert and sent them spinning in a dirt devil around her body. I tried to sit up, pushing my hands against the armrests, but my head spun, and I felt woozy and fell backward.

Then suddenly Juana's laugh turned into singing, and she sang a song that made me very sad and happy, so I both cried and laughed. The tune wrapped me in a blanket, and then quickly pulled that blanket away, leaving me caught in a state of longing and belonging.

She raised her hands above her head. I caught every movement, every twinkle in her dark eyes. Juana's singing slashed through the night air, and the bones wriggled in delight. I tried to stand up, hoping it would make everything stop, but I couldn't. A large weight held me down in my seat. I strained stubbornly against the heaviness.

Juana kept singing, her hands still outstretched. The bones vibrated with her song, moving together by an invisible force, connecting at the joints. I stopped trying to stand up but succumbed to the weight and settled back in the chair.

Ligaments sprouted from joints, muscle grew between the bones, blood rushed through veins, and the bones disappeared. Her song sped up as fur appeared, and the shape became clearer. I leaned too far forward, and as I did the vision before me slowly began to fade. Shadows crept from my peripheral vision, reaching for each other, blocking my view.

I fell forward out of the chair just as the wolf looked up to the sky and howled.

9

Dodge met me, Eddie, and Billy at the burger place. His hair was wet, but he smelled better and had on new clothes. No one mentioned how Billy yelled at Dodge at the house or kicked out the woman he'd been with. He didn't look at me as I ate my french fries, but only down at his meal. Billy and Eddie spoke about things like "routes" and making schedules for them, but I didn't understand so I ate my food silently.

That evening, Dodge and I returned home alone in his truck. When we got inside, I walked to the couch and got under the covers, tired from being out so late. Even though I hadn't wanted to touch the couch on my first day here, I'd grown used to the sticky stains that covered it. They kissed me lightly on the shoulders and legs when I slept, and sometimes I pretended they were guardian angel kisses protecting me from bad things.

Dodge went to the kitchen and grabbed a soda from the fridge. He was about to walk past me but stopped.

"You brush your teeth?"

It was the first time he'd asked me such a thing since I'd moved in. I shook my head no and rubbed my tongue over the slimy film on my teeth.

"Well, go on. Brush them."

I sat up on the couch. "I don't have a toothbrush."

"They didn't bring your toothbrush?" His voice rose like it did when he was angry. I shook my head again. He swore under his breath and muttered to himself as he popped the top of the Coke. He stood there drinking from the soda for a second before looking at me again. I shrunk into the couch, hoping the stains might save me from his anger.

After groaning in disgust, he walked over and sat on the coffee table in front of me. He set his forearms on his knees and looked down at the Coke between his hands.

"I heard Eddie call you 'Raqi,'" he said.

I nodded. Maybe he wasn't angry. The couch pushed me to sit up straighter.

He took another drink. "That lady said your name was Raquel."

I shrugged. "Mama and Dad called me Raqi."

He nodded and mumbled, "Raqi." Dodge took another drink of his Coke and then cleared his throat.

"You're going to live here," he said. "So, I guess I need to make some changes. Tomorrow, I'll clean out that bedroom across the hall and you can move in there."

I sat back on the couch and nodded. He looked up for a second then back down.

"And we'll get you a goddamn toothbrush. Can't believe that bitch didn't bring you one."

He took a drink. "I—" He paused and cleared his throat. "I'm sorry about your mama. She was my sister, you know. You should be with her, not me." He sighed. "But here we are."

Dodge looked up at me and we locked eyes for a few seconds.

"What the hell did you do to your lip? They thought I hit you."

My hand went to my lip. "I bit it on accident."

"Hmph," Dodge said. "Don't do it again. I don't need someone calling Social Services on me. You hear?"

I nodded.

He took another drink and studied me for a second. "How old are you again?"

I held up four tiny fingers and wiggled them. I still had two flecks of purple nail polish on my left forefinger and right pinky finger. Mama had painted my nails weeks ago.

"Four years old," he said quietly, before standing up and walking to his room. I waited for him to turn around and say "goodnight," but he never did.

10

1990, thirty-one years old

I woke up to the taste of dirt on my tongue. I tried spitting out the grit and grime, but I didn't have enough saliva. A bright light shone through my eyelids, and I knew if I opened my eyes, it would hurt. My head pounded, and I lay on something hard. Suddenly, the bright light dimmed as if something shielded it from me. I slowly opened my eyes to Juana's warm brown face hovering over mine.

"Are you awake?" she asked.

My temples throbbed and I felt something rising quickly in my throat. Faster than I thought I could move, I turned onto my side and dry heaved, but nothing came up.

"Puke if you have to," Juana said.

She . . . last night. Knew Dodge. Sang something weird. Singing. The bones. I heaved a few more times; jagged flashes of the previous night came back to me with every contraction of my stomach and throat muscles. I tried to piece it all together, but it didn't make much sense. The heaves eventually stopped after a minute or two and I panted, laying my head in the crook of my arm.

A shadow came in view. I looked up. Juana held a mug out to me.

"Here. This will help."

Black coffee. Before I grabbed for it, I sat up and reached behind me for the chair from last night. My hand finally found it, and I pulled myself up with little grace. I took the coffee from her.

"Fuck," I said. I took a drink and looked up. "God, I feel like shit."

Juana put her hands on her hips. "I imagine." She chuckled.

"Why'd you let me sleep out here? Aren't there snakes and coyotes?"

Juana shrugged. "They don't come close to the house, and besides, how was I going to pick you up and carry you in? I tried to wake you, but you were out like a light."

The coffee was almost gone. I leaned back in the chair, my whole body screaming in soreness. I didn't know if I was sore from yesterday's bike ride or from sleeping on the desert floor. Probably both. Still, last night had been . . . not right.

"Did you drug me?" It was the only thing that made sense.

She laughed. "I wouldn't waste drugs on you."

This sobered me up quickly. "What—no, you had to—" Raising my voice sent a sharp pain through my head. I grabbed my skull until it subsided.

She ignored my anger and instead asked, "Why?"

"What do you mean, 'why'?"

"Why do you think I drugged you?"

"Uh . . ." I paused. How could I explain what I saw? It seemed like a hallucination. Maybe it had been a dream . . . But it had felt different from any other dream I'd ever had. In my dreams, my senses—especially smell and touch—were dulled. But that didn't happen last night. It was almost as if I had been awake. That couldn't be possible.

"Well?" she asked.

"Must have been a dream," I replied.

She smirked. "Fine, what was this dream?" I could almost see the air quotes when she said the word "dream."

It was a jumble in my mind. "You looked different, and the bones came together—"

"Into what?"

I shrugged and looked for the bones on the ground. But they were gone.

"Where'd they go?"

Juana looked in the direction of the missing bones then slowly back to me. Ignoring my question, she said, "What did the bones turn into?"

"I don't know," I whispered. "A wolf or dog or something." It wasn't possible, but where were the bones? Uh-oh. I leaned over my chair just as nausea hit again. I spit up a clear liquid this time, but nothing more substantial. I couldn't remember anything else after that.

"What happened to me? What did I do last night?" Blacking out was not something I took lightly. It happened twice in college, and it drove me insane the next days, weeks, not knowing what had happened to me, what I'd done. I refused to let it happen again, until now.

"I grabbed the cup out of your hand and took the plates inside. When I came back out, you had fallen forward, and I couldn't pick you up off the ground."

"But I—" I swallowed another wave of nausea. I didn't remember any of that.

A young woman about my age came around the corner of the house. She wore blue jeans and a white T-shirt that stood out against her smooth tawny brown skin. Her black hair was shiny and long and a few wisps floated in the breeze. In her hands were my duffel and a brown paper bag.

Juana stood up. "Can't stay long; I need to go out and administer those pills."

I scoffed. "Not a drug dealer my ass."

She sighed. "As I said, I help people in pain, but only when they want it." Juana took my things from her companion. The woman smirked and crossed her arms. I scowled.

"As for your vision, dream, whatever you want to call it," Juana added, "You should be thankful. Such visions can help people figure out those things in their life they don't want to examine."

"It didn't do that," I said.

She shrugged. "Then at least it gave you a taste of what Dodge felt, what he did to get clean."

I coughed. I must have inhaled some dirt while sleeping on the ground because my throat itched. "This—" I coughed again. "He got visions out here and that helped him get off drugs? That's the most absurd thing I ever heard."

"He saw something of his soul, and it changed him from the man you once knew."

"Yeah right."

She smiled sadly. "I think your friends are leaving soon."

Juana made me get up and follow her to the front of the house. The young woman walked behind us. Juana handed me my bag and I fished inside for my sunglasses. They gave me little relief when I put them on.

"I put Dodge's urn in your bag," Juana said as I placed it on my shoulder. "Come back when you're ready."

Fuck, my head hurt. "Why would I ever come back?"

The young woman, who had been silent all this time, answered for Juana, "To let go of it all and finally move on."

Move on from what? I stared at the mystery woman for a second. She seemed so familiar, yet also wasn't. Who was she and how was she mixed up with Juana?

I shook my head and turned away. "I'm good," I called over my shoulder. The woman laughed, and it sounded like a stone splashing into a still river.

I trudged over the red earth under the crowing of birds I could not see. Steps from the bar, the howl of a wolf pierced the air somewhere nearby. I yelped in surprise and turned around, but I was alone.

I stumbled into Bones searching for more coffee. I left my sunglasses on, because the dimly lit bar lights were too bright for me. During my walk to the bar, I'd inhaled the breakfast of dried fruit, meats, and a granola bar in the brown bag. It had done little to help my aching head or growling stomach.

The bartender eyed everyone in distaste as he cleaned a mug.

"Coffee," I said bluntly.

He handed me a cup and it smelled on the shitty side, but I didn't care. I took it and stumbled to a wooden table in the corner. The Lawless were moving through the place, heading in and out to their bikes, loading up. Few paid me any mind.

I had taken a couple of sips of the coffee and was starting to relax, when a gravelly woman's voice said, "God, you look like shit."

I looked up. Dodge's piece of ass. What's-her-name gave me a sly smile.

"Go away." I took another drink and grimaced as she sat down.

"I'm surprised is all," she said, leaning back in her chair. She wore a turquoise bandanna today.

"Look, Rebecca—"

Her smiled disappeared. "It's Lenora."

"Whatever. Could you shut up? My head's pounding."

"Hmph" was her reply. Lenora remained quiet for a second as she watched my face. After a few moments, she leaned forward and placed her elbows on the table, cradling her face in her hands. It was a youthful movement for a woman in her fifties.

"Odd is all."

I slammed the coffee cup down. A little bit sloshed onto the table.

"God, Lenora. What is odd?"

"Dodge made it sound like that Indian lady was some miracle worker."

"How do you know she's Native American?" With a name like Juana, I assumed she was Mexican.

"Guess I don't. Just going off what Dodge thought." She shrugged. "Dodge said he left her feeling brand new—cured and all. That's why I don't get why you look strung-out."

I hated to admit it, but Lenora had caught my interest.

"Dodge said that lady cured him?"

"Mm-hmm. Or close enough. Called her the Bone Lady or the Wolf Lady—"

The bones. The wolf. My stomach twisted. "Why did he call her that?"

Lenora leaned forward. "He said the locals tell a lot of stories about her. It's weird enough she gathers animal bones, but Dodge said she's real keen on wolf bones. People round here say that when she's gathered all the bones of a wolf, she can bring it back to life."

My mouth felt dry and my hands hot.

Lenora lowered her voice. "But these ain't regular wolves. They can turn into women."

My hands shook around my coffee cup. That was ridiculous.

"Raqi, you look as white as a ghost. Did you see something like that?"

I shook my head and wouldn't meet Lenora's eyes. I'd seen something, but I—No, I hadn't. I couldn't have. I had been drunk and hot from a full day of riding. It had to be a hallucination or a dream.

"After his experience with the Bone Lady, Dodge stopped cold turkey and started getting help by going to meetings. That's where we met."

So, Lenora used drugs too. Didn't surprise me one bit.

"He claimed it wasn't the meetings that helped get him off the drugs. He always said it was her."

"Right," I said sarcastically.

Lenora leaned back from the table, and her eyes squinted in annoyance. "I ain't lying to you. Dodge wasn't using, Raqi."

"I don't care."

She looked to the front door. I hoped she'd get up and leave, and I'd have a chance to sit quietly with my headache.

Quiet was too much to ask from Lenora.

"You know if it hadn't been for her, he would have overdosed."

"You don't know that," I spat. I closed my eyes behind my sunglasses and leaned back in my chair, hoping the pounding in my temples would ease up.

"He told me so. He had been thinking about doing it himself, instead of accidentally doing it one day," she said.

"Dodge would never have committed suicide. That's bullshit."

She slammed her hand on the table, and I jumped, losing a bit more coffee. I shook the brown droplets from my hand in annoyance and wiped it on my jeans.

"Goddamn it, Raqi. He didn't have anything after you left. Just drugs and these guys." She pointed with her thumb over her shoulder. "That wasn't enough anymore. They might be brothers, but"—she lowered her voice—"they got too much damn pride to get anyone the help they need."

I felt a little knot form at the base of my throat. Dodge would never.

Lenora's shoulders sagged and she sighed. "I wished I could have met her. Dodge said she was into some weird things, but—"

I interrupted Lenora. "Weird how?"

She shrugged. "Like a witch or something. You sure you didn't see her do magic?"

"No," I said quickly.

Lenora opened her mouth to say something, but a sharp whistle pierced the air. My temples pulsed in anger, yelling for silence. I gripped the mug tightly, surprised it didn't crumple in my hands.

Billy stood framed in the doorway by a soft, heavenly light.

"Five minutes."

Before we left, I asked Billy about our next destination.

"New Mexico."

"Please, tell me I can sleep in a fucking motel this time."

He chuckled. "Whatever the princess wants."

I punched him on the arm without thinking—playful but hard. Growing up as a teenager, it was something I would do when things felt uncomfortable. I hadn't done that in years, preferring not to touch most people, playful or not. Billy didn't seem to notice, but grinned and walked to his bike.

The ride was about as horrible as I expected it would be. My head pounded in the heat and my stomach growled. But at least we were leaving the town and Juana behind. I didn't know what to think about her and her cryptic message of returning when I was ready to "let go."

Let go of what? I wasn't on this ride to "let go" of anything. I was here to grab an address and be free of them all.

11

A month after I had moved in with Dodge, I turned to him and asked, "What's a spic?"

Dodge had been spreading peanut butter on a piece of white bread but paused at my question. We had had peanut-butter-and-jelly sandwiches for lunch the past three days. It was strawberry jelly since Dodge didn't like grape. Now, my sweat smelled nutty one second and sweet like strawberries the next. I sniffed near Dodge. He still smelled like cigarettes, but if I concentrated hard enough, I thought I smelled peanuts.

"Where the hell you hear that?" He looked at me from beneath his gray baseball cap. I no longer flinched when Dodge said bad words that my parents never said.

I stood next to the counter, one foot on top of the other. I swayed a little bit, trying to balance. "That guy yesterday. The one who came up to your window at the gas station."

Dodge made an "*umph*" sound, something between a grunt and a "hmph," and continued spreading the peanut butter. He often made the sound when he didn't want to speak to me. Usually, I didn't pester him with questions, but new words filled this new life and I wanted to know what they meant.

"So, what does spic mean?"

"Don't say that word," Dodge snapped. He grabbed the jelly jar and set it a little too forcefully on the cabinet.

I had also learned that Dodge liked to yell and be rude, but he wasn't mad. That was how he was.

"But that man—"

"His name's Gray, and it ain't no word you should be saying."

I stood on my tiptoes and tried to peer under his hat.

"But why?"

"Because it means the Mexicans." He slapped the jelly piece of bread on the peanut butter piece and slid it over to me. I took a bite. I didn't even like peanut-butter-and-jelly sandwiches.

"My dad was Mexican, so that means I'm a spic, right?" I said through mouthfuls.

Dodge pulled off his hat, wiped his black hair down, and then put his hat back on. He tried not to look at me.

"Goddamn it, girl. Stop saying that word."

"But you said—"

"Look." He finally turned to look at me. "It ain't a nice word. Stop saying it."

"Then why did Gray say it?"

It didn't seem like Gray used it in a wrong way. Gray had said, "Billy says it's about time you get that girl in school. He needs you to meet the spics about a load and go on a run."

I thought it was weird that Gray told Dodge to go on a run. He didn't seem like someone who worked out. My parents exercised when they were alive. Mom would go on long runs, while my dad, rocking a bandanna around his head, lifted dumbbells in the garage. I used to sneak into their room and steal my dad's lime-green bandanna. I would try to wrap it on my head like he did, but it never came out right. He would adjust the bandanna, then let me lift small weights with little number twos on the side until Mom returned from her run.

As I finished eating the sandwich, Dodge leaned his elbows on the counter. He looked at me and chewed the inside of his cheek.

"Look, don't go saying that word, okay? And don't let anyone say that word to you, you hear me?"

I still didn't understand, but if Dodge said it was bad, it must be, since he said bad words all the time. I wondered if it was as bad as the word One-Tooth Boy called me.

I nodded. "What do I do if someone calls me that?"

Dodge stood straight. "You knock him out." He hit his right fist into his open left palm and a large slapping noise rang out. I grinned because it was kind of funny. Still, it didn't make much sense. He was mad I had fought that boy but was okay with me hitting anyone who called me that bad word.

After finishing my sandwich, I watched Dodge eat with his mouth open. Mushy breadcrumbs stuck to his gums as he chewed.

"Dodge?"

He made the "*umph*" sound again.

"Do you run?"

Dodge pulled off a piece of crust and threw it down on the counter. "Run?"

"That Gray man, he said you needed to go on a run. Mama ran a lot. Do you run too?"

Dodge took another bite of his sandwich and chewed it for a long time before he swallowed. He stared hard, searching my face for something, but I don't think he ever found it.

A week later, we saw Gray again. He came by the house with a bag for Dodge. When Dodge opened the door and saw Gray, he turned and looked at me. I sat on the living room floor, drawing on a piece of paper. He stepped outside with Gray and closed the door. I ran to the window and looked out. I couldn't hear what Dodge said, but his hands flew about so fast that it made him look like a rollie pollie on its back, kicking its legs in fear. Gray looked to the house and tried to calm Dodge down by patting his shoulder, but Dodge pulled away and continued yelling and spitting.

When Dodge took me around the Lawless after that, I didn't hear people say bad words that meant "Mexicans" anymore. The few times I thought an adult might say it, I saw them pause, look at me, and then change the subject. Just because "spic" and "beaner" were off the table, didn't mean I didn't hear other things that made my stomach hurt and my neck turn hot—like when they said the Mexicans were taking over California and debated accepting a hit on Cesar Chavez for getting those "illegal grape pickers all rallied up."

Maybe people like them could only change so much.

12

1990, thirty-one years old

As I refueled my bike at a gas station outside of Albuquerque, Jackson walked up, bringing the smell of sweat, unfounded anger, tobacco, and teenage sexual tension with him. I fought not to groan. My headache had just disappeared.

"What do you want?"

Jackson pushed a wad of tobacco from his lip to his cheek. "You're to meet a guy at a café in Albuquerque."

"Why isn't Billy telling me this?"

He stretched his long, thin arms behind his back and popped his joints. "Because you're going to follow me there."

I heard the gas spill over as soon as I smelled it.

"Fuck," I said pulling out the nozzle and thrusting it into the holder. Jackson laughed. That shithead had distracted me so much I hadn't been paying attention to how high the gas level was in the tank. The gas pooled around my feet, staining my boots with its iridescent oils.

I sneered. "To hell I am. Tell me where to go and I'll figure it out."

He moved closer to me and put his hands on the back of my bike's seat as I screwed the nozzle onto the gas tank.

"You know Billy won't allow that. Besides you could get lost—"

"You mean leave," I interrupted.

He shrugged. "Whatever. It's the way Billy wants it."

"We'll see about that." Jackson moved out of the way when I swung my leg over the seat and kick-started the engine. I drove to an empty parking spot, parked the bike, and went in search of Billy. I found him looking at the packaged doughnut selection inside the gas station.

"Hey," I said. He didn't respond. "Me and Jackson riding together is not going to work. Find somebody else to take me to the café."

Billy leaned forward and grabbed the cinnamon-powdered dough-nuts. He looked them over in his hand.

"I don't think so."

"Why not? It doesn't matter who does it."

Billy walked past me toward the checkout counter.

"It does. Jackson's going to take over Dodge's old route, and he needs to know who to meet and where."

I rolled my eyes. Could this ride get worse?

"Fine but tell him to keep his fucking distance."

Billy chuckled and glanced at me sideways. "What, Raqi? You scared you gone catch feelings for old Jack again? Things ain't all paradise with your colored boy?"

At that moment, Billy stepped up to the checkout counter. The cashier was a Black woman. I didn't know if she had heard him, but I felt my face get hot from Billy's words.

"Don't say shit like that to me," I said.

Billy grumbled something under his breath, but I couldn't make it out.

I glanced at the woman who tried not to look at us as she rang up Billy's items. I grimaced and walked away.

Billy's racist remark wasn't the only thing that had pissed me off. His mention of Trevor hit a little too close to home. I hadn't spoken to him since I'd left. I could go days without speaking to Trevor, but Trevor wouldn't like that at all. It wasn't that he was the jealous type. Trevor was the kind of person who genuinely worried about the people he cared for. We were very different in that regard. I found a pay phone outside and dialed Trevor's work number.

The phone rang and rang as my stomach twisted in knots. His

assistant Nancy answered, "Smith and Associates. This is Trevor Johnson's line."

"Let me talk to Trevor." I didn't like Nancy. She was one of those LA girls who arrived eight months ago from the Midwest hoping to make it as an actor. Instead of going on casting calls, she went to clubs on Sunset to convince coked out agents and casting directors to give her a big break.

"One minute, Ms. Warren," Nancy said before she put me on hold. I wanted to punch her in the face for refusing to call me Raqi.

My heart sped up a bit and I shuffled nervously as the hold music played.

"What the hell, Raqi?" Trevor said as he picked up the call.

I cringed. "I know, I know."

"You didn't call last night. I don't know where you're at or what you're doing with Billy's gang—"

"Club."

"What?"

"Nothin'."

Trevor sighed. "See. You're starting to sound like them."

"God, I know, Trev. I'm sorry, shit." I looked behind me hoping none of the Lawless were around to hear, then cursed myself for even caring what they thought.

"Where are you?" he asked.

"Outside of Albuquerque."

"And you'll be gone for how long?"

I sighed. "Another seven days—"

"What? Are you serious?"

I groaned. "Look, I know. It's bullshit. But this is it—after this, I'm done. Free. They're going to be out of my life. It's not like I have a choice—"

"Bullshit, Raqi." Trevor was not usually harsh. I winced. "You have a damn choice. You choose to give into them. You're never going to be fully rid of the Lawless until you put your foot down."

I hadn't told Trevor about my grandfather. Why, I wasn't sure. Maybe

I wanted something for myself. Or perhaps, I was scared that if I told anyone back home about my grandfather, it would make it too real, too hopeful. If something happened and Billy really didn't have the address, or I couldn't find my grandfather, then the disappointment wouldn't hurt as bad. And perhaps I wouldn't seem as pathetic for believing a criminal like Billy.

I rubbed my forehead. "I'm sorry, Trev. I'll make it up to you when I return."

He sighed, and I felt the cold breath of disappointment against my cheek. "Sure." He was shutting down, which meant he was pretty pissed off. Shit.

"I have to go. I'll call you tomorrow," I said.

"If you say so."

I needed to pull out the big guns. "Bye, love you."

I thought I heard him say, "You too," before there was a click and then dead air, a silence roaring in my ear, bringing on another headache.

13

1970, eleven years old

"Raqi, get up!" Dodge yelled from the living room. A quick look at the alarm clock on the bedside table told me it was 10:00 a.m. Dad used to make me wake up at 7:00 a.m., even on the weekends. He always said, "Time in bed is time wasted."

Dodge wasn't like that. He didn't care about sleeping in on the weekends. He didn't care what I did during the week either. I had to wake myself up in time to catch the school bus, and I was lucky if there was anything to eat for breakfast. Not like the mornings Mom made me eggs and pancakes before she or Dad took me to pre-K.

"Raqi, damn it. I ain't asking again. Get out here!"

What was Dodge doing up so early? In the seven years since I lived here, Dodge never woke up before me unless it was to take one of his trips. Sometimes, he'd let me join, and other times I had to stay with God-knows-who for a few days. I always begged to stay with Eddie. He was the cleanest and the nicest of the Lawless, but sometimes he'd be on his own trip.

I padded barefoot into the living room, wiping the sleep from my eyes. Dodge stood by the door, his hands on his hips.

"Why ain't you dressed?"

"I just woke up," I replied.

"Hurry up and get your butt to the garage," Dodge said.

"The garage?"

"I didn't stutter. Now hurry up, girl." Dodge walked out the front door.

He never let me go to the garage, which wasn't a garage, but more like a separate shed. It's where he kept his bike and tools and other things I wasn't allowed to get into. A month after I moved here, I walked too close to the garage, and he flipped. Told me to keep my filthy hands away from his stuff. So, I had.

I went back to my room and changed into a pair of jeans that were a little short around the ankles and a white tee with dirt stains. Now that I didn't have Mama to wash my clothes, I had to do them on my own— and Dodge's for that matter—and I wasn't good at getting stains out.

The garage doors were open. It sounded like Dodge was moving tools and kicking metal boxes this way and that. I slowly peeked inside and got my first look at why Dodge was behaving differently. There was a motorcycle, or more accurately, a minibike called a Taco. I wasn't sure why it was called that because it didn't look like a taco, but many of the boys my age had one and that's all they talked about in school.

Caked in dirt, the minibike had flat tires and missing parts, even to my untrained eye. The metallic purple color was chipped and faded away. The bike looked at me, not seemingly impressed by what it saw in me either.

"Finally," Dodge said. I walked into the garage.

"Well?" he growled impatiently.

I waited for him to say something else, but he didn't. He put his hands on his hips and then dropped them, then did it again. He bit his lip and watched me carefully by looking down, then sideways at me, then down again.

He huffed. "Ain't got nothing to say? I do something nice, and you just stand there?" His face twitched, and I could tell he wanted to yell, but he fought against the urge. He crossed his arms, then uncrossed them quickly.

I didn't realize that the bike was for me, though I guess it was my size. Dodge had never bought me anything, besides food for the house, and even that was random and involved boxes of mac n' cheese, peanut butter and jelly, and cans of soup or chili most of the time. I had grown to despise Hormel.

Quickly, I said, "Thanks," because I didn't know what else to say.

All the sons of the Lawless were excited when their dads bought them Tacos. I had never seen the appeal in the metal contraptions or heard of a girl with a minibike. Motorcycles were big, loud machines that I had to sometimes ride with Dodge. I didn't like to ride with him, because it usually meant holding onto Dodge so I wouldn't fall off, and touching him wasn't pleasant. He smelled and always tensed.

My thanks satisfied Dodge, at least for a bit.

"We got to fix it up. Bought it off one of the guys. His kid got too big for it." Dodge looked at the bike and moved from one foot to the other. I nodded and wondered how it had gotten so worn out.

"It's the Frijole model," Dodge said, pronouncing the *j* in frijole so it sounded like "free-jolie." "Think it means 'bean' in Mexican."

I shrugged, but Dodge didn't notice. He smirked then pointed at a table. "Go over there and grab me that socket kit. We'll pull off the tires first."

I walked to the table and stopped. "What's a socket?"

Dodge grabbed some contraption from the wall and took it back to the bike. "That one." He pointed to a table covered in a scrap yard of metal tools in varying stages of rust. I tried to guess and reached for a thin metal tool, but Dodge stopped me.

"No, not that. To your right. Not that either. It's a box kit. Yes."

The socket kit felt heavy in my hand, yet also warm. I shook off a few flakes of dust and rust and the slight clanging in the kit sounded like a song I recognized. I held it out to Dodge after he placed the bike on a stand, so it was slightly off the ground.

"What you giving me that for? This ain't my bike. It's yours. You gon' take it off," he said.

I looked at the bike. "But I don't know how."

"No shit, girl. Take off them bolts there." He pointed them out.

I paused, not sure how to do it. The socket kit became warmer in my hand, happy that it might finally be of use to someone. I must have taken too long to move because Dodge said, "Grab that socket there and put in in the ratchet handle, then put it in the bolt. Come on. What do I send you to school for?"

I put the socket wrench in the bolt and waited.

"Now turn it to the left." His voice sounded rougher, a sign he was growing more frustrated with me. I twisted the wrench, but the bolt wouldn't budge. I grunted and twisted again. The bike glanced at me disapprovingly, while the wrench cheered me on.

"It won't move." I pulled the wrench away and held it out to Dodge, even when it begged me not to give up.

"You ain't trying hard enough," Dodge said. He squatted on the other side of the motorcycle. This close, I could see the red veins in his eyes and the stubble of his chin. His breath smelled like Fritos.

I refit the socket wrench and twisted again, but the bolt wouldn't move. The minibike chuckled at my failed attempts. I let go of the wrench, my hands burning from gripping the metal so tightly. Again, again, it chanted.

"It won't move," I said, my voice rising a bit.

"Not if you're going to quit like a little bitch." His words stung, and I felt a ball of anger and tears form at the base of my throat.

I pulled, and pushed, twisted, and shoved. Almost there, the socket wrench said, even though the bike fought against me, refusing to give in.

"Come on, Raqi," Dodge goaded me.

I pulled again, furrowing my eyebrows in concentration. The bike's taunts were worse than Dodge's. How dare it not let me do this.

"You're barely doing anything."

I repositioned my throbbing hands and tried twisting with both together. My arm muscles screamed with the effort. Give up, the Taco said. You're just a girl.

I squatted and tried to pull the wrench toward me. You're never going to do it, the bike whispered. Again, the wrench repeated.

"God, girl, I didn't know you were this weak. You ain't even trying, Raqi."

The ball of tears at the base of my throat hardened and rose, until they spilled out in a yell.

"Goddamn it, I AM!" It was then I felt the bolt give and the socket wrench move all the way to the left. I looked at the bolt and back at Dodge, realizing that it was the first time I'd ever yelled at an adult or cussed for that matter.

Dodge smiled.

"Attagirl, Raqi."

14

Albuquerque was hot but at least it was a city, unlike the town we left in Arizona. A motel bed called to my aching body, but it would have to wait. On the ride there, I stewed over Juana and the vision and Trevor's anger. After I hung up with Trevor, I called Lisa to tell her I wasn't going to be home by Sunday before calling David at home. He was, not surprisingly, pissed. Thankfully, Clay and Smith managed to get the Brown son's bail lowered, but that did little to appease David. There was really nothing David could do though, and he knew it. I was a partner, and I got more leeway than low-levels at the firm.

I was more worried about my experience with Juana. Had it been a dream? If so, what did it mean? I hadn't done well interpreting the meaning of symbols in texts in literature class. I didn't imagine I would be able to figure out the psychedelic dream I'd had the night before.

Then there was Trevor. We'd been dating for two years, but about eight months ago, he'd moved in, with the hope that it would make us closer. I had been fine living separately, but Trevor was not. He wanted us to be emotionally and physically closer because I wasn't giving him enough intimacy when we lived separately. He'd even said that I treated him like a "booty call boyfriend," which meant I was faithful to him but only wanted him around when it fit my needs. I hadn't wanted to break up, so I invited him to move in. Maybe that hadn't been a good idea. The only reason I felt bad about our last conversation was because I knew Trevor was a good guy with good intentions. I wasn't used to people worrying about me and I wasn't sure how to come to terms with that.

Jackson and I pulled up to Good Café and parked. It was the kind of place where two Harleys, a drug-dealing biker, and, well, me wouldn't fit in. The patrons were the creamy types with polo shirts and button-ups, cowboys that didn't work on a ranch, and old white ladies with soft blue hair freshly permed by the salon.

I hopped off the bike and stretched my arms behind me, my left hand pulling on my throttle hand, which burned from strained muscles. Jackson got off his bike and grabbed a cigarette from his pocket immediately. I had once smoked, but I stopped ten years ago. Seeing the cigarette between Jackson's lips reminded me that his teeth would soon yellow before rotting.

I wanted to get to the motel as soon as possible, so I headed straight in, not bothering to wait while Jackson lit his cigarette. I looked around hoping I could pick out whoever it was Dodge wanted me to meet..

"That's him." Jackson tapped my shoulder and pointed to my right. His touch burned through my shirt, past my skin, and left a mark on my bone. I grimaced thinking how I'd once liked him touching me. He blew out the smoke near my face and I made a sound of disgust before quickly walking to a white man who sat in a booth.

He wore a chunky silver watch with turquoise stones and a bolo tie with a black leather string that circled around the collar of a white short-sleeved button-up shirt. His fingers bore silver rings inlaid with red and turquoise stones. A silver pendant of a hawk held the tie together at his chest. The turquoise accents on its silver wings glittered in the light as they flapped back and forth.

I walked toward the man. When he finally caught sight of us, he frowned and looked sideways at those sitting near him. He wasn't the only one. The other patrons stared at me with my boyish haircut, but most eyes went to Jackson. He looked greasy, wore leather, and flew his colors; all things that signaled trouble.

I sat opposite the man, on the edge of the booth. Jackson nodded his head for me to move over, but I pretended like I didn't notice. He muttered something I couldn't hear and spun to grab a chair from a nearby table.

The man stopped him midturn by saying, "You're not staying."

Jackson paused. "Mr. Sand, I'm Jackson, I'm supposed to—"

The man interrupted him with a wave of his hand. He leaned slightly toward Jackson so that he wouldn't have to talk too loudly.

"I said you're not staying. Go wait outside."

The words weren't even directed at me, and I felt the sting of them. I knew Jackson did, too. No matter how nonchalant he played it, Jackson wanted to reign over Dodge's route. He'd been vying for a route of his own since he was a kid, something that would make him a "real" Lawless member. Not interacting with the client during their first meeting wasn't a good sign.

Jackson looked at me, but I pretended once again not to notice. He shook his head and muttered curses under his breath as he walked out the door. I smirked and looked at the man in front of me. He didn't seem as amused as I was because a scowl remained on his face.

"Hi," I said.

"Hello," he replied very formally.

Time stretched uncomfortably. I had to say something. But what? The hawk's wings on Mr. Sand's bolo tie fluttered again and made me think of something I'd been wondering since I'd walked in. "What's with all the Indian jewelry?"

The man's brow furrowed. "What kind of question is that?"

I shrugged. "Just a question."

A waitress appeared with two glasses of water and set them down. He waved her off. It was the kind of gesture that said they knew him well here.

Mr. Sand *hmph*ed and said, "My mother was part of the Santa Ana Pueblo."

"What's that?"

"It's the home of the Tamaya people."

"So, like a reservation?"

He grimaced. "The Pueblo people call them pueblos."

I took a sip from the water. "You're like half Native American then?"

Mr. Sand narrowed his eyes. "You make it sound like you don't believe me."

"I—I—Uh . . ." His hair was light, his eyes green, his skin as pale as the rest of the folks in the diner. "I just assumed . . ."

His eyebrows narrowed. "Dodge said you were a lawyer."

I sat up a little straighter. "I am."

"Ain't lawyers supposed to be smart? I got to be dark-skinned, shirtless with a tomahawk in my hand, to be *Indian* to you?" He said "Indian" like he despised the word.

My face turned hot, and it was hard to swallow. He was right. Skin tone wasn't a clear-cut indication of ethnicity or race. I was living proof of that. Most people didn't realize I was half white. I shifted uncomfortably in the booth. Not to mention, I'd used the term "Indian" instead of "Native American" or more specifically "Tamayan." Mr. Sand had made it clear what he thought about that. I fucked up. Had a day with the Lawless brought out those stereotypical thoughts I'd fought so hard to get rid of? Shit. I had to make this right.

I took a deep breath. "I apologize." I paused. "Of all people, I should know better. I'm sorry."

"You should," Mr. Sand huffed.

"Again, I'm sorry."

He studied my face for a few moments, then sighed. "It's fine. I've heard worse." I was sure he had, but even so I was still mortified by my careless statement.

Mr. Sand took a drink and looked at me expectantly. I took a drink of water and looked around, then back at him. The moments ticked off.

"So . . ." I said.

"So, what?"

"What am I doing here? Do you have something to tell me or . . . ?"

He fumbled with his watch. "Why would I have anything to tell you?"

I leaned back in the booth. "I don't know. They said Dodge wanted me to meet you."

"And you think I know why? That boss of his called me a few days ago to tell me Dodge is dead, and I have to meet you if I want to maintain my deal."

"That was it?"

"Yes."

I took another drink of water. Mr. Sand did, too. The weird silence crept in again.

"I didn't even like Dodge," Mr. Sand blurted out.

I chuckled. "Who did?"

Mr. Sand tried not to smirk and continued, "It was hell trying to work with him those first few years. When he found out about Carlos—"

"Carlos?"

"My boyfriend," he replied.

Shit. I could guess where this was going. Dodge was homophobic. Big time.

"What did Dodge do?"

Mr. Sand placed his hands around his water glass. "Carlos is a cook here. We were talking on the side of the building one day when Dodge arrived. Carlos had his hand on my arm for two seconds too long and Dodge saw it and blew up on me."

He took a quick drink of water. "Made a huge scene. Called me a fag in front of everyone, and other unmentionable words."

"Sounds like Dodge." I shook my head.

"I guess you would know. Everyone knows about Carlos and me, but as long as we don't show affection in public, the people here are polite."

Next to us sat a man and woman in their seventies. The woman chewed her eggs slowly and looked past her husband's head.

"What happened after that?"

"The next time we were supposed to meet, he was a few days late. Pissed off my customers."

For a moment, I had forgotten Mr. Sand dealt drugs.

"Then when we did meet, he was always quick to hurry away and made sure to get in some demeaning word each time."

"He's such a dick," I said.

"Was." Mr. Sand smiled. I did, too.

I looked at my glass. "So, what? You kept working with him?"

He nodded. "Too much trouble to find someone else, and we had a good deal."

"But he called you all that shit. Didn't you get tired of it?"

Mr. Sand's laugh was a short, harsh bark. "Of course, I did. But most suppliers think the same way, some are even worse. If it wasn't Dodge, it would have been another small-minded macho asshole."

I didn't doubt it, but I grimaced at the thought of Mr. Sand being harassed for who he loved.

"I chose my career, and I knew what I was getting into. Dodge thought I'd take it, but I didn't. There were a few times we almost got to blows."

"Oh shit," I muttered.

"I've been boxing since I was five, and I'm good with a knife. There isn't much that can scare me. Least of all Dodge," he said coldly.

Shit. Dodge was scrappy, but he wasn't much of a fighter. Mr. Sand had the kind of steeliness that Billy had. I had a feeling that Dodge wouldn't have stood a chance against Mr. Sand.

Mr. Sand leaned back in the booth. "But things changed. A few years ago, he stopped."

"What do you mean he stopped?" I asked.

He picked up his glass like he was going to take a drink and paused. "I didn't notice it at first. It started out slowly, until one day, I realized he had stopped calling me names. Then the next few times, he stayed around a bit longer. Eventually, we were having meals together."

Mr. Sand took a quick drink. "Then one day he asked how Carlos and I met, and I nearly fell out of this booth."

I shook my head. "Dodge would never. No way."

Mr. Sand chuckled. "Never figured it out myself. I'm not one to ask too many questions, so I took it in stride."

Homophobic Dodge becoming friends with a man who's gay? Couldn't be.

"Was he high?"

He smiled. "Couldn't tell. He was still kind of a jackass."

I smirked. Of course, he was.

"So how did you get caught up with Dodge? All this?" I twirled my left hand and lifted my eyebrows.

"You mean, why do I do what I do?"

"Yeah. I don't remember Dodge meeting with people like you back in the day." Mr. Sand didn't take shit, but he wasn't particularly sketchy or scary. If I saw him on the street, I'd think he was a straitlaced, upstanding citizen of society. Hadn't I said something similar about Juana?

Mr. Sand shook his head and smiled. "There you go again with your assumptions."

"Wha—" I raised my hands, confused.

"There is good money in selling pot, and I make my own hours," he said. "Plus, I don't have to worry about anyone firing me because I'm dating Carlos."

He was right, but selling drugs seemed like a risky job nonetheless if you asked me. I merely responded with "true" before taking a drink.

Mr. Sand watched me closely.

"What?" I asked.

"He talked about you a lot."

I looked down at my water.

"It started out slow with stories about you as a kid. He'd say, 'My Raqi once did this or that' and for the longest time I thought you were a boy."

My stomach turned at the thought of Dodge telling stories about me.

"Nope, definitely not a boy," I said sarcastically.

Mr. Sand looked thoughtful. "When you walked in here, I did wonder . . . Maybe Dodge warmed up to me because you—" He raised his eyebrows.

I shook my head. "No, I'm not—"

"It would make sense."

"Trust me. I'm straight."

Mr. Sand held his hands up. "Okay, okay." He chuckled. "I'm just saying, the only women round here with hair that short—"

"A hairstyle doesn't make you a lesbian any more than wearing turquoise jewelry makes you Native American."

"Touché." Mr. Sand laughed.

Nothing about Dodge's sudden change of heart with Mr. Sand made sense. For that matter, nothing about this entire Grieving Ride had made sense. What had happened to make Dodge less of an ass?

Mr. Sand interrupted my thoughts. "He talked a lot about you."

"You said that already."

"Want to know what he said?"

I looked away and shrugged.

"It was mostly about how well you knew bikes. The way you were better than boys at everything. He said you could outride them all. And you were smart."

My lips twitched, trying not to smile.

"He was a little torn about you being a lawyer. A little proud and a little disappointed. He couldn't seem to make up his mind."

Mr. Sand leaned forward, so that the ends of his bolo tie laid on the table. The hawk pendant flapped its wings harder.

"He even brought a newspaper clipping about some case you'd won for one of his friends. He wouldn't shut up about it."

I scoffed. "Was it the one about Ray slicing some guy's throat or Hammond kicking some guy into a wheelchair?" As I said it, my mouth became hot, which was usually a precursor to vomiting. It took two deep breaths through my nose to make the feeling disappear.

Mr. Sand paled. "No, another case, I think."

I shook my head. "Who's proud of someone who gets guilty men off? Twisted son of a bitch."

Mr. Sand didn't seem to know how to respond.

"This is why—" Acidic vomit shot up my throat, but I swallowed it down quickly.

"This is why," I began again, "I didn't speak to him for thirteen years."

Mr. Sand tilted his head. "Thirteen years? Really?"

I nodded.

"The way he talked about you, I would have thought y'all had Sunday lunch every week."

I couldn't do this anymore. I stood up quickly, startling Mr. Sand.

"I, uh, got to go," I said.

"What—Okay, well—" He didn't seem to know where to place his hands, and even moved to stand up, then sat down.

"Nice to meet you," I said. I paused, unsure of whether to shake his hand or not, so I settled on nodding once and walked to the front doors. I glanced over my shoulder. Mr. Sand pinched his eyebrows together as he raised his glass to his mouth, unaware that it was empty.

15

1974, fifteen years old

"I can't believe he stole your dad's bike," I said as I removed some nail polish from the crease of my left big toe with my fingernail.

"He didn't steal it," Bethie said. "Only borrowed it." She was on her first layer of bright orange polish, while I applied my second layer of Spark Pink.

I placed the brush inside its bottle and twisted it shut, then shook it back and forth between my forefinger and thumb. It was nearly empty, and this was the best way to get more paint on the brush. "Still, your dad's going to be pissed."

Bethie bit her lip as she concentrated on painting her pinky toe. When she finished, she leaned back and put the brush in the bottle.

"You're not doing a second coat?" I asked.

She shrugged. "Eh, takes too much time."

"What do you—" I stopped, hearing the rumble of a bike.

We looked at each other, our eyes widening. "Shit!" Bethie whispered before bouncing off the bed and to her window. I followed right behind, pulling down one of the blinds for a better look.

It was Jackson, all right. Even though all three of us were fifteen years old, Jackson appeared older on the bike, especially with his black leather jacket. He'd had an early growth spurt that made him taller than all the other boys our age by a foot. With his broad shoulders, he looked like a football player. I squeezed my thighs together, suddenly feeling uncomfortably hot in a spot lower than my belly.

Jackson parked the bike, got off, and sauntered to the front door.

"Quick!" Bethie whispered. We ran to her door and cracked it so we could peek out.

Bethie's dad, John, sat in his armchair in the dark living room. The lights of the TV danced on his face and the walls behind his head. The volume was too low to make out which program was on. An empty bottle of whiskey and a glass of half-melted ice sat on the TV tray next to the armchair. Bethie's mom must have been in her bedroom.

We heard Jackson enter the house but couldn't see him yet. John picked up his glass and took a drink of the watered-down whiskey. I looked at Bethie who chewed on a piece of hair. Keys clanged on the kitchen counter, but still, I couldn't see Jackson.

"Where've you been?" John's words slurred.

"Out."

I heard the fridge open and close. John placed his glass back onto the TV tray.

"That's not an answer," he said.

A cabinet door opened and shut, and I heard Jackson sigh.

"Who said you could take my bike?"

A drawer opened. "Not like you were using it," Jackson said.

Heat rose into John's face, turning it strawberry pink, then, quickly, the color of maraschino cherries. Jackson appeared with a piece of cold pizza in his hand. He walked toward us down the hall, but had only taken a step past his father, when John stood up with the whiskey bottle in hand and smashed it against Jackson's head. The glass exploded and paused for just one second in the shape of a razor-sharp halo before raining onto the brown carpet below.

Bethie yelped as Jackson fell to the floor, somehow missing the jagged shards of glass that stood like spikes in a moat.

"Asshole!" Jackson yelled, pushing himself up. John stood above him, swaying with the broken glass bottle in his hand. He dropped it when Jackson yelled, then bent down and grabbed Jackson by the jacket collar and pulled him up.

"The fuck you say to me?" Spit flew from John's mouth.

Jackson pushed John away, breaking them apart for a second, before John came after him again. Bethie stood up, opened the door wider, and took a step out. I grabbed her from behind.

"No!" I yelled, knowing full well that she shouldn't get between them. She struggled in my arms.

"Let me go!" she said.

Jackson tackled John into the armchair, knocking over the TV tray and lamp. Without the small amount of light that the lamp had provided, the room darkened and the bright colors from the TV played on the father-and-son fight like stage lights at a theater.

"What the hell is going—"

Bethie's mom, Grace, stood in her cotton muumuu next to us. She must have been asleep, and the fight woke her. As soon as she saw her husband and son struggling on the ground, she rushed to the living room. I let go of Bethie, but she didn't move forward.

"Stop it! Stop it!" Grace yelled, grabbing at John. He pulled his arm out of her grasp and smacked Jackson on the side of his head. Grace tried a different tactic and went after Jackson, grabbing him from behind and pulling him away from John, who finally stopped his attack.

"Don't hurt him," Grace yelled at John, who swayed again, catching himself on the wall.

Jackson fought for a second against his mother, then allowed her to carry him away. She opened the front door and pushed Jackson outside. "Goddamn it, John!" she yelled before grabbing a set of keys and her purse that hung by the door. She slammed the front door shut.

John looked at the door with glazed eyes. He rubbed his chin and surveyed the room. He looked up and saw Bethie and I in the hallway. He took a step toward us. I grabbed Bethie's forearm. She fought to pull it away, but I yanked on it hard.

"Get in!" I hissed, before throwing Bethie into her room. John took another step, and I shut the door quickly. I locked it, then pushed my backside against the door and planted my feet into the ground. Roots from below the house sprouted from the carpet and wrapped around my legs, offering some help in our time of need.

Bethie stood in front of me, her mouth slightly open.

"Bethie!" I hissed, and she snapped out of it. She got in the same position next to me and grabbed my hand.

His footsteps got closer and closer. Each step made the house shake. Please, pass by, please, pass by. The footsteps paused and the house stopped moving. It was quiet for one second before the sound of his hand sliding across the door made Bethie and I jump. She squeezed my hand so hard my bones cracked. John's footsteps continued until a door opened down the hall and then shut. It was over for now.

The roots returned below the house, leaving behind crude, uneven lines in the pink polish on my toenails.

I couldn't sleep that night.

Ten minutes after John had gone to his room, Bethie and I had deemed it safe to move away from the door and sit on her bed. She cried for a bit, while I held her. When she was done, I convinced her to pull out a few Cosmopolitan magazines. We'd already read them before, but it was something to keep us occupied.

When we heard the front door open, Bethie jumped up, and ran to the living room. I stayed on the bed.

"Mom!" Bethie said seconds before Jackson stomped by the open door of Bethie's room and into his room across the hall. He closed the door quickly. I didn't get a good look at him, but I swore his face looked bruised. Minutes later, Bethie came in with a paper bag filled with chicken fingers, fries, and gravy. We ate on her bed.

Bethie had fallen asleep at eleven. I usually fell asleep before she did, but I couldn't tonight. I'd managed thirty minutes of sleep but had woken quickly from a nightmare I couldn't remember, and now I was wide awake. My watch said it was 2:00 a.m. I pulled the bed covers away and got up. Maybe if I ate something, I'd be able to sleep.

I tip-toed down the hallway, hoping not to wake anyone, which was something I felt like I'd been doing my entire life. I'd seen John hit Jackson before but never to this extent. I couldn't help but think that I was always holding my breath for something like this to happen. I never knew what Dodge would do when he was high or drunk, so sometimes I locked myself in my room or took a blanket outside and slept in his truck, another place I could lock. Being around the Lawless wasn't any different. I had a sixth sense that told me when the drugs and alcohol were becoming too much and I had to disappear into a room that locked, catch a ride home, or else witness some dangerous blowup that might get me hurt. Other teens didn't live in a perpetual existence of flight or fight.

When I got to the kitchen, I opened the fridge and grabbed turkey deli meat, a jar of pickles, mustard, and slices of American cheese. I placed it on the counter and opened the cupboard to grab the loaf of white bread.

When I turned around, I jumped at the sight of a figure. "Fuck!" I whisper-yelled. It took my brain a second to realize it was Jackson. "Jesus, you scared me." My heart slowed down a few paces but quickened again at the thought of being alone with him.

Jackson shrugged as if to say sorry. "What are you doing?"

I held up the loaf of bread. "Can't sleep?"

He shook his head. "Fucking headache the size of California. I think it's the staples."

"How many?"

"Three," he said.

We were quiet for a second, but I broke the silence with, "Want one?"

"Sure, with mayo though."

"Gross," I said.

"Gross," he mocked in a high voice. I rolled my eyes and smiled.

I made us both sandwiches while Jackson went to the fridge and grabbed a beer. He held one out to me and I shook my head no, instead filling a glass with tap water. I handed Jackson his sandwich in a napkin, before taking a bite out of mine.

"Want to sit outside?" he asked.

I shrugged. "Sure."

Jackson and I weren't exactly friends. We'd always been competitive with one another, especially when it came to racing bikes. Sometimes I won, sometimes he did. We never really talked alone because Bethie was always around. Plus, Jackson's recklessness and impulsiveness didn't make me like him that much. He got in trouble at school all the time and never thought before he did anything. I suspected he dealt drugs, which wasn't unusual for a lot of people I knew, but that didn't make it any less dangerous or reckless.

We went outside and sat on the porch. I looked up as I ate my sandwich. There weren't that many stars in the sky, most likely hidden by clouds. One of the pickles in Jackson's sandwich had dropped onto his lap. He picked it up and placed it back in the sandwich.

It felt weird, hanging out with Jackson without Bethie. My eyes had adjusted to the dark and I could see now that Jackson had a busted lip and his right eye looked darker around the edges than his left one. His blond, shaggy hair must have been hiding the staples because I couldn't see them. My hand wanted to reach out and move his hair around until I found the staples, so I could run my fingers over them, maybe even push them in a tiny bit deeper.

"What?" he said between chews.

I looked down. "Nothing." When I glanced up, Jackson scowled. I knew he didn't believe me.

"I'm sorry about what happened." I wasn't sure why I told him sorry. I hadn't done anything.

Jackson shrugged and looked up at the dark sky. "Shit happens."

Too often.

16

I didn't give Jackson much time to gather himself when I left the diner. I got on my Ironhead and started riding, until I realized I didn't know where to go. I slowed down, while Jackson's bike growled in fury as it caught up to me. He pulled up a few seconds later, motioning for me to follow him with a scowl on his face. His bike snapped at mine, but my Ironhead bared her teeth, not showing any fear at the mild threat. I let Jackson lead the way, while my mood grew darker and called upon shadowy clouds to form in the sky.

On the way to the motel, I tried to keep my mind blank and let the conversation melt into the past, but I couldn't. Dodge's pride for my most shameful work as a lawyer. Dodge leaving out that we hadn't talked in years. His sudden comfort around gay men? I tried to make these new revelations fit into boxes that made sense, but the logic resisted and became a thicker web of confusion.

Finally, Jackson pulled up to a motel, the kind with two floors and a variety of low-budget cars in the parking lot. Lenora sat on a bench smoking a cigarette. When we pulled up near her, I felt Jackson's anger pulsing out in waves. Once we hit the kill switch, he'd want to talk.

He turned his motor off first and opened his mouth, but Lenora was quicker. "Your dad got y'all a room, 154. We're all cleaning up and taking a rest."

Jackson ignored her. He looked at me and opened his mouth again, but Lenora beat him to it.

"I need to talk to Raqi," she said.

Jackson's head whipped back to her. "*I* need to talk to Raqi." He turned to me again, but Lenora interrupted him once more.

"Maybe you should check in with Billy first."

Jackson's knuckles tightened around his handlebars. "I will after Raqi and me—"

"Saw some of the guys and your dad heading up to his room for a meeting," Lenora said. "I think it's 257."

Damn, she was good.

Jackson looked down, fighting every urge to yell at Lenora. I wasn't sure what made him fire back up and head toward his room on the other side of the building, though not before spitting on the ground near my feet. His saliva bubbled and hissed on the asphalt, then evaporated into thin air. I refrained from saying anything. It was better that way.

I let go of a breath I'd been holding and finally got off my bike. As soon as I did, I felt exhausted, ready to crash into a bed, a floor, anywhere I could let my mind go blank. I headed to the front office to get a room.

"Ain't no more rooms, sweetie," Lenora called out to me.

I paused for a second, then kept walking. We'd see about that.

Lenora was right. There weren't any rooms. I begged the front-desk manager, an old lady with leathery skin, to find something—a closet even. She raised her hands in the air and said, "Some kind of accountant convention in town. Sorry, sugar."

I left the office and headed to my bike. I'd find another hotel. There had to be one room left somewhere. I wanted my own room tonight.

Lenora still sat on the bench. I walked past her to my bike, my blood boiling with annoyance. I thought I might start crying I was so tired and frustrated. I hadn't thought this ride would be easy, but this was far more than I expected. Visions of bones turning into wolves, hangovers, soreness, Trevor's anger. It was becoming too much.

"Ain't any more rooms in town."

"So I heard," I snapped back.

She took the last drag of her cigarette and dropped it to the ground. "You can stay with me. I have another bed in my room."

I laughed harshly. "Yeah, right." I started the engine of my bike.

She yelled over the noise. "It seems ridiculous to go looking for something that ain't there."

I paused. I didn't want to stay with Lenora, but what if I did go around town and discover that there weren't any rooms? Honestly, I'd break down. The conversation with Mr. Sand had created a small crack in my outer shell, and with poor sleep, it was getting larger by the second. Had my perception of Dodge been wrong this whole time? I knew that if I stayed with Lenora, she'd want to talk about Dodge and that's exactly what I didn't want to do.

I turned off the engine. "I want to sleep. I don't want to talk. At all." I narrowed my eyes.

She considered it for a moment, even looked like she might argue. "Fine," she said. "For now."

It felt like a bad idea when I followed Lenora to her room. And maybe it was. But when she opened the door to a room perfumed by decades of smoke and must, I didn't care. I saw the bed, pulled back the covers, burrowed into a landscape of bodily liquids that no amount of detergent would ever clean away, and let myself escape from Dodge and this hell of a ride.

I woke to the sound of gun shots popping in quick secession, followed by screams then shouts. I kept my eyes closed. They weren't actual gunshots. I knew that sound all too well. Probably something on TV.

Maybe I could go back to sleep. It couldn't be the next morning yet. The stale smoke smell had turned fresh which meant Lenora was smoking. I tried to fall asleep again but the noise from the TV mixing with the smoke was starting to piss me off. I pushed myself up, opening my eyes at the same time.

As I guessed, Lenora watched a TV show as she smoked. The edges of her mouth turned slightly down as she slouched against the headboard.

"You're awake," she said.

Waking from naps put me in a poor mood. I tried to run my fingers through my hair but stopped. I had no hair. The realization made me angry all over again. Why the hell did I cut my hair? I thought of the time it'd take for it to grow back and how each passing day would remind me of why I cut it in the first place. How could I have been so easily manipulated?

"Everyone went to a bar," Lenora said.

I stood up quickly. The secondhand smoke entered my pores and charged through my mouth and nose. It filled me up and expanded, pushing against my brain, my heart, my organs, looking for more space to exist. I had to get away. I found my jacket placed over a chair and put it on.

"Where are you going?"

I didn't respond. I couldn't breathe and wanted out of the room. She repeated her question as I opened the door.

"Food," I said. Just a whiff of fresh air eased the pounding in my head.

She moved off her bed. "I'll join you." She didn't ask, so I didn't feel the need to reply.

There was a Mexican restaurant across the street, so I figured that would do. The verifiable hole-in-the-wall smelled of beans and tortillas. It reminded me of Diego's, a small joint that Trevor and I visited on the weekends sometimes. Shit. I was going to have to call Trevor again soon.

There were four orange booths, and thankfully, one was empty. I slid in and Lenora followed suit, her eyebrows furrowed.

"What?" I said sharply.

She looked around at the other patrons, all who were Mexican. "I don't like Spanish food."

"It's not Spanish food," I said. "It's Mexican."

"Same thing."

I fought to say it wasn't. She grabbed a plastic menu from behind the sugar shaker and ketchup bottle.

"You don't have to eat here," I said.

She grumbled before looking down at the menu again.

A young woman about my age appeared and said something to me in Spanish. This happened all the time, so I knew she was probably asking what we wanted to drink.

"I'll take a beer. Cheapest is fine." She nodded, not seemingly surprised by my reply in English, then looked at Lenora.

Lenora replied, "Same," and the waitress walked off.

"You speak Spanish?" Lenora asked me.

"No."

"You are half Spanish."

"Half Mexican," I said, "And that doesn't mean I know how to speak Spanish. Not like Dodge taught me."

"I meant your paren—" The waitress appeared with our drinks, cutting Lenora off. She asked us if we were ready to order. I hadn't even looked at the menu.

"Tacos?" I asked. She nodded. "I'll take three, with steak," I said.

I looked at Lenora. She squinted at the menu like it might change. The waitress swung her pen between her forefinger and middle finger as she waited for Lenora.

"We can do hamburgers," the waitress said.

Lenora grumbled. "That's fine." She handed the menu to the waitress, forgetting that we got the menu from the table. The waitress walked off with our orders and I was stuck again with Dodge's girlfriend.

We sat silently, purposely trying not to look at each other, though I caught Lenora studying me a few times. I couldn't believe Dodge dated her. He'd always gone for girls much younger than him. The floozie-type who were ditzy and less into bikes than what Lenora seemed to be. What did he see in her? Or more importantly, vice versa?

When our food appeared, I began eating immediately, scarfing my tacos down so quickly that I didn't care when grease dripped down my cheek and seeped into my skin. Lenora inspected her burger for two minutes. I wanted to hurl the plate at her face and tell her to fucking eat already. By the time I was close to doing so, she finally took a bite. Unfortunately, food gave Lenora courage to speak.

"You know Dodge would have been happy you joined the ride," she said.

I shrugged. I could give a damn about Dodge's feelings. This angered Lenora a bit. She chewed a piece of hamburger faster and swallowed quickly so she could speak again.

"Why are you even here, Raqi?"

The way she said my name irked me.

"It's a means to an end, *Lenora*."

"What does that mean?"

I took a drink of my beer. "It means, after this, I'm done. Done with all,"—I waved my hand toward the motel—"that shit. Free of it." And free to meet my grandfather. Lenora didn't seem to know about him, or she didn't want me to know she knew. Both of which were curious.

She looked toward the motel and then back at me, still holding one of the last bites of her hamburger in her hand. And then she laughed—loudly. It made a few customers turn their heads. My cheeks grew hot.

"Oh, honey," Lenora said through her laughs which were starting to quiet down. "You can't escape them."

"I can—"

She interrupted me by taking a bite of her hamburger and talking with her mouth full. "You can't escape the Lawless no more than I can escape the fact that I've struggled with drugs most of my life." She took another bite. "Hell, those people are worse than drugs. They're family."

Lenora started in on her french fries, chuckling a little. Was it true? Was I never to be free of the Lawless and everything they did and stood for? I couldn't eat my last taco after that. The thought of being stuck with them forever made my stomach churn. They would always be the type of people who didn't think twice about selling drugs to teenagers, beating up someone for looking at them wrong, hating anyone who lived differently than them, using women as sex objects, and leaching off my career.

"Then why am I here?" I asked Lenora.

She took a drink of her beer and realized it was empty. "What do you mean?"

"I mean, what the hell does Dodge want with me meeting all these people? Why does it matter?" I couldn't help but think maybe Dodge wanted me to come back to the Lawless. His end goal couldn't be to connect me with my grandfather, right?

Lenora set her beer down and sighed. "I have a theory or two."

When she didn't reply right away, I asked, "What is it?"

She leaned back in the booth. "I don't think Dodge rightly knew what he wanted you to get out of this trip."

"For fuck's sake—"

"I meant—" Lenora held a finger up to calm me down. "Loved the man, but Dodge wasn't no thinker."

That was true.

"He probably thought you meeting all these people could help you see how he was a changed man."

"Meeting a few people isn't—"

"Damn, Raqi, let me finish." There it was again. The way she said my name was like a punch deep in my chest. It sounded like Dodge.

"I think Dodge did something—you know—subconsciously. Is that the right word?" She bit her lip.

"God, Lenora, spit it out already."

She narrowed her eyes. "Maybe this trip wasn't meant for you to see how Dodge had changed, Raqi. But to show you how you hadn't."

17

1970, eleven years old

It took Dodge and me the whole weekend to fix the minibike. It was the most time that we had ever spent together, and it required learning a new language, one that Dodge didn't know he was speaking. I came to understand his moods, guess when they'd change, and adjusted what I said or did so that he wouldn't yell, kick things, or disappear into the house and come out with a glazed smile.

Eventually, I had to go to school on Monday, but when I got off the bus in the afternoon, there was Dodge waiting with his hands on his hips, elbows pointed out, puffing a cigarette in his mouth.

"Hurry up!" he yelled between pursed lips. "Been waiting all day."

My eleven-year-old heart fluttered at the thought that Dodge was happy to see me. It felt both unnatural and nice.

"You goin' to ride today," Dodge said as I walked up the stairs to the porch. He smiled, lips still tightly holding his cigarette. I paused, a sudden cold sweat erupting on my neck. It was a minibike, sure, but to my small frame, it was loud and big, and dangerous. Tim, a boy at school, had his arm in a cast from falling off his minibike. What would happen if I fell?

Dodge patted my backpack and scooted me toward the house, where I dropped my bag on the couch and walked back outside, nervous but not wanting to show it. He pulled out the bike and set it in front of the garage, aiming the front wheel toward the empty lot behind the house.

"Start her up," Dodge said. We had practiced starting the bike the day before. It required a strong pull and sometimes I'd have to yank it a few times before it growled to life. This time, it took one yank. Dodge let out a long whoop. I couldn't help but smile.

"Don't that sound good, Raqi? Sweeter than a dog's tit, I tell ya!"

My smile lessened a bit as the reality of what Dodge wanted me to do gripped my insides.

"This right here is your throttle on the right hand and this here," Dodge pointed near the foot, "is your brake. Don't slam on that pedal or you'll break your neck."

I gulped.

He stood up straight. "Now, make me proud."

Engulfed in so much fear of disappointing Dodge, I fell a lot that first day. And the next. It pissed off Dodge to no end. I became so familiar with the dirt ground, covered in faint patches of grass and weeds, that it invited me to stay, promised to cover me over time with dirt, roots, and weeds so that I would never have to fall again. When I refused its proposal, it put large rocks and holes in the path of my tires so that I would crash and be tempted by its offer. Each time my body hit the dirt, the small blades of grass and weeds tried to grab me, keep me there for good. It became harder to stand up each time.

At the end of my second day of riding failure, Dodge griped, "Why did I get you that damn thing if you can't ride it?"

Before I left for school the next day, he said, "I ain't raising no scaredy bitch. When you get home, you're going to ride that Taco like you're a goddamn pro."

Maybe it was his threat, but on the third day, I finally rode. My arms and legs were sore from falling and fighting against the pull of the ground, and my heart tired of hearing Dodge cut me down. After a really nasty crash caused by my fear of speeding up, I got back on the bike quickly, wanting to drown out Dodge's yells. I hit the throttle hard, and the bike sped off so fast that instinct led me to grip the handles tight and manage the machine or be flung backward. As the bike flew farther away from Dodge's voice and I stayed on, I realized that one day this machine might take me away from here, from Dodge, for good.

Dodge was in a better mood after that, but for the next few days, he made me keep practicing. He pushed me to turn quickly, adapt to unexpected bumps or dips, and stay on even when I lost balance. No longer afraid of falling, riding soon turned into something thrilling. My speed stripped away the landscape like old wallpaper, leaving me alone and surrounded by white walls. The roar of the minibike engine faded softly until it became soundless in that colorless hall. This would go on for a few moments until my heart burst with happiness at freedom and the arterial blood and guts splattered the walls in color, painting the world that moved around me.

After a week of riding, Saturday afternoon arrived, and Dodge loaded my bike into the truck and told me to hop in.

"Where are we going?" I asked.

"To the Richie Field."

My fear of riding returned immediately. The boys in my school raced their minibikes at the Richie Field. They'd come back on Monday, bragging about wins, and picking on one another for a loss or a wipe out. As far as I knew, no girl had ever raced.

When we pulled up, the races were already underway. Fathers cheered their sons on raucously with shouts of "Better win, boy!" that held the sharpened edges of a threat. Boys who weren't racing stood on the sidelines screaming and jumping on each other to get a better view.

Dodge jumped out of the truck, but I stayed in for a moment, looking out the window, suddenly nauseous. He knocked on my window.

"Let's go."

I got out of the truck slowly, willing my body to melt into the ground, past the earth's lava and to the hard center core. Dodge wouldn't be able to find me there.

Dodge took the Taco out of the truck bed and placed it on the ground. He held it out to me. I grabbed it and pushed it along as I followed him to the field. We walked up to the starting line where a few men handed cash between each other. A race had just ended, and Jackson had won. His dad smiled gleefully at the other end of the track with a beer in one hand and a wad of cash in the other.

It didn't take long for the crowd to catch sight of Dodge and me. They didn't stop what they were doing, but the boys my age started nudging and whispering to each other. A few laughed and pointed at me and my bike. My cheeks grew warm, and I felt my back start to sweat. Dodge walked up to a group of men, and I slowed down to stay some ten yards back.

"Bane!" Dodge yelled at a short stocky man with long black sideburns, a thick black mustache, and a shiny bald head. He wore small round sunglasses colored blue by the reflection in the sky. Standing in the thick of the men, he moved between them, collecting cash. Bane turned when he heard his name, and walked toward Dodge. He smirked, then went back to counting the cash in his hands, his lips moving silently as he did. When he got in front of Dodge, he chuckled and stopped counting.

"I want in," Dodge said. He pulled out a wad of cash from his back pocket and grabbed a few bills from the rubber band tied around it.

Bane looked at Dodge and then at me. "Dodge, you know you ain't got no reason to be here."

Dodge moved closer to Bane. "Just a right as any of you assholes."

Bane laughed. "Come on. Really?"

That made Dodge fidget, which I knew wasn't a good sign.

"You gon' get this little girl killed and then Social Services will be down our throats. Take her home and buy her a doll." Bane turned around, putting his back to Dodge.

Dodge looked over his shoulder at me, breathing heavily. He was mad, but I wasn't sure if he was mad at Bane or mad at me for being a girl. Before I could figure out which it was, he turned and grabbed Bane by the arm.

"Hey." Dodge's voice lowered. "I ain't asking. Get me in, now." He pushed Bane, who stumbled a few steps. Bane looked shocked for a moment, then shook his head and laughed.

"Don't say I didn't try." Bane turned his attention to me. "Let's throw you to the wolves, girl. You're up."

My breath shortened and sweat quickly spread to my underarms and stomach. Boys lined up at the starting line, Jackson included. Some looked over their shoulders at me. The men handed Bane money and pulled out fresh beers from small coolers. Tree roots and rocks appeared on the field and the earth gave way to holes. The racing field was prepared to knock me off my bike and break my neck.

Dodge swiped at his nose a few times and pulled up his pants, though they weren't falling. He glanced at his friends, then walked back to me. He didn't look as mad as he had been a few seconds ago, but his eyes held some type of intensity.

After looking over his shoulder once more, he spoke low. "Now you listen to me, Raqi. You're going to win this. You hear me?"

I nodded, even though I didn't feel so confident.

"I said, do you hear me?"

"Yes," I whispered.

He stepped closer and his vinegar breath made me dizzy. "Because I'll be damned if you embarrass me out here."

Dodge looked at the finish line, and I did, too. He moved closer and grabbed my upper arm, pulling me slightly toward him. It hurt, but I didn't pull away. His sour breath was a paralyzing gas that entered my bloodstream and froze me in place.

"Win, or else," he whispered hard.

He let me go and I was suddenly able to feel my body again. I struggled to right myself and keep my bike from falling. Dodge quickly turned and walked to the other men.

I moved toward the race line even though my insides screamed, "Don't! Turn away!" I watched Dodge with the other men. Someone had given him a beer and he had a cigarette in his other hand. His eyes never left me as he sipped and dragged.

I had to push the bike through a group of boys who weren't racing. They smiled mischievously and moved closer to me.

"Stupid girl," one said.

"She'll crash hard, watch."

"Look, a beaner riding a Taco."

"Ain't no girl gonna beat Jackson."

On they went, crowding me so that a few had to jump out of my way at the last second or be hit by my bike. There were four boys on the white starting line. I pulled up on the end near a boy named Lee. Kids made "oinking" noises around him because he was a chubby and ran behind them like a piglet to a sow. That's not to say he was kind. He knew that it was better to be a boy than a girl, so when I pushed my bike to the line, he laughed and pointed at me.

Jackson leaned over the front of his minibike a few riders down. His brow furrowed, and his lips curled in a snarl. Though the boys made me nervous, I was more preoccupied with Dodge. His words echoed in my head. *Or else.* Or else. What did that mean?

Bane stood in front of us. Dodge walked with the fathers and the boys who were not racing to the end of the field to get a good spot next to the finish line. I started the engine when Bane told us to, then straddled the bike.

The smell of gasoline and the buzz of the five engines made me feel sick. My mouth turned warm, and before I knew it, I leaned over the side of my bike and threw up. I wiped my mouth and fought not to cry. The laughter of the other boys sliced through me like a knife through a tomato, while the Richie Field absorbed chunks of my breakfast like an offering.

When I stood back up, Bane looked over his shoulder at Dodge as if saying, "Come get her." Dodge squatted down, his lanky elbows resting on his knees. His hands clawed at grass at the ground. He would not save me. Someone nudged him and laughed, but Dodge didn't stop looking at me with hatred in his eyes. I had messed up. Dodge didn't move, so Bane turned around.

"All right, you know the rules. Whoever crosses the line first, wins. I'll count down, 'three, two, one,' and then when I say, 'go,' you go."

He pointed at a kid with a scab on his nose. "That don't mean go on one, Westin." The boy smiled and shrugged his shoulders.

My whole body felt like it was shaking, but when I looked down at my arm, it wasn't moving.

"All right, then," Bane said. "Let's do this."

Bane walked to the side of the field, and I looked at Dodge. He stared at me, and I heard Dodge's threat again in my head.

"Three!" Bane yelled out.

I don't know if it was Dodge's stare and the fear that it caused in my chest . . .

"Two!"

Or the fact, that I was embarrassed for throwing up in front of the boys . . .

"One!"

Or because some part deep down wanted to make the only family I had in the world a little proud of me . . .

"Go!"

But I won the race. Hit the throttle hard and fast and didn't look back.

When I crossed the line, I kept riding a few more paces, stopping far enough to remove myself from everyone. I looked over my shoulder and saw a few of the dads gleefully slapping Dodge on the back. Westin's and Lee's dads grabbed their sons by the shoulders and shook them hard. Jackson's dad pushed Jackson to the ground and pointed his finger inches from his face as he yelled at his son for losing.

Bane reluctantly handed Dodge a wad of cash, which made Dodge smile. He raised the bills and saluted me with them, and for some reason, I smiled, too, having suddenly forgotten the echoing words, "Or else."

18

I didn't want to talk to Lenora anymore. She had hit me with too much truth in too little time. It made me want to drink. A lot. So, I ordered another beer. When Lenora moved to leave, I told her to go back to the motel without me. She must have picked up on my mood because she paid for her meal and left.

"We ride at nine tomorrow," she said before heading out.

Of course we did. Could I get one fucking day to sleep in?

I ordered three more beers after she left and downed each with more fervor than the last. The other patrons of the restaurant eyed me, a lone female intent on getting drunk. By the third beer, I stared back until they looked away, and I felt triumphant in my ability to be in control again.

Lenora had opened Pandora's box. Even if I was physically free of the Lawless, were they still inside of me? I kept being thrown into shitty situations and it was all Dodge's fault, and the bastard wasn't even alive. As I took a drink from the last beer, I cursed Lenora. I was not like the Lawless, nothing like them at all.

I paid my bill and walked out of the small restaurant, almost tripping on a curb. I was a little tipsy but fuck it. I deserved to let loose for all the shit I'd been through in the past two days. Hell, my whole fucking life.

The parking lot between the restaurant and the motel didn't have much lighting. I leaned my head back to look at the stars in the sky. They were so bright, taunting me like pinpoints of hope in a hopeless world. I raised both hands and wiped them back and forth against the sky, erasing as many stars as I could. But no matter how many I wiped away, they flicked back to life after a few seconds, ruining all progress I made. Frustrated, I tried wiping harder, but lost my balance and fell over, catching myself with one hand on the pavement. My head spun as I stood back up. I scowled at the stars, said "fuck you," and kept walking to the motel.

As I approached the building a shadow man, surrounded by hazy wisps of cigarette smoke, moved. I faltered in my step for one second. Dodge, back from the dead? The shadow man moved into the light. It was Jackson.

"Pretty fucked up what you did today, Raqi," he said. I tried to move around him, but he sidestepped in front of me. The air around Jackson was so hot it singed my skin. I stepped back.

"I didn't do—" I began.

"You knew I was supposed to be there to talk to him. He's my goddamn point."

My head felt light and dizzy. I wanted to go to sleep, wanted to be alone, wanted to be in Los Angeles in the court room, my head not spinning with thoughts.

"Always my fault," I taunted, rolling my eyes, and waving my hands in the air. "Never Jackson's fault. God, I'm tired of your pussy-ass bullshit."

I tried to walk around him, but he blocked me again. His anger was so hot it made breathing difficult.

"It is when you get in the way of my job." He bared his teeth. One flick of my finger and they would crumble from their rotted insides. I laughed and the air around him became a little cooler, allowing me to breath normally.

"Job?" I laughed again. "You're a fucking drug dealer, man. Wake up, it's not a real job."

I used my shoulder to push him aside. The five beers weren't making it easy, so I used my hand to push him away, too.

"Get out of my way." I was almost past Jackson. If I could get to Lenora's door . . .

Jackson grabbed my arm and I hissed in pain at his scalding touch. "Why do you always have to be a fucking cunt?"

That was it. I'd had enough. I punched toward his face but hit the side of his ear instead. His eyes widened in surprise. He drew his arm back immediately. I didn't see his punch as much as felt it go through my eye and out the other side. My eye throbbed and my sight disappeared for a moment. I stumbled backward into a bike, not quite falling. I righted myself. My eye watered and throbbed, but the shadows retreated as I blinked rapidly.

I stood up slowly, feeling thirty years of anger spill through a hole the size of Jackson's fist. His mouth hung slightly open, as if shocked by his own action. Tipsy or not, I ran at him with a guttural yell and tackled him at his waist. My linebacker move surprised him, or else it might not have been a success. We fell onto the asphalt in a heap, making an imprint of our bodies on the ground.

I punched furiously. "Asshole!"

He tried to grab my arms but failed.

"You ruined my life!" I yelled. Our hands pushed at each other's faces and throats. "I hate you!"

Jackson hit me in the gut, and I lost my breath for a moment. He pushed me off him. I scrambled to my feet and ran at him again, swinging with both arms. I was off balance from the beers and Jackson's initial punch to my face, which meant my hits didn't land the way I wanted. He was trying to push me, but I kicked his shin and he doubled over. "Bitch!"

I pulled my fist back to swing again when someone pulled me away.

"Raqi, stop!" I struggled, but they had their arms around my waist and swung us both to the ground. I rolled away when I hit the asphalt. It was Beth. She pushed herself up, panting. The girl was skin and bones—how the hell had she done that?

Seeing her face, I suddenly grew tired and fell on my back in the middle of the parking lot. My breath came in rapid, deep pants. I steadied my heart rate to the twinkle of the stars that taunted me above.

"Go to your room, Jacks," Beth said.

"She fucking started—"

"I don't care!" I'd never heard Beth yell at Jackson like that. "Go away, asshole!"

Jackson swore a few times and walked off.

I smiled and then started laughing. The laughter didn't stop. It came in heaps from the bottom of my stomach. I'd packed those laughs deep inside me for the last thirteen years. I'd not deserved to feel them, to enjoy them, to share them with the world, but the box had been broken and now they were spilling out and causing little bursts of pain from my now bruised and sore body. I rolled to my side and curled into a ball as my body shook uncontrollably in squeals.

Beth knelt in front of me. She placed her hand on my arm and the laughter quieted down.

"Bethie," I said, smiling. "My savior."

She smiled a little bit, the first I'd seen since we started the trip.

Oh, no . . . I turned and threw up the beers and tacos.

"Good God," Beth whispered.

I wiped my mouth and groaned.

"Come on." She grabbed my hand and helped me up. "Let's get you to bed." As she pulled me up, I felt dizzy.

"Hold on," I said, turning away and pausing. I thought I might throw up again. Was this another concussion? I didn't throw up but spit out a chunk of what was probably steak meat that had lodged itself behind one of my teeth.

"Gross," Beth said before pulling me to the motel.

I shook my head and dug my heels in the ground. "I don't want to go in there right now."

Beth looked around the parking lot, back at me, then at the motel. "Where do you want to go?"

"Anywhere besides here."

She bit the side of her mouth and looked at the bikes. "You got your key?"

"I'm a little tipsy to ride right now."

She held out her hand. "Not you. Me."

I handed her the keys and she walked to my bike and kick-started it to life with one kick. I paused before getting on the bike behind her.

"Since when do you ride?" I asked.

Fire erupted from her shoulders and fanned around her head in a glorious halo of ferocity. "What else was I going to do the last decade without you?"

I fell asleep at some point on the ride. Not the best idea, but anybody who grows up in biking families has done it at one point or another. It probably wasn't for long because I woke when I felt my balance tipping on a turn and quickly bolted up and grabbed for Beth. It wasn't a move that I was proud of—when you know how to ride a bike, you don't have to hold onto anyone. But I was tipsy and had been in a fight and it was nighttime and who the hell was around in Albuquerque to see.

Eventually, Beth pulled into a park, next to a few picnic tables. She waited for me to get off the bike, but I moved slowly. The bruises on my face and ribs pulsed. When I swung my leg over, I felt dizzy and there was a sharp piercing pain in my side. God, I hoped Jackson felt the same way. I disembarked and made my way sluggishly to the picnic table, Beth right behind me. We climbed on top of the table.

"How'd you know about this place?" I cringed as my butt touched the wood. I tried to find a comfortable position, but it was no use.

She stared ahead. "Came here earlier. The guy at the motel told me about it, so I borrowed Garrett's bike and came out here for a bit."

"I didn't know you liked"—I searched for the words—"outdoor places."

Her voice didn't hold any emotion when she replied, "You don't know me, Raqi."

One more punch to the gut, and this one hurt the worst. I was quiet after that, wrestling with feelings I couldn't quite name. A few minutes passed.

"Look, I'm sorry, Beth—"

"You should be! You abandoned me, Raqi. Me."

Tears formed around the edges of her eyes. She could never yell without crying. Her tears fell onto the wooden picnic table forever staining them with circular blots that tasted of salt and betrayal.

"You left the Lawless and you left me. You were"—She struggled to speak—"my best friend and you threw me aside like I was nothing."

My pounding head and bruised body didn't compare to the guilt that stretched, twisted, and pulled my insides like a never-ending game of Jacob's Ladder.

"Fuck, I know. I wasn't thinking. I needed to get away from it all."

"That meant me, too?"

Beth wiped her eyes with the back of her hand, and I was transported to when we were fourteen. We had caught Walter, a junior Beth had been dating, locking lips with some girl from another school at the carnival. Beth cried for fifteen minutes by the Porta-Potties. When she'd finally had enough crying, she wiped her eyes with the back of her hand and asked me how to get back at him. We spread a rumor that he was talking shit about Jackson and his friends, and they beat him up the next day after school.

"God, Bethie, I've messed up a lot in my life, but what I did to you fucks with my mind. I'm so sorry."

There had been moments when I'd tried to call her, even picked up the phone. But I knew that being friends with Bethie would bring me closer to the Lawless and Dodge and that made me quickly put the phone back on the receiver. Besides, life without the Lawless had sped up when I removed myself from them. I met new people and ran in circles that Beth would never fit in. Without her around, I could be someone new with a different past.

Beth shook her head and wiped her nose on her shoulder. "You're shit, you know that?"

I smiled. It was something we used to say. An old Lawless, Rick, said it after every other sentence. We mocked him until it became our own overused inside joke.

I looked away. "Yeah, I am."

We sat quietly. I felt Beth look at me after a few moments.

"You look like shit, too," she said.

"God, I feel like shit." I laughed.

Bethie shook her head. "When I saw you two going at it, it reminded me of when we were kids. Raqi and Jackson fighting again. Felt like nothing had changed."

The thought made my stomach hurt. Jackson and I had been a volatile combination since the first time we met, and it hadn't gotten much better when we'd fallen in love as teenagers. Yelling matches were frequent between us and sometimes it got physical. But that's how we were taught to love in the club. We didn't think anything of it.

A Lawless hitting their Old Lady wasn't a given, but it wasn't abnormal either, especially if she let her mouth run and didn't respect his authority or club matters. For Mamas and Sheeps—it was expected. Better to keep your mouth shut, appease the men when you could, and never expect that to be enough. Even Bethie, who had been the sweetest girl, had been backhanded by her dad and boyfriends many times. I may have been treated a little better than some of the other girls, because I raced with the boys and Dodge took me along on rides with the club, but it wasn't enough to protect me from everything. I had to learn when to be quiet and when to fight back—because the wrong choice could be the end of me.

It wasn't until I separated myself from Dodge and experienced the real world that I learned to let go of my false belief that passionate violence equaled love. But look at me now. I had been with the Lawless for just a few days, and I'd fallen right back into my old patterns with Jackson tonight.

"Things have changed. I've changed. I shouldn't have let that happen tonight," I said.

"My dickhead brother shouldn't have come at you like that." Beth sighed. "You're going to have a black eye."

Great. Just what I needed.

"At least, tell me I got a good hit or two in."

"It was a little dark, but he could have had a busted lip."

I sighed. "Lost my touch."

"Seems like it."

From my peripheral vision, I saw her smile.

I stood up slowly and climbed off the table. "Can we get a burger? I'm starving." I had thrown up all those tacos, so my empty stomach craved to be replenished.

Beth jumped up, much faster than me. "You're paying, rich-ass lawyer." She jogged to the motorcycle like we were kids again. I moved a lot slower but smiled.

"I'm not rich. Still paying off student loans."

"Oh, boo-hoo," Bethie taunted and kicked the motorcycle to life.

19

I knocked hard on Eddie's door twice. Bethie stood by my bike. She'd been too scared to come onto the porch. I shook my sweaty hands by my sides then stood on my tiptoes, before lowering down. Eddie finally opened the door.

"Hey Raq, what's going on?"

My heart beat rapidly, but I had to stay calm for Bethie.

"Eddie! Hey." I put my hands in my pockets so I wouldn't grab my hair or wave them around nervously. "Can I borrow your truck?"

Eddie's eyebrows furrowed. "My truck?"

I nodded quickly. "Yeah, Bethie and I want to go into the city and grab this new album."

Eddie looked behind me at Bethie.

"An album?"

I put my weight on my right foot and my hand on my hip. "Yeah, the Saints. They're this punk band."

He rubbed the stubble of beard on his chin. Did he believe me? He had to believe me. His forearm tattoo, a fiery skeleton on a motorcycle, looked between me and Eddie. The skeleton shook its head 'no' at my request and crossed its arms. I narrowed my eyes at it.

"Wh—"

I interrupted him. "Look, Eddie, please let me borrow your truck. I have my license and I'll get it back to you in the morning. I'd ask Dodge but, it's Dodge, so you know how that will go."

My stomach did somersaults as I watched Eddie think about it for a second. He turned around and grabbed something off the coffee table. When he got back to the door, he handed me the key.

"Here," he said. "I'm trusting you to be safe, yeah?" The skeleton tattoo threw its bony arms in the air, annoyed by Eddie's decision.

I smiled and hugged him. "Yes! Yes! I promise." I stuck out my tongue at the fiery skeleton tattoo, and it shot me the middle finger surrounded by a burning flame.

"I'll bring it to you in the morning. Thank you!" I yelled the last bit as I bounded down the steps to Bethie, who smiled nervously. The smile disappeared when we got into Eddie's red truck and started driving to the city.

Two weeks earlier and a few days after her seventeenth birthday, Bethie had found out she was pregnant. At the beginning of last year, Bethie and I went to Planned Parenthood in Los Angeles and got on the pill, even though Bethie had already had sex a few times. I'd waited to get on the pill before doing it with Brice Michaels, a boy I liked who was a grade older than us. Even though Brice and I had only done it a few times after that, I always made him wear a condom except for the third time. For a month after, I obsessed incessantly over the thought that I had contracted something, or I would be that small percent that still got pregnant. The fear was so overwhelming I told myself I would never have sex without a condom and the pill again.

Since getting on the pill, Bethie had slept with three different guys, most recently with Peter, one of Jackson's best friends. Jackson didn't like that they were seeing each other, but he preferred Peter over Bethie's last boyfriend, Frank. Bethie and Peter never used condoms and Bethie wasn't as good about remembering to take her pill like I was, so she got pregnant.

Bethie leaned against the door of Eddie's truck, staring at the quickly passing scenery of the highway. She looked sad. I wanted to say something, but I wasn't sure what. She was scared that her parents would find out. Her mom would be cool with it, but her dad—no way. She hadn't even told Jackson, her twin, what we were doing, though she had asked him earlier for the money we needed.

"What do you need that much for?" Jackson asked her. He was taller than her, but even then, they looked so much alike with their thin straight noses, blond hair, and high cheekbones. We were the only ones in the house, but they spoke quietly as if their voices might linger until their parents returned home.

"I can't say," Bethie replied. Tears formed in her eyes. "I just do." She stomped her foot. "Please, Jacks, I'll owe you big time."

Jackson looked at his sister for a second then gave her a hug. She wrapped her skinny arms around him, and they melded into the same position they'd been in inside their mother for nine months. Sometimes I forgot they were twins, bonded by a unique experience of birth. Jackson could be an asshole to most people, but to Bethie, he was kind and gentle. It made me a bit jealous. If I'd had a twin, life would be more bearable.

When they pulled apart, Jackson went into his room while Bethie wiped her tears away. Jackson dealt weed to the rich kids at school, so he always had a ton of cash on hand, which was good for us since we didn't have any.

"Here," Jackson said. "You sure you don't need more?"

Bethie shook her head. "This is good. Thanks, brother."

When we arrived at the clinic in Los Angeles, Bethie sat up and looked at the building. Defeat pulled at her face, pulling her puppy-dog eyes farther down.

"Hey," I said. She chewed on her lip when she turned to me. "We don't have to do this if you don't want to."

She smiled weakly. "No, I do. I'm not ready—" She looked down at her stomach. "I mean, can you see me being a mom now? Hello, no thank you."

I chuckled. At least her humor wasn't gone. Still, she was right. Bethie with a baby was a bad idea. She was seventeen, with no skills, job, or even a high school diploma. Granted, plenty of girls had overcome those odds, but Bethie had one more glaring problem: the Lawless. I knew what being raised among them was like and I wouldn't wish that on a child.

When we got out of the car, I grabbed Bethie's hand. She squeezed it. We would do this together, and it would forever bind us.

As we walked up to the building, a skinny white woman in jean shorts and a floral top who sat in a metal foldable chair stood up. She looked older than Bethie's mom and held a white poster the size of a billboard. We weren't ten feet away when she walked hurriedly to us, sign raised high. The words, "Don't kill your baby. Be saved by God," had been written in thick red lines of judgment that dripped from the carcass of letters, down the handle, and over her hand.

"Girls, you don't have to do this!" she said. Bethie and I paused as she rushed up to us.

"Don't kill your baby. I can help you, take you to our church. Have your baby put up for adoption," she rambled. "Your baby has hair, a heartbeat!"

I pulled Bethie away from the woman. "Hey, back off," I said.

The woman smelled the pregnancy on Bethie. Her pupils constricted and she hissed at my best friend, "You'll be a murderer, go to hell. Do you want that? Jesus forgives whores, look at Mary Magdalene."

I let go of Bethie's hand and pushed the woman away. "Shut up, bitch!"

She stumbled back, shocked for a second before opening her lipless mouth to yell. "Whore! God sees you. Baby killer!"

She shook her huge sign at us. Before I could react, Bethie grabbed the sign and pulled it from her hands. The woman was as surprised as I was when Bethie threw it into the parking lot. My best friend got three inches from the woman's face and yelled, "Fuck off, bitch! Or I'll beat your ass!" I'd never seen Bethie so angry before. Sure, we'd gotten into fights with girls at school, but Bethie's face had never turned that red and her body had never vibrated with so much strength. Not a single tear formed in her eyes. The woman ducked her head in submission and slinked off to pick up her sign.

"Come on," Bethie said.

She stomped through the front door. I caught up with her, quietly screaming in triumph. Bethie walked to the attendant at the front desk and said in an unwavering voice, "Bethie Cook. I'm here for an abortion."

I hugged her then, proud of her for being such a badass. We probably seemed off to the front-desk attendant, but I didn't care. When I pulled back, Bethie beamed, and her golden hair twinkled from a light she'd found within.

"I'm so fucking glad you're here," she said.

Hours later, Bethie leaned on me as I guided her into Dodge's house. She winced in pain, but never cried, never called out. When she gritted her teeth, I felt the dull ache in my back molars. Inside, Dodge grabbed a beer from the fridge.

"What's with her?" His voice sounded too friendly, and he bounced on his toes, floating a few inches off the ground. Great. An upper high, the kind that made him creepily kind and attentive in ways I didn't need him to be right now.

"Cramps," I said, as I rushed Bethie into my room. She would stay the night tonight so that her parents wouldn't know what happened. Dodge was so high or drunk all the time that I expected him to barely take notice of us, or at best, be at some chick's house the whole evening. Guess we couldn't be that lucky.

I settled Bethie onto my bed. She whispered "fuck" as she laid down.

"You okay?" I asked. She nodded and sighed when she settled in. The ride home had been a little bumpy in Eddie's old red truck. Even though I had actively tried to stay away from potholes, the pain medication had worn off and each bump had sent vibrations of discomfort through her body.

Dodge opened my bedroom door suddenly and sang, "Raqi, Raqi." He hiccuped and a star glided out of his mouth and floated through the ceiling. "What are you two doing?" He pointed at Bethie. A light shot out of his finger bathing her in a spotlight. She chuckled nervously and tried to hide under the sheets as I ran over to Dodge and pushed him out, closing the door behind me. He laughed and the unfamiliar notes made me cringe.

"Always so serious, Raqi. I came to ask if you wanted a pizza." He downed the rest of his beer and then lifted it up like a telescope, pointed it at me, and peered through the open end. I put my hand up and covered the bottom of the bottle so he wouldn't be able to see through my bullshit.

"And . . ." He drew out the word and pulled the bottle away from his eye. "Billy's coming over." Fuck, fuck, fuck. Not Billy. Could this night get any worse?

"Sure, yes, whatever," I said. "Yell and I'll come grab it, okay?"

He tried to stop smiling, but his cracked lips rebounded wide and up into a maniacal smile. "You're up to something, Raqi." He shook his finger mockingly like a concerned parent.

"I'm not, Dodge," I said, my voice gaining a tract of annoyance. "Where's the Tylenol?"

"I don't know; my room maybe." I went into his room, and he called out, "Keep your hands off those serious pain killers. You can get high off them." No shit.

After I found the Tylenol bottle in an ash tray filled to the brim with a decade of burnt tobacco fragments, I ran back to my room and gave Bethie a few.

"Thanks," she said. I turned on the small box television on my dresser and we flipped through the channels until Bethie stopped on *Happy Days*. Not much later, I heard the front door open, and Dodge exclaim, "Billy!"

Bethie and I didn't speak much, mostly because I had a feeling that she wanted to rest, and I didn't quite know what to say anyway. Bethie had been pregnant and now she wasn't. There was nothing shameful about what Bethie had done today. Women had been having abortions since the beginning of time. Yet, I wondered if it might change her, in small ways at least. Only time would tell. But I'd be there if she needed me because I was proud to be her friend.

Half an hour later, Dodge yelled at me when the pizza had arrived. I ran outside to the front porch where Billy and Dodge sat smoking cigarettes and eating slices of pizza between puffs. Puff, puff, pizza bite. I tried not to look at Billy when I grabbed the pizza from Dodge, even though I felt his black eyes sear the back of my neck.

"Thanks," I said quickly and ran back inside to get two Cokes from the fridge.

Bethie ate one and a half pieces before saying she wasn't that hungry. My worries increased. I needed my best friend to be okay.

An hour later, Bethie turned to me. "Hey, I need to pee."

I jumped up and ran to her side. She put her right arm around my neck, took a deep breath, and stood up, grunting as she did.

"You okay?" I asked.

"Yep," she said through gritted teeth. "Let's get this over with."

We walked slowly to my door and then out into the hall. We'd only taken a step toward the bathroom when Bethie groaned and leaned over, grabbing her stomach. She put her knees on the floor and held the wall with one hand.

"What is it? What's wrong?"

She groaned again, but not as loud this time. "Cramp, major cramp. God, I don't think I can get up."

I heard a noise behind me and turned to find Billy.

"Uh, Billy, hey—"

"She okay?" he asked. His deep voice turned the slight sheen of sweat on my back into an ice sheet.

I nodded. "Yeah, she's fine. Major cramps."

Bethie looked up and nodded. She moved to stand but whimpered and reached for the wall. I grabbed her to prevent her from falling, but Billy moved in front of me. He was so big that it didn't take much for him to hold her up. Her small hands wrapped around his waist.

"Bathroom?" he asked.

She nodded, and he led her to the bathroom slowly. When they got to the toilet, she said, "I'm good," and sat down.

Billy walked out and closed the door. I stood beside him as we waited for Bethie to finish. He stared at my face, and I tried to look anywhere but at him. I stood on one foot and then the next, walked a few steps away and then back.

"I've never seen cramps do that to someone," Billy said.

I shrugged, looking at my feet. "Cramps are different for everyone. She gets them really bad sometimes."

"Hmph," Billy said. I grabbed a piece of hair and chewed it, hoping that Bethie would hurry up.

We heard the toilet flush, and then Bethie call out, "Okay."

I opened the door tentatively and looked in. She was dressed and sitting on the toilet, smiling weakly. "Help me back?"

I nodded, but before I could get to her, Billy said, "Move." I did as he said. He picked up Bethie, a small, blond, blue-eyed doll, and like any good doll, she curled into his chest as he carried her out the bathroom and into my room, laying her gently on the bed.

"Thanks," she said as he set her down.

He stood up, looked at me, and replied, "Anytime."

20

1990, thirty-one years old

"So, you're rich," Beth said.

I laughed. "Not rich." She took a sip of her chocolate shake. "Well, you have more money than me. I'm a bartender with two roommates."

Life was so different for me and Beth. It made me feel sad, and a little bit guilty. We were the same age and had grown up similarly, but I'd left while Beth had stayed behind.

"That sounds kind of nice." I took the last bite of my hamburger.

Beth flicked her straw at me, sending flecks of chocolate shake onto my face.

"Hey!" I exclaimed, laughing.

"Oh, come on. 'That sounds kind of nice.' Who are you?" she teased.

I ate another fry. "Okay, fine. That sounds awful. I'm struggling as it is living with my boyfriend."

"Ah yes." Beth raised her hands and touched her fingertips together. "Boyfriend, tell me more."

"Mm-mmm." I shook my head. I still hadn't called Trevor. Just another thing I'd royally fucked up in the past few days. "You first. Boyfriend?"

"Ha!" Beth chewed on her straw. "I was married a few years ago."

I stopped chewing the fry I had just popped into my mouth. "No way, to who?"

Beth covered her face. "Barry."

I gasped. "No! Not Barry boy!" Barry Smith was three years younger than us, and he had the biggest crush on Beth growing up. We teased him endlessly about the crush, but he didn't care. He always said, "Just wait. One day."

"How did that happen? Why did that happen?" I leaned forward.

Beth looked down for a moment, before raising her eyes. She sighed. "The only thing I can say is . . . Barry boy became one hell of a hottie."

We laughed so loud the people next to us told us to hush—which only made us laugh louder.

When we finally quieted down, I said, "So, you and Barry then . . . Life's good?"

Beth rolled her eyes. "We got divorced six months after we married."

"Why?"

She huffed. "Oh, you know. Girl cheats on boy, boy retaliates by cheating with girl's work friend. Same old story."

"I'm sorry," I said.

She shrugged. "Shit happens."

I'd heard that before. We stared at each other for a few moments, before I reached out, grabbed her hand, and squeezed.

Thirty minutes later, we returned to the motel. I quietly made my way into Lenora's room, hoping not to wake her, but quickly realizing that wouldn't be a problem. Lenora's loud snoring shook the walls and furniture and sent the floor rolling under my wobbly feet.

When I got in bed, I winced from the pain of what I assumed would be fresh purple bruises in the morning. Staring up at the ceiling, I thought about how the last few hours with Beth had felt like the old days. The guilt I felt from abandoning Beth was all but gone, but it was being replaced with a nervous feeling in my stomach. If I let Beth in my life again, could I keep our relationship separate from the club? I closed my eyes and turned on my side. It wasn't a question I could answer tonight.

Something hit my face, sending a ripple of fire through my body.

"Ouch!" I opened my eyes and cringed again. Oh, God, my body hurt—bad.

"Get up," a gruff voice said.

I pulled what I soon discovered was my jacket off my face and sat up slowly, looking around for whoever had spoken. It was Billy. Lenora's bed was empty.

The clock on the nightstand said "7:00 a.m."

I fell back on the bed slowly. "Lenora said nine."

Billy stripped the covers off me, and I sat up too quickly. Ouch, that hurt. I was only wearing my T-shirt and panties, so I reached for the comforter but that sent pain through my shoulder and side. Fuck it. Billy had never been inappropriate toward me, and as we talked, his eyes never left mine.

"Lenora and the others will take off for Oklahoma at nine. We have a side stop to make," Billy said.

I fought the urge to slam my fists into the bed. Instead, I fell back and rolled over, burying my face in the pillow, and groaned. "Fine," I yelled into the scratchy pillowcase. I added a muffled, "I'll meet you outside in ten."

"Don't make me wait." A moment later, the door clicked, signaling Billy's departure.

I turned on my back and looked up at the ceiling. The mold that sprouted along the edges of the ceiling was just a shade darker than the green wallpaper with white flowers that had been plastered on it. I thought about the night before when Beth had asked me about Trevor. I knew I had to call him. But shit, I didn't want to. I looked at the other bed. Lenora was gone, and I was alone in the room. It was now or never.

I picked up the phone on the wooden nightstand between the beds and moved the cord so I could push the numbers. The phone rang and rang. Was it too early in the morning? I couldn't recall if there was a time difference or not.

The phone continued to ring. My call was clearly going to voice mail. Either Trevor was ignoring my call, or he wasn't home at six or seven in

the morning. Both were probably bad signs. Trevor's recorded voice came
on the line, and the phone beeped.

"Hey." I paused for two beats.

"It's, um, me. I'm in New Mexico. Heading out in a bit to Oklahoma. I'll call soon to check in." What else should I say? "Look, I'm
sor—I want to be more open with you. Being around these—"

The phone beeped. The recording was over. The silence pressed
down on me like a blanket, and I ached for it to suffocate me to death.
I let the phone fall from my ear to the pillow. With no one watching, I
felt less childish for hitting the bed with my fists and feet like a toddler
who didn't get her way.

Billy waited by his bike, smoking a cigarette. He stared at my right eye.
I tried to adjust my bangs to cover the bruise, but it was hopeless. I'd
forgotten to bring makeup and could not cover it one bit. Black and
blue would be my look for the day.

"Looks like you can still take a punch," he said.

"And give them too."

Billy made a noise in his throat and shook his head. "Just had to
neg him . . ."

"What? Should I have kept my mouth shut like a Sheep? He started
it—"

"That's not—"

"—so I finished it. That's what you and Dodge taught me, right?"

Billy stared at me for a few seconds. His jaw twitched. I wanted to
say more. I wanted to yell at him for how his club members thought
they could do whatever they wanted and get away with it. They treated
women like shit, and I wasn't going to let any one of them do that to
me. Not anymore.

He growled low in his throat, bent down, and picked a small Styro-
foam cup off the ground. He handed it to me, along with a bear claw
that sat on his bike. Billy wasn't going to get into it with me. The coffee

and doughnut were his way of saying the conversation was over. I took a deep breath in and let it out, before taking a bite of the wiggling doughy claws.

His eyes flicked to my black eye occasionally as he watched me chew. When I swallowed, he sighed and shook his head. Billy stood up and walked to one of the doors on the first floor. He knocked. A second later, a man in boxers opened the door. Billy said something to him. I couldn't hear the words over my chewing and the distance. The man's head turned toward me and then back to Billy. It only took a few minutes and then Billy walked back to his bike.

"What was that about?" I asked.

"It's a Grieving Ride. The boy knew better than to quarrel with the family."

"Hmph." Jackson was in trouble now. Served him right. Though I was sure he wouldn't see it that way. I finished the doughnut and took a sip of coffee. I wasn't sure what Billy had planned for Jackson, but I didn't really care. I just needed to get through a few more days, a few more meetings, and then I'd be free.

"So where are we going?"

"Amarillo." Billy kick-started his bike to life.

I shook my head. "We're going through Amarillo, right? Not stopping?"

Billy smiled, revealing rows of gray teeth. "Oh, we're stopping."

"Not at—"

He nodded.

I looked up at the heavens. "Why are you doing this to me?"

Billy laughed over the roar of his bike. "You have no idea why that's funny."

I downed the rest of the hot coffee in one gulp. It scalded my throat, but the pain was nothing like what I was about to experience. Nothing could be worse—and I mean, nothing—than having to stop and see Charles.

Charles was Dodge's oldest friend. They grew up together and had both been shipped out to Vietnam. Unfortunately, Charles's time in Vietnam didn't end so well. He stepped on a land mine and both his legs had to be amputated above the knee. During my childhood, Charles visited us on occasion in California, but more often Dodge stopped in Amarillo when he was out on his route. That was fine by me because having a conversation with Charles was hell on earth.

He never let you get in a word. And instead of finishing his thought, he'd veer off to another topic and then another and another until you wanted to pull your hair out. There was no subject that Charles didn't have an opinion about and claimed to be an expert on. His laughs were loud, and his breath always smelled like sulfur, but it was the fact that he never—ever—got angry, that made me despise him the most.

Someone would invariably put him down, outright insult him, and he'd laugh it off like they didn't mean it. But oh, they meant it. Charles got on everyone's nerves, even his own club. He was part of a regular old motorcycle club in Amarillo, and since he didn't have his own bike, everyone took turns attaching a side car so he could join in on the ride.

As a kid, I'd been immediately put off by Charles. It wasn't like I grew up with saints, so I could normally get along with the worst of the worst of them, but Charles's inability to get upset infuriated me. Something told me that neither Charles nor I had changed much, which was going to make this meeting a living nightmare.

Halfway to Amarillo, Billy and I stopped at a gas station. I bought us two bottles of water while he filled up the tanks. He was done by the time I returned. I tossed his bottle to him, and we sat against the bikes rehydrating.

"Charles? Really?"

Billy nodded. He didn't seem too pleased either.

"Dodge knew I couldn't stand him."

Billy chuckled. "Maybe that's the point."

"Asshole."

I took a sip of my bottled water and looked at Billy from my peripheral vision. He watched the road, taking a sip of water every now and then.

"So, my grandfather . . ."

"You're not getting his address yet."

"I know." I sighed. "At least tell me his name."

Billy shrugged. "Don't know it."

"How do you have his address but not his name?"

"Dodge didn't tell me."

So, it was Dodge who had found my grandfather, not Billy. How the hell did he get it? I'd never even thought to look for any other family members because I'd been told there weren't any left. As for finding extended relatives, it seemed pointless. My last name had been Gonzalez before it was changed to Warren to match Dodge's last name. There were a million Gonzalezes in the world. I didn't have an earthly clue how to go about sifting through them all.

"How did Dodge get the address?"

Billy shrugged again. I felt my patience slipping away.

"Then how long has he had it?"

Billy shrugged.

"That's not an answer," I said through gritted teeth.

"Some years. Why does it matter?"

I stood up off my motorcycle. "Years! That matters." I paced in front of him. Years! How could Dodge do that to me? Keep my grandfather from me for so long?

"Why didn't he tell me?"

Billy drank the last bit of his water. "He tried to tell you, but you wouldn't take his calls."

It was true. I praised the gods when caller ID was invented, because it meant I didn't have to hang up on Dodge anymore when he called. If Dodge's number or some other number I didn't recognize appeared on the caller ID, I wouldn't pick up. It annoyed Trevor greatly. "What if it's an emergency? Or someone from the office?" he would say. "They'll live," I always replied. Nine times out of ten, it wasn't an emergency. Just Dodge. He rarely spoke when the answering machine picked up. Most often, I heard his breathing, though on occasion he grunted or sighed. Once he muttered, "fuck," and another time he said, "Goddamn it, Raq," before hanging up.

"So, it's my fault that I don't have his address? That what you're saying?" Was it? Could I have known my grandfather all this time? I didn't want to think about that, think about all the time I'd lost because I hadn't picked up the phone and given Dodge a chance. Now, it seemed petty and immature, but at the time, I had been protecting myself from the boogie man of my youth.

Billy finished his water and twisted the plastic bottle between his hands. "You know, when, uh, your folks passed," Billy said, "I didn't want Dodge to take you in." My body stilled and my jaw tightened.

He chuckled. "I looked at a picture the Social Services sent, and I told him you didn't belong with us."

I looked away and bit my lip hard enough to feel the pain I felt in my heart. When I looked back our gazes locked.

"But Dodge didn't listen. Said family don't abandon family." He chuckled. "I think he wanted to be a dad."

"Ha. Right." I shook my head.

"He wasn't a saint, that's for goddamn sure," Billy said. "And he didn't always do right by you."

I opened my mouth to say something, but Billy said, "Don't."

He untwisted the water bottle. "He took you in when he could have sent you into the system. You think that shit's better?"

It couldn't have been worse. I crossed my arms and looked down. Billy sighed.

"A couple years ago, Dodge got a letter from Social Services. They didn't know how to get a hold of you, so they reached out to him. Then he got a letter from your grandfather. You were in a pissy mood and wouldn't take his calls, and he wouldn't let anyone but him tell you." He ran his hand over his facial hair. "And when it seemed like you weren't going to ever speak to him, Dodge went out to that address after a run to see if it was true."

The news felt like a punch to my chest. I gritted my teeth. "Dodge met my grandfather?"

Billy nodded. My fists clenched. "And you let him? You didn't think *that* was a bad idea?" I spat.

Billy shrugged, unperturbed by my anger. "They seemed to get along okay."

What could those two have possibly had to say to each other? And 'they got along'? Bullshit. That couldn't be true.

Billy walked to the trash can to throw away his water bottle. As he walked back, I noticed for the first time how slow he moved, how he favored his left leg over his right, how many wrinkles were etched on his face. Billy, this monster of a man who had lived in my mind as a larger-than-life figure, who embodied strength and danger, had somehow become old.

"What about my grandfather? Didn't he ask for me? Didn't Dodge give him my number or address? It's not like he didn't know it." Sure, I'd changed my phone number a few times, but the Lawless knew where I worked, and they had ways of getting information they needed.

Billy swung his leg over his bike. "Dodge didn't give it to him."

I threw my water bottle at the trash. It bounced off and hit the ground.

"And why the hell not? He's my grandfather!"

"We are your family, Raqi. Don't you forget that."

He kick-started his bike. It was his way of telling me to shut up and get moving. We stared at each other, me breathing heavily and Billy, as cool and composed as ever.

Eventually, I looked away and got onto my bike. The vibration of the engine caressed my legs, a secret message to not give up hope. The sooner I got through this, the sooner I could leave. Real families didn't treat each other this way, no matter what Billy said.

21

Every night, the smoke swirled and danced languidly below the ceiling, putting on a picture show. The white wisps coalesced and dissolved into images of men drinking to unconsciousness, fights that resulted in overturned tables and broken chairs, men and women dancing too close, and the hiding of guns in the walls. The smoke, expelled from the lungs of the Lawless, witnessed everything that happened in Scoot's, a Lawless-owned bar. It had taken on the role of historian, always on the lookout for a new story to tell. Anyone who stared long enough could see this magic at work, but no one ever did. No one but me.

I stood next to Missy, Billy's older sister, and watched as she played a hand of poker against Dodge, Eddie, and Gray. Even though Missy wore a lot of eyeshadow for an old woman and had pocked skin, she was always nice to me. She'd explained the game and why she played each card that she did, and how some hands were better than others. Missy even went as far as playing a few rounds with me when the guys went out back for thirty minutes to talk business with an associate who stopped by.

The game was Five Card Draw and Missy was good at it, much better than Eddie and Dodge. Gray was Missy's biggest competition. Missy gave me the job of placing her quarter bets in the pile, pulling out her winnings, and stacking them in little towers next to her.

"The thing is, Raqi," Missy said as we waited for Eddie to hand over his third card. "I'm not luckier than any of them, I'm just better at reading their tells."

Dodge grunted and scowled at this, while Gray took a drink of beer. Eddie moved his cards around as if that might make them a better hand.

"A tell is kind of like a hint that tells you what someone is thinking?" I asked.

She smiled. Her teeth were yellowed like everyone else in the club. "Yes, smart girl. Sometimes it's a nervous twitch or the way they move their lips. Anything can be a tell. If I can spot it, then I can figure out if they have a good or bad hand and how I should bet."

I knew exactly what Missy meant. I was good at seeing tells; I had to be. If I could judge Dodge's mood based on the glaze over his eyes, the tone of his grunts, or even by how bad he smelled, I could stay out of his way and avoid getting yelled at or even pushed. I'd taken those skills and used them in other parts of my life. At school, around the Lawless, and sometimes for fun in my own mind, to see if I could figure out what someone would do or say before they did it.

Eddie finally placed a card down and Gray handed him a new one.

"Bet," Gray said.

Dodge sucked his teeth while he looked at his cards and Eddie wiped sweat off his forehead. Gray took a sip of beer before putting a quarter in.

"What should I do?" she asked me.

I studied the men. Eddie had folded, but Dodge was placing a quarter in the pile. Standing on my tiptoes, I whispered in Missy's ear, "Gray's going to win."

When I pulled back, she smiled and playfully grabbed my nose. "Smart girl," she whispered before folding.

Gray and Dodge looked at each other before showing their cards. Dodge had a full house, which may have won him the pile if Gray didn't have a royal flush. I was right. I turned to Missy who said, "Hah!"

Dodge threw his cards down on the table. "Damn it!"

Gray, in his usual silence, pulled the pile of quarters to him. He rarely showed emotion and talked as little as necessary. I'd heard other

Lawless speak about Gray's penchant for silence and why it made him the best hitman of the club. He was methodical, quiet, and he attacked when calm. That's how he caught his victims in surprise. These stories made Gray sound scary, but I'd never seen that side of him. I hoped I never would.

"Dodge, you got yourself a smart one here. She can read people as good as anyone," Missy said as she took a cigarette out of her pack.

Dodge turned his hard eyes on me. "Then why the hell you ain't helping me? I'm the one that feeds you."

Eddie snorted. "Only peanut butter and jelly."

I fought to hide a smile. If I smiled, it'd piss Dodge off.

"If it's good enough for me, it's good enough for her," Dodge replied and took a drink of beer. Eddie shook his head and Gray smirked.

"I'd replace your sorry ass with her and let her bring home the bacon," Missy said. I stilled. Missy was known to let her mouth run and it sometimes got her in trouble, especially when she was drinking.

Dodge's head turned to the side, and he said, "Huh." That wasn't what I was expecting. He turned his attention to me. "You as good as she says?"

I shrugged.

"Either you are, or you aren't. Which is it?"

I looked up at Missy and then at Eddie for help.

"Don't look at them. Look at me, damn it," Dodge said. I did, and what I saw there surprised me a little. He was serious.

I found some courage deep within and said, "Yeah."

Dodge regarded me for a second as he took a drink of beer. He nodded his head and pointed to an empty chair at the next table where Grim and his girlfriend Aubrey talked.

"Pull up a chair and let's see then."

I waited. Was this a trick? Dodge said, "Go on. We ain't got all day."

Missy clapped her hands together in glee, while I walked over to grab the chair.

"If she's so damn good at reading tells, you can spot her some quarters," Dodge said.

Missy stopped clapping and smiled mischievously. "Sure, but when she wins, she'll pay me back, plus twenty-five percent."

"Taking money from a kid," Dodge said, shaking his head.

"Girl's got to eat," Missy replied.

I scooted the chair to the table and climbed up.

"You two are the worst," Eddie said. "Here, Raq. Take my quarters. Anything you win is yours."

He slid over his meager pile of quarters, then dug into his front pocket. He pulled out two more and added it to my pile.

"Thanks, Eddie," I said. He winked at me.

"I can't win for shit anyways," he said.

"Now that's right!" Missy said. She grabbed the deck from Gray and shuffled the cards.

Just as she was about to pass them out to us, Billy walked into Scoot's.

The Lawless greeted him with nods and "Hey Billy!" A few even got up to shake his hand. Billy looked around the room and saw us. He walked up to the table, while pulling up a chair from another. He placed it between Gray and Missy.

"What are we playing?"

"Five card draw," Missy said as she began dealing around the table, skipping over Eddie. I was the first card she dealt to her left, but it wasn't until Billy got his first card that he seemed to notice me.

"The kid playing?" He looked at me when he said it, but he wasn't quite asking me. He did this a lot, and I wasn't sure why. Billy rarely spoke to me, but when he did, it was as if he didn't want to speak to me.

"What—you scared, little brother?" Missy said as she kept dealing.

Billy didn't smile a lot. His wife and Missy were the only two who seemed to be able to make the ice giant's lip turn up in slight amusement, and that's exactly what they did now. He looked at me through his bushy eyebrows, studying me for a second. I looked down at the three cards that lay on the table, trying not to meet his eyes. A second later, he yelled at Scoot, the bartender who stood behind the bar, to bring him a beer.

When Missy finished dealing, we picked up our cards and examined them. I had two aces, a three, a king, and a seven.

"Remember the rules?" Missy asked me. I nodded and pulled my cards closer.

Dodge was the easiest to read. He couldn't hide anything from me. Living with him for four years, I knew every twist of his mouth, every crinkle of his eye. Gray took a sip of his beer when he had a good hand. He didn't touch his drink, so he probably didn't have anything. Missy was the best at hiding her tell because it seemed so natural. She lightly licked her lips when she had a good hand and sniffed when it was bad. At that moment, she was about to lick her lips and then stopped and looked at me.

"Are you reading me, little one?"

I blushed and looked down.

"She better damn well be," Dodge said.

Eddie countered, "Why? Out of peanut butter?"

Everyone chuckled.

"Ready?" Missy asked. I was to her left, so I had to put my first card down. I handed her the seven face down and she slid me another from the deck. Another ace. I tried to keep my face neutral.

While she went around the table, I looked at Billy. He was the hardest to read, always had been. Was it the twitch of his whiskers? The way he held his cards? How he hunched over? Took a long gulp of his beer? I wasn't quite sure, but something inside me told me he had a pretty good hand. Missy said to trust my instincts. Maybe this is what she meant.

We went around a second time. I put down the three and got a king. By the time everyone exchanged their cards on the second round, I was pretty sure that Billy was the one to beat. As Missy replaced one of her cards from the deck, Lenny appeared behind Billy. His eyebrows pinched together, and his mouth was set in a line. He was angry, but the way he moved between his feet, rubbed his chin over and over again, it was clear he was nervous too. He had bad news and he didn't want to share it with Billy.

Billy placed his cards on the table and leaned back so that Lenny could whisper something in his ear. Billy wasn't a warm guy. He radiated ice-cold stillness. But whatever Lenny told him was making him colder, stiller, harder . . . and I didn't think that was good. The pit in my stomach grew, and fear clawed its way from there to my heart, gripping tighter and tighter. I looked around at Dodge, Eddie, Missy, and Gray. No one seemed to notice what was happening.

When Lenny was done, he stood up, his hands bunched into fists at his side. Billy looked down at the floor, sniffed, and stilled again. Then he turned and scooted his chair back from the table. No one blinked an eye, but I knew that something was wrong—really wrong.

"Okay, boys—" Missy said. "And ladies." She winked at me. "Last round."

I didn't move. Didn't put down a card.

"Pass, Raqi?" Missy asked.

I nodded because I couldn't take my eyes off Billy. I could feel the pressure building inside of him. Lenny stood behind him, rolling his shoulders forward and his neck side to side.

Gray put his card on the table, and as Missy reached for it, I saw Billy's tell. His nostrils flared and his eyes turned slightly toward Missy, and it all clicked. I opened my mouth to warn her, but I wasn't fast enough. Billy grabbed the back of Missy's head and slammed it into the table.

Missy screamed in agony, and Dodge, Gray, and Eddie jumped back from the table. The bar grew silent. Billy pulled Missy up for one second—her nose dripping in blood, her face a tangle of anguish—and then slammed it back into the table. His forearm shook as he pulled her head back up.

Tears and blood ran down her face. "Billy—" she wailed.

Billy stood, dragging Missy up by her hair.

"Snitch," he growled.

With one word, the bar's energy changed from confused to angry, and everyone seemed to take a step closer to our table.

"I—" Missy cried. "The cops made me! I didn't want to."

Billy wrapped his hand around her throat and squeezed. The blue veins in his arm pumped with blood. Missy clawed at his hand.

"Please!" Her voice strained. "I didn't have a choice."

Billy's black eyes flared with ice-cold hatred. The cards in my hands shook.

"I'm sorry, brother—" Missy choked out.

Billy pulled her closer and let out a guttural roar of a lion who had nothing left to live for, before throwing her on the ground. Missy landed on her side and tried curling into a ball. Lenny kicked her in the stomach. "Snitch!" he yelled. Grim came up beside him and kicked Missy in the face. Her head whipped back, and she groaned. Blood covered her teeth.

Eddie stood up and put his hand on my shoulder to guide me away. Billy stopped him with a look. "She stays. She needs to learn you don't betray family."

I didn't look up at Eddie for his reaction, but I trembled when his hand slipped away from my shoulder. Every Lawless member in the bar, including Dodge, Eddie, and Gray, kicked Missy and yelled, "Snitch!" They kicked her all over. Her head, her back, her stomach, her legs, her chest. Kick, after kick, after kick. Missy cried out with the first few kicks, then whimpered, before growing silent and still. She eventually passed out.

Standing above it all was Billy. The ethereal cloud of smoke that filled Scoot's every night moved around his head. It was churning, transforming into the scene that played out below. Billy watched as his brothers kicked his sister to unconsciousness for being the worst thing someone could be in the club. And I stood there among it all. Watching. Witnessing.

22

1990, thirty-one years old

"Brownie!"

For fuck's sake. I'd forgotten Charles had nicknamed me "Brownie" when I was a kid. Not because I loved brownies, but because I was brown. A sick racist pet name.

Charles grabbed my hand and squeezed it. His hair had been gray for as long as I'd known him, but now it was shaggier. In an odd way, it complemented his long white scraggly beard yellowed along the edges.

"Oh, Brownie, you're so grown up. I swear you used to be no taller than me."

I groaned and looked at Billy. I wanted him to know that this was his fault, since Dodge wasn't there for me to yell at.

"Charles—" I said.

He looked up at me with a smile on his face, unaware of having done anything remotely wrong.

"Don't call me 'Brownie.' It's inappropriate, to say the least."

He squeezed my hand again before letting go. I wiped my hand on my jeans.

"Listen to you. 'Inappropriate, to say the least.' You sound like a damn good lawyer," he said. "I mean, 'good lawyer.' I don't cuss anymore."

My anger prickled across my skin. He didn't get it. He never would.

"Billy, man, so good to see you," Charles said, extending his hand to shake. Billy shook it and gave him a nod.

"Come on," Charles said as he turned around. "Got us a seat over here."

The dimly lit sports bar had a few TVs tuned to various sports channels. Even though the lunch hour had already started, only a handful of customers were there, so most of the tables were empty. Charles led us to the back to a table that seemed shorter in height than the rest of them. I was right, because when I sat down, my knees hit the table. I smirked at Billy, who was unable to fit his gangly legs underneath and had to splay them out to get comfortable. It was exactly what he deserved.

"Ilene!" Charles yelled at a waitress in her fifties with maroon lipstick that was far too dark for her complexion. Ilene walked over with a smile. Small curly strands of brown hair framed her face, while the rest had been pulled back in a bun.

"My friends came all the way from California to see me, Ilene," he said.

"Well, ain't you special," she joked and gave him a wink. "What can I get y'all?"

I opened my mouth to speak, but Charles beat me to it.

"We'll have a round of beers to start. Two burger specials for Billy and I and a basket of chicken fingers for this pretty lady."

Ilene didn't have to write anything down, which meant she'd probably been working here since this place opened decades ago. She nodded at everything Charles said.

"Actually, I'll have the burger special, too," I said, never taking my eyes off Charles. Usually, I'd prefer chicken fingers, but I didn't like Charles ordering for me. Hell, I didn't even like Trevor ordering for me. Charles didn't seem to notice my annoyance, but only smiled and thanked Ilene before she walked away.

Charles turned to me. "I'm so glad you're here. When I heard Dodge had died and returned to his maker, it broke my heart."

Maker?

"I'm so blessed to have had him as my friend and I praise God every day that you were brought into his life, Raqi. You really made him a better person." He reached out to grab my hand, but I pulled it away and sat back in my seat.

"What's with all the praise God shit?" I asked. Charles was acting weird, even for him.

He clapped his hands together then spread them wide, revealing two bloody holes the size of nails in the middle of his palms. "I was saved a few years ago. Found Jesus and it has seriously changed my life."

I looked at Billy, suddenly realizing why he'd laughed when I mocked God for putting Charles on this Grieving Ride. Charles was a born-again Christian. This was worse than I could have imagined. Billy smirked. Dodge was a shithead for including Charles on his list.

Ilene returned with our drinks in ice-cold mugs. As she passed them out, Charles rambled about his new religious journey.

"—He spoke to me, actually spoke aloud to me one day. Told me that I had a gift, and I was the best person to share His love with others, starting with my club and expanding to the community at large. So now, I volunteer at the church, work on fundraisers, and sometimes I even preach at the local prison."

I took a long gulp of my beer. God, I was going to need this drink and another before the conversation ended.

The Lawless were not church people. Some of them believed in God, if tattoos of crosses were any indicator, but they never spoke about it. It wasn't something most people talked about in California except to joke about the Church of Scientology and the wack jobs that lived behind the walls. I wasn't surprised that Charles had found God. It seemed like something Charles would do and with the fervor that Texan Christians had, he'd fit right in trying to convert the masses with his garrulous chatter.

"The other day, I was witnessing to a—"

I interrupted him. "Charles, do you know why Dodge put you on his Grieving Ride?"

Billy grunted in amusement. The only way to get Charles to focus was to be direct, and the sooner we got this over with, the better it would be for my sanity.

Charles leaned back, glowing brightly in holier-than-thou light. His mouth opened so wide in shock that I could see the chewed-up bacon and eggs he'd had for breakfast stewing in his stomach.

"Of course, he put me on the ride, Raqi! I'm his oldest friend." He emphasized his words by touching his chest with both hands.

"I was there for everything. The day his mama ran off with some banker. You know he never knew his daddy. I was there when Mee-Mee beat him and that time we put a dead cat in the principal's car. When—"

I'd been taking a big gulp of beer but sputtered at his words. "Wait, Charles stop talking—" I wiped the beer that I'd spit up on my chin. "Who's Mee-Mee?"

Charles scooted closer to the table. "Didn't he tell you anything? Mee-Mee was Dodge's grandma. She raised Dodge, and—"

"What about my mom?"

Charles took a drink. "Jean went to live with some family friend, the Collettes, I believe. Mee-Mee didn't much like her own daughter and she didn't want to raise another."

That was fucked up.

"Mee-Mee was the meanest woman I ever met," Charles said. "Used to make Dodge clean the house every day, even sent him to work on farms when he was a kid. He couldn't mess up for nothing, or she'd beat him good." He shook his head slowly. "And I mean, *beat him good*."

"Shit." No wonder Dodge had been so messed up. I looked at Billy. He sat back in his chair, listening. He always seemed to be listening to conversations and rarely engaged in them. I don't think I ever saw him let loose, be spontaneous. I wondered what he thought about Dodge's childhood.

"Did you ever see my mom growing up?" I asked Charles.

"Sure, sometimes at school. Dodge didn't really have much to do with Jean. They didn't run in the same circles and the Collettes were strict. Jean was a good girl, didn't get in trouble much. Not like your uncle and I. We were rascals. Drinking beer in the teacher's lounge, sneaking into bars when we were sixteen . . ."

Charles continued listing vile and reckless teenage acts he and Dodge had done, getting further and further away from what I really wanted to know: more about my mother.

Memories of my mother were limited to smells and touch. I felt her sharp fingernails scratch my back softly, lulling me to sleep. Sometimes on chilly days—which weren't often in California—I smelled her chicken and dumplings stewing on the stove. My fingers became sticky thinking about how I ran them through her thin blond hair that rose high with volume from four rounds of hairspray.

"Charles," I said. He kept rambling. "Charles," I repeated, harsher. He finally stopped. "I want to know more about my—" I paused because Ilene returned with baskets of burgers. Charles reached forward for the ketchup to drench his fries.

"Thanks," I said to Ilene. Billy had already taken a few bites of his burger before she'd even finished setting the other baskets in front of Charles and me.

"My mother, Charles, what else can you tell me about her?"

Charles stuffed two fries into his mouth. "She sang in choir. I remember that." He thought a second. "She hung out with Barb, Laura, Elaine . . ." He paused. "And . . . Sherry, Brenda, and Sonya. Used to date this guy named Rob. He was a football player. Dodge didn't like him. I remember this one time—" Charles laughed, and a few bits of ketchup flew from his lips and landed on the table.

"Rob was pissing in the bathroom and Dodge came up behind him, grabbed him by the neck, and pushed him against the wall. He told him if he didn't stop dating Jean, he'd beat him so bad that he wouldn't be able to walk." Charles chuckled and shook his head, remembering the disturbing "good ol' days."

"Doesn't sound like Dodge at all," I muttered before taking a bite of my hamburger.

When I looked up, I saw something on Charles's face that I had never seen before. He bit his lip and his eyes flittered back and forth. Had he suddenly realized for the first time the shit he and Dodge had done had been dangerous and cruel? What was even more, the look on his face didn't leave. He stared at his burger, his face turning pink.

"We didn't do good things all the time, Dodge and I," he said. "Jesus has shown me that."

It was about the most honest and sane thing Charles had ever said, minus the Jesus part.

He looked up at me. "But he was my best friend and stayed my best friend all these years."

The bite I'd just taken suddenly seemed harder to swallow. I took a drink of beer.

"I know I talk a lot and Dodge . . . maybe he didn't talk enough to you. But he loved your mama, even after they stopped talking," he said.

"Why did they stop?" I asked.

Charles shrugged and took a sip of his beer which was slowly turning into red wine. "They were different people. She had a pretty good family who took care of her, and Dodge had mean ol' Mee-Mee. When we joined the army, Dodge didn't look back, didn't stay in touch with anyone. Jean tried to. She sent a few letters when we were overseas, but he never wrote back."

"Because?"

Charles stroked his white beard. "Dodge didn't share his feelings with anyone, not even me. But I tell you, since becoming Christian, I've become pretty good with interacting with people. I don't think he felt worthy of having Jean's love. So, he pushed her away, before she could hurt him."

Charles looked off in the distance, seeing Dodge and he in a time that no longer existed. Billy sat next to me, eating the last of his fries. His eyebrows rose when he caught me looking at him, indicating that he was a bit surprised by Charles's insight.

Charles laughed. "I'm going to miss your uncle." Small tears pooled at the corner of his eyes. Oh, God, Charles was starting to make me feel sorry for him. Dodge had been friends with him for so long, and now he wasn't in Charles's life anymore. I wondered what that felt like, to have someone you cared about deeply for most of your life suddenly die and never be there for you to see or speak to again.

Charles wiped at his eyes. "I'm thankful he's with Jesus now." He took a sip of the Blood of Christ, then slapped his mug playfully on the table. A few drops sloshed out and stained the table in the image of Mary.

"Let's talk about better things," he said as the heavens above shone a light on their disciple. "Now tell me, Brownie. Have you taken Jesus Christ into your heart as your Lord and Savior?"

23

Our mouths consumed each other, searching for the other's soul. My hands touched Jackson's abs; his hands were under my shirt. We fell back on my bed, with Jackson on top of me. He had just unbuttoned my shorts when the door opened. We froze. Teenage desire hung thickly in the air but not thick enough that we couldn't see Dodge swaying in the doorway, bloodshot eyes growing redder by the minute, lips pulled back in a snarl.

I pushed Jackson off and he rolled to the side. No one moved for about a half a second. Jackson and I watched Dodge. He looked between Jackson and me as if trying to decide who he would go after. He chose me.

"You slut!" Dodge ran toward me. I wasn't sure what he was going to do once he got to me, but I didn't want to find out. I bounced behind the bed, so that it was between Dodge and I, and quickly buttoned my shorts. Jackson ran at Dodge and pulled him from behind.

"Get off!" Dodge yelled. "Raqi, get over here!"

Dodge's bloodshot eyes bulged from his head, and his thin graying hair stood straight out like a Halloween wig of a mad scientist.

"Run!" Jackson yelled. He pulled Dodge away, leaving a small opening for me to run past and out the bedroom.

"Whore! Opening your legs for this piece of—" I didn't hear any more as I closed the front door behind me. I jumped on my Ironhead and sped off, breathing hard and fast. It was still light outside, and I wasn't sure what to do. I had a few bucks in my pocket, so I went to a burger joint.

"Whore whore whore" appeared in scraggly red letters on the backs of my hands and forearms as I ate chili-cheese fries. I wiped the words away, but they kept appearing. Dodge was with different women every week, and he thought I was the whore? I wasn't like those girls or even him for that matter. I loved—or liked—or something—Jackson. We were dating and had been for seven months. I wasn't messing around with other guys. And even if I was, it didn't make me a whore.

When I was about done with my fries, I wondered where I should go next. I usually went to Jackson's if I needed to get away from Dodge for a night and shared a bed with Bethie. The thought of seeing Jackson right now made me squirm. I could go to Eddie's. It wasn't the first time I had to stay with him. Sometimes, Dodge went on runs that I couldn't go on because of school, and Dodge wouldn't let me stay at his house alone. One of the few "normal" parental things he'd ever done.

I paid, got on my Ironhead, and rode to Eddie's.

When I knocked on Eddie's door, Mike—Eddie's friend—answered. He swayed in the doorway with a beer in hand then leaned on one arm against the door frame. Mike's breath smelled like deception and oranges left to rot on the ground. I took a step backward.

"Hey, Dodge's little Mexi-girl." His eyes went straight for my boobs.

Crossing my arms, I tried to look past him. "Where's Eddie?"

He stepped forward, and I stepped back. "Why do you want Eddie? Mike's here. You're old enough—"

Suddenly, Eddie appeared behind him. "Get out of here, Mike. Dumb shit." Eddie pushed Mike onto the porch. I had to move quickly to get out of the way of Mike who stumbled forward and dropped his beer. Half of it spilled on my left leg. Eddie held the door open and motioned me to get inside. I breezed by him quickly and went to the kitchen for a paper towel.

"Eddie, come on, man. You can't kick me out," Mike said before Eddie shut the door in his face.

Something sizzled in a frying pan. Eddie returned to the stove, barefoot, in jeans and a black shirt. I wiped the beer off my leg with a napkin and plopped onto the couch. *The Carol Burnett Show* played on the TV. The sizzle increased when Eddie moved something around the skillet.

"What happened with you and Dodge this time?" he asked.

Dodge and I had been getting into it a lot lately. I was tired of the drugs and his mood swings and at seventeen years old—we made for a volatile situation.

I covered my face with my hands. "I don't want to say."

Eddie looked up at me. "Suit yourself."

A few minutes later, Eddie had two steaming plates filled with rice, butter beans, collards, and fried pork chops. Eddie was from Georgia, and it showed in his cooking. Then again, anything was better than the fried bologna or peanut-butter-and-jelly sandwiches Dodge made.

"Chef Eddie-r-dee," I sung. It was a common joke anytime Eddie fed me.

He smiled and returned to the kitchen to grab a beer for himself and a water for me, before settling down on the couch.

"Dude, you should be a chef," I said through forkfuls.

He laughed, getting a bit of greens in his brown beard. "I like making food for me, not for bitchy customers who won't appreciate it."

I rolled my eyes. Who wouldn't appreciate this?

"Besides, I'm a Lawless. Ain't no other life for me."

I didn't believe that. Eddie wasn't like the rest of them. He wasn't always drunk or high. He didn't have a wife he beat or kids he yelled at. His house was nicer than most. Sure, it was a trailer, but it was clean and homey in a way that even Billy's house was not, and he had a wife who compulsively cleaned.

We ate and watched TV in silence. When we were done, I washed the dishes and Eddie dried them. A few plates in, I noticed he was trying to say something every few seconds but stopped himself. Finally on the fifth try, he spoke.

"Raqi, you're at that age where you got to watch for guys like Mike."

My face turned hot. I was well past *that age*. In junior high, boys started looking at me differently, as did their fathers. I felt their eyes on my butt when I walked away, my breasts when I walked up. Now I crossed my arms often and deferred to pants and a baggy shirt when I knew I might be around the club.

"Yeah, I know," I said. "Most guys are like Mike."

Eddie stiffened, and I realized my mistake. He thought I meant him, too.

"Ah, shit. Not you, Eddie," I said quickly.

I scrubbed the dish in my hand a bit harder, ashamed and embarrassed. It was true though. I never saw Eddie making out with random women, never knew him to date anyone. I'd heard a rumor that he had been molested as a kid and that shit messed with his head.

Eddie ignored my screw-up, probably embarrassed, too. "I'm serious," he said. "About Mike and others. You're older and it's on you to make sure these guys don't do something foolish."

I stopped washing for a second.

He continued, "Watch how you dress and act around them. Men can't help themselves. Don't need to give them any more reason to not do right by you." My eyes unfocused and refocused as I tried not to release an anger that had quickly flared.

The plate I held in my hand was a mass of soapy bubbles. One bubble showed a Lawless running his hand lower and lower down my back, another floating bubble showed a boy in school grabbing my butt. A bubble on the right side of the plate recounted a man in a grocery store pushing his crotch against my hip in the checkout line. A large bubble that threatened to pop replayed two men leaning out of a white truck to yell lewd things they would do between my legs. Why couldn't boys, and men, leave me alone? There was nothing I could wear or not wear, nothing I could do or not do. I'd never given them any reason to not do right by me because society had already given them a reason *to*—there were no consequences for their behavior because "boys will be boys."

I pushed my anger down into a stone box inside my chest, then put the plate under the running faucet and wiped away the bubbles of harassment.

My only reply to Eddie was, "Mm-hmm."

That night, Eddie made up the couch with a few quilts that used to belong to his granny and even gave me cookies and milk before I crashed. I knew Eddie was looking out for me. His words came from a fear that I could be hurt, and because of that, I wasn't super mad at him. I was disappointed. He was different from most guys, but like he'd said, he was still a Lawless.

24

Row after row of motorcycles guarded the tan building of the Red Roof Inn in Oklahoma City. It was seven in the evening by the time Billy and I arrived.

Two Sheeps stood outside smoking cigarettes. When we pulled up, they looked my way, whispering to each other. Billy nodded before walking up the stairs. I wondered how he knew which room was his. I grabbed my duffle bag and walked up to the women. One had long stringy blond hair and blue eye shadow, the other had curly brown hair and a cropped black top.

"Hey."

"Yeah?" The brunette asked with a bit of attitude. The skin around her mouth shriveled with ten more wrinkles after each drag of her cigarette.

"You know where Eddie's room is?"

They looked at each other and smirked.

"You mean Jackson?" The brunette opened her mouth wide when she laughed. Her back molars were blackened with rot and decaying to a nub as the seconds passed.

I sighed. Fucking Sheep.

"Or is Eddie your man now?" The blond asked while the brunette knocked her shoulder as if to say, "I can't believe you went there."

"Look, I'm tired. Do you know or not?"

The brunette said, "I think it's 202." She smiled and looked me up and down, her eyes pausing at my dusty black pants and black eye.

I walked to the stairs, telling myself to let it go, that they couldn't help being born with brains the size of mice.

"Give Eddie a kiss for me!" one of them yelled as I walked away.

I flipped the bird and kept moving.

At 202, I knocked on the door and Eddie answered. "Thank God," I said as I walked past him.

"Just arrive?" His room was clean with a single queen-size bed, a small armchair, and a TV.

"Yeah."

Eddie sat in the armchair and let me have the bed.

I flopped on top of the bed comforter, not caring that it was probably covered in invisible bodily fluids. My body was tired but more so my mind. We were quiet for a few seconds. Some cop show played on the TV.

"Did Billy tell you where we went?" I asked.

Eddie shook his head.

"Do you want to know?"

He put his hand to his beard and stroked it, an unconscious habit he had never broken.

"You clearly want to say," he replied.

I leaned back, looked at the ceiling, and sighed.

"Charles."

He scowled. "Shithead."

"Yeah, but now a Saved shithead."

Eddie seemed puzzled by that, but he didn't ask for an explanation and that's what was so great about Eddie. He didn't intrude, just let me be. Eventually, I crawled under the sheets. I knew Eddie would sit in that armchair and leave me alone, and at least for the night, that's all I needed.

I woke to knocks on the door. When I opened my eyes, Eddie was in the armchair still, his hands resting on his potbelly and his head leaning back, mouth open, lightly snoring. The man could sleep through anything. I could picture it then: a mega-quake hitting California and mountains and civilization falling into the sea, and Eddie would sleep through it all. He'd sink slowly into the water and be preserved for all eternity as the snoring man under the sea.

The alarm clock said "10:00 a.m." Damn, I'd slept over thirteen hours. I never did that, but the long ride combined with a lack of sleep the past few nights had really worn me out.

I got up quickly to answer the door, so Eddie wouldn't be woken. It was Billy. His mouth was set in a firm line and his eyebrows furrowed.

"What?" I whispered.

Billy looked me up and down. I was fully clothed with no shoes. He pushed the door open to look inside. He grunted when he saw Eddie asleep and snoring in the chair.

Me and Eddie? Gross. "Are you done examining the decency of the room?" I whispered sarcastically.

His eyebrows furrowed again, and he nodded for me to come outside. I turned the inner deadbolt to the right so that I wouldn't get locked out and joined Billy on the landing. He had one arm on the railing and the other placed on his hip.

He rubbed the bottom of his chin and scowled. "Get ready. You got someone to meet here. We'll leave at eleven."

I sighed. "Of course, I do." I turned away and reentered the room. There was no point in arguing. I was too tired.

Eddie was awake when I returned.

"Breakfast?" he asked.

"I wish." I rolled my eyes. "The Lawless king demands I meet someone in an hour. I'm going to take a shower then go."

Eddie stretched his arms out and yawned. "I'll see you when you get back." He grabbed his wallet and left. I showered and changed clothes before running to the front desk where they had enough free coffee left for three-fourths of a cup.

When Billy saw me, he whistled hard. The ears of four Lawless perked at attention and they came running to their bikes. One nipped at the neck of a blond he had been talking to, leaving a faint impression on her skin so others would know she belonged to him.

"Why are they coming?" I asked.

"We'll show you where to go, but then we got some people to meet. You can make it back here on your own."

We went to our bikes. Billy took the lead, three of the Lawless puppies followed next, then me, and the fourth Lawless rode sweep. We turned north on the highway. As we passed a red Explorer, a small girl with thick black curly hair pressed her nose against the window in the back seat. She waved at me. I smiled and waved back.

It was a short ten-minute drive up the highway and down a few streets, until we turned into an area where the building's architecture was clearly influenced by traditional Asian styles. Golden roosters on red banners announced our approach with screechy caws, while Chinese Foo dogs growled and lunged at our tires with a snap of their stony teeth. The red glowing eyes of dragon statues that lined the tops of the buildings followed us as we rode. With a snort of smoke and a flick of their tail, they threatened to attack if we stepped out of line.

Billy pulled up to a small hole-in-the-wall restaurant—Phu Loc's—in a cramped shopping center. Someone peeked through the blinds of the front of the store then closed them quickly. I parked the bike and turned it off. Billy pulled up next to me.

"You're meeting some boy named Lee," Billy said.

"Any other information about this guy?"

Billy shrugged. "Some small-time chink that Dodge worked with. Not worth the trouble if you ask me, but it's Dodge's ride."

"Why do you have to call him that?" A flood of anger hit my stomach, shooting acid into my throat. I swallowed it down.

Billy frowned. "What else would I call him?"

I wanted to punch the confusion off his face. "A guy? Anything else but *that word*." I uttered the last bit through gritted teeth.

Billy only replied with "hmph" before adding, "We're off. Be back at the motel before nine," he added. "We're taking off for Arkansas at ten."

"Wait—tonight? We're doing a night ride?" I asked, my heart pumping a bit faster.

"Picking up the product now," Billy said. "No point in losing an opportunity."

He took off before I could argue.

"Fuck," I said under my breath. A night ride meant we'd be moving product—drugs or guns. I inwardly groaned. Lawless often moved their product at night when there were fewer people and cops on the road. And if we ran into any trouble, the Lawless always carried enough cash to pay people off. They usually didn't move product on a Grieving Ride. It was supposed to be holy, or as "holy" as the Lawless could get. I couldn't recall anything like this happening when I was young and went on Grieving Rides with Dodge. Then again, I hadn't been allowed on the multiday Grieving Rides because of school. Maybe things had changed since I'd been gone. Whatever the case was, I didn't like this.

I thought about leaving then, getting on my bike and heading back to California. But we were so close to being done and I was so close to holding my grandfather's address in my hand. Was a night ride worth it? I thought about all the bad things that could happen—jail, losing my job, never meeting my grandfather. Fuck. This wasn't fair, wasn't how it was supposed to go.

Before I could decide, someone tapped me on the back. I turned around and saw an Asian woman with curly black hair cut to her shoulders. She must have been fifty or so, though her face had barely started to wrinkle. She wore a short-sleeved pink top, a pair of khakis, and gray sneakers.

"You are the lawyer?" Her accent made me think English was her second language.

Hadn't Billy said Lee was a man? I nodded in reply, and she smiled before clapping her hands together.

"Good! Come in. We are waiting for you." She waved her hand

toward the door and walked quickly inside without holding the door open for me. I caught it before it slammed shut.

"Lee!" she yelled out. "Lee! The lawyer lady is here!"

There were a few patrons in the restaurant, but none gave disparaging glances when she yelled. An Asian guy about twenty or so walked out of the kitchen door. He had on a white tee, faded blue jeans, and a white apron over his clothes.

When the woman saw Lee, she moved to him quickly. "Lee—" she began, before switching into another language. Whatever she said made him smile.

He moved past her and held his hand out to shake. "Oh, hey! You're Raqi, the lawyer?" We shook hands.

He leaned back as if to assess me. "Your uncle didn't say you were so pretty."

The woman slapped the back of his head. He exclaimed, "ow!" and looked over his shoulder and said something to her in another language. The woman narrowed her eyes at him, and he stopped speaking immediately. Oh, to be young and overly confident again.

I tried not to laugh when I said, "So, Lee?"

"Yeah, I'm Lee Loc. This is my mom, Linh." He pointed over his shoulder at the woman, who smiled and nodded. I smiled in return. She lightly pushed his shoulder and said something rapidly.

"Yeah, Ma, that's good," he said before Linh left us and went to the kitchen.

Lee turned to me. "Want to sit down?" He sat in a booth next to us and I followed suit.

"My mom's going to bring some fried spring rolls. They're the best. She's famous for them."

"Oh, no, she doesn't have to—"

"Like, for real, people come all the way from Kansas for these babies. Trust me, you'll love them." He smiled, showing off a glittering gold cap on the tooth one over from his incisor.

"What kind of food is this?" I looked around, trying to get a glimpse of other people's dishes.

"Vietnamese. Mom and Dad are from Vietnam. Lot of Vietnamese people moved to Oklahoma City after the war. Mom runs the restaurant and Dad runs a grocery store around the corner."

"Cool." How the hell did Dodge get connected with Vietnamese people?

"So . . ." Lee began.

"So?" I hoped he would be able to explain why I was here, and it wouldn't be another Mr. Sand fiasco.

"Can you really get me into UCLA?"

What? Before I could ask him what he meant, Lee took off in what was obviously his natural speed of speaking—ninety miles per hour.

"Man, my parents are so excited. I've always wanted to be a lawyer, you know, and California seems more dope than Oklahoma. I'll go to the beach in the morning, Hollywood at night, and then get some killer study time on the weekend at UCLA's library. Live the Cali dream."

I pushed my palms out toward Lee. "Hold on, hold on. Wait a minute."

Lee finally shut up, which gave me a second to think.

"Dodge told you that I could get you into UCLA?"

Lee nodded. "Yeah, he said that—"

I shushed Lee, or else we'd never get through the conversation.

"Start from the beginning. How do you know Dodge? You deal for him?" I said, lowering my voice at the end, though that didn't satisfy Lee who hushed me loudly.

"Man, keep your voice down. Can't have my mom hearing, you know?"

I smirked and shook my head. "Unbelievable."

Lee looked down at the table, cheeks turning a light shade of pink. "Look, I didn't want to do that, but it was a tough time, and I didn't want my mom to lose this place. Dodge helped me out."

Dodge "helped" by putting the kid in a position to get in trouble—why was I the only one who saw the irony in that?

"Whatever. How'd you meet?" I asked.

"He came in one day with this other tough-looking white dude who was all about mom's fried spring rolls."

Mentioning the fried spring rolls called forth his mother with a plate of fresh hot ones. She set them on the table. Behind her was a waiter with a few bowls of fried rice, which he placed in front of us, too.

"Oh, no, I'm good, really," I said.

Linh wasn't having it. "Eat. It's very good and you are so skinny."

Across from me, Lee had already begun eating. I grabbed one of the fried spring rolls and dipped it into a sauce in the middle of the platter. It was a damn good spring roll, and the sauce had the right balance of sweet and salty flavors, and something else . . . It coated my tongue and seeped into my taste buds until I finally figured out what it was: passion with a touch of confidence.

Linh watched me closely, and I could tell that if I didn't play this up, she wasn't going to leave.

"Mm, wow. That's amazing," I said to Linh, smiling as wide as I could. The smile hurt my jaw, it was so unnatural, but it made Linh happy. She patted my shoulder.

"I'm so happy you will help, Lee. He will be great lawyer like you," she said.

Why did everyone think I could get Lee into UCLA?

"Thanks, Mom," Lee said, and then added something else in Vietnamese.

Linh nodded her head. "Yes, I'll go. You talk." She patted my shoulder once more and walked away.

When she was gone, I took another bite of the spring roll. "So, Dodge came in for spring rolls?"

Lee nodded with a mouth full of fried rice. "Yeah, and mom overhears him talking to the guy about how his badass lawyer niece got one of his friends off for murder. Said she's the best lawyer in Southern California."

God, it was probably Chip. The thought made my stomach churn, as it does any lawyer who knows they are representing a cold-blooded murderer who will probably do it again. Lee smiled as if this was something I should be proud of.

"And then?" I asked.

He took a bite of rice. "Then they try my mom's fried spring rolls, and she can tell your uncle loves them. She starts talking to him about the rolls, then you, then gives him another order on the house."

Lee spoonfulled more rice into his mouth and grabbed for a spring roll. "Then she tells him to come back the next time he's in town and she'll give him another plate of fried spring rolls for free."

"And he came back?" I asked.

Lee took a drink and swallowed. "Yeah, this time alone. So, mom sits with him and talks to him and—"

"And Dodge let her?" I asked, not quite believing this story, and yet impressed by Linh's persistence.

Lee nodded. "Yeah, your uncle is a pretty cool guy, and mom goes after what she wants."

Dodge had never been called a "pretty cool guy."

"—and so, the third time he comes by, my mom introduces me and tells Dodge I want to be a lawyer. Long story short, Dodge said you could write a recommendation letter for me since you're an accomplished lawyer and everything."

I sat back in the booth. This didn't make sense. Well, some of it did. Dodge promising things he couldn't deliver—that made sense. But how did Dodge think he could get me to do this?

Which made me wonder . . . "When did this all happen?"

Lee shrugged and looked away as if thinking. "Mm . . . maybe like six months ago? But don't worry, I don't need the letter now. I still got a year at the University of Central Oklahoma before I can start applying to law school."

He dove into his fried rice again, eating as fast as he spoke which was great, because I needed a moment to put this all together. Dodge had called me 'stupid' for wanting to go to college when I told him I had been accepted into UCLA. Granted, he was high off his ass, but it took all the excitement out of my body and pushed me to rip the acceptance letter to shreds later in my bedroom.

I looked at Lee. "You want to be a lawyer?"

He nodded. "Yeah, crime law and all. Like you."

I shook my head. "You don't want to be like me. Trust me. Defending those guys . . ." I sighed. "That shit ain't worth it."

"But Dodge said you have a big-ass house and you're well-known and all."

I laughed. "That's not—I mean, I do. But I'd take a small house and no respect if it meant I never defended those types of guys. Besides, I didn't have a choice."

Lee snorted.

"What?" I asked.

"Nothing." He smiled. "It's my dad. He always talks about Vietnam, you know? He likes to say, 'Even during the war'"—Lee deepened his voice and mimicked a thick Vietnamese accent—"'when we had no food and illness was widespread, we made honorable choices.'"

Lee chuckled, and his voice returned to normal. "Dad, this isn't Vietnam in the war." He rolled his eyes. I couldn't imagine what Lee's parents had gone through in the Vietnam War, and while Lee's mocking of his father wasn't the greatest, his dad's words stuck out to me. Isn't that what Trevor had said—that I had a choice? Could I have refused to go on the ride and demanded my grandfather's address from Billy? Or had I said yes, so I wouldn't have to stand up to Billy once and for all?

I squirmed in the booth and changed the subject. "Are you even smart, kid?"

Lee sat up, finally done with his fried rice and all the spring rolls. He interlaced his fingers and pushed them out in front of him as if stretching.

"All As in college so far. I'm bilingual, studying government, and head of the college debate team. Valedictorian in high school. Not to mention, I tour regionally with a local improv group." He wiggled his eyebrows.

I chuckled. "Impressive." And it was. I was smart in high school, but I had downplayed my intelligence. It wasn't "cool" to be smart, and so I never made it a big deal, never spoke up in class, and I wasn't Valedictorian. But I was near the top of my class and that, a good essay, and a lot of luck got me into UCLA.

Linh walked up to us just then. "You will help Lee?"

I folded my hands and placed my elbows on the table. Hell, why not? This was probably one of the least "bad" things Dodge had ever cornered me into doing, and with that, another crack in my idea of who Dodge was splintered farther down the middle. Who had my uncle become?

"Yes, I'll help him." I pointed my finger at Lee. "But he has to stay out of trouble, and I mean, *stay out* of *all* trouble."

Lee turned pale, and I knew he understood what I meant. No drugs. This kid couldn't afford to get involved with the Lawless again. Hopefully without Dodge around and my promise of a recommendation letter, Lee would stay on the straight and narrow.

I gave Lee the number and address to my office and told him to get in touch with me when he needed the recommendation. Linh thanked me with a long hug and wouldn't let me pull away until she was done. She signaled to one of her employees who brought a to-go box of fried spring rolls and shoved them into my hands.

Before I left, Linh moved closer to me and whispered, "I know my son is not perfect, but thank you for giving him a chance." When she winked, I had a feeling Linh knew what her son had been up to with Dodge all along.

25

1977, eighteen years old

I graduated from high school third in my class out of five hundred kids. That meant I would be the third person to walk across the stage. It was a mortifying thought, but secretly, I felt a bit honored and excited.

Graduation was held outside on the soccer field. The school had set up a stage and rows upon rows of white chairs on the green grass for parents, families, friends, and the graduating seniors. Most of my friends didn't show up for graduation. They laughed at the blue gowns and square hats with gold tassels and skipped out.

Jackson didn't want to go, arguing that he'd rather get drunk or smoke pot in celebration. Bethie joined me in walking the stage because she knew her mom wanted a picture of her daughter with her diploma, something she had never received and always regretted.

Dodge had seen my graduation gown and knew about the cookout that Bethie's family was hosting for the Lawless kids who had graduated that afternoon. I hadn't asked him to come to my graduation because I couldn't picture Dodge, in his gray holey jeans and black leather vest sitting among moms and dads who lived in manicured houses with picket fences and drove Sedans instead of motorcycles. Besides, he wouldn't want to go. I knew him well enough to know that.

During the ceremony, the principal talked on and on about "where we go from here" and "remembering where we came from." It wasn't the most interesting of ceremonies, and I sweated profusely in my black jeans and gray T-shirt under the blue gown. The gold tassel kept sticking to my lip gloss when the wind blew.

As our principal spoke, I wondered why I cared about walking the stage. Lately, I had been thinking about my mom and dad. Graduation was one of those big life events, and it sucked that my parents weren't there for it. If they could be, I imagined my dad might cry, perhaps shyly by blinking his eyes quickly so the tears wouldn't fall. My mom would gush over how adorable I looked, wanting to take pictures of me with my diploma from five hundred different angles. Maybe they'd have given me a graduation present like the ones the kids in my class talked about—a car, money for college, a trip to Europe. The fantasy made me happy and sad, and I squirmed in my seat as the emotions rolled through me.

When my name was called, I took two steps onto the stage just as a symphony of motorcycle engines revved in unison. The crescendo rolled across the field and reverberated through my organs like soft caresses and warm hugs. I turned toward the parking lot. Two lines of Lawless revved their bikes in a symphonic tune led by their conductor, Billy, and his first chair, Dodge. I laughed as I grabbed my diploma from the principal, whose mouth hung open at the Lawless performance. My jaw hurt so hard from smiling as I sat back down in my seat.

Bethie got an engine rev, too, as did Tony, the only other Lawless kid who walked in graduation. Afterward, Bethie and I took a bunch of silly photos with our diplomas for Bethie's mom. We stuck our tongues out, threw our hats in the air, and held up peace signs and our pinkies and forefingers in true "rock on" fashion. Finally, when Bethie's mom had taken enough pictures, we headed to the parking lot.

The Lawless had left, but there was Dodge, sitting on his bike next to mine, smoking a cigarette.

"Hey, graduate," he said. I looked closer at him. Something was different. His hair was combed and pulled into a ponytail at the nape of his neck. He had shaved, and it made him look younger. There were a few beads of sweat on his forehead, but the same could be said for mine. And then it hit me—he wasn't high.

"See you later, Raqi!" Bethie yelled. She and her mom got into their white car to head home.

I waved and turned back to Dodge.

"So, you came?" I posed it as a question, not quite believing he was there.

He nodded, took a drag of the cigarette, and blew out the smoke. "It's a big deal, I hear."

This was weird. I went to my bike and stuffed my gown, cap, and diploma into the swing arm bag.

Dodge got on his bike and started the engine. "Follow me." I quickly kick-started mine to life before he left me.

I couldn't stop smiling as we rode. I had graduated, and Dodge wasn't high. Dodge took the Pacific Coast Highway, and we rode north along the coast. I had taken the ride a thousand times, but our tires had never floated so far off the ground and over the sea so blue. Dodge and I raced like kids in the sky, and a few times, when I got too close to the blistering sun, he flew in front of me and guided me down. Was this how real freedom would feel when I went to UCLA in a few months?

After about thirty minutes, I realized Dodge was going somewhere in particular. He exited the highway, and we made our way toward Malibu. Eventually, we pulled into a shopping center with a pizza shop, Chinese restaurant, jeweler, tattoo artist, and an antique store. Dodge parked, and I followed suit.

"Chinese?" I asked, feeling a little hungry suddenly.

Dodge smiled and nodded his head toward the tattoo shop.

"Ain't it tradition to get the graduate a gift?"

Dodge showed up for my graduation *and* was getting me a present? What the hell was going on? I followed Dodge into the shop, waiting for him to turn back into an asshole at any minute.

Inside, a short stocky guy with a long, peppered beard and ponytail prepped a chair and inks on a tray. He nodded at Dodge as we walked over.

"Ron, this is my niece, Raqi," Dodge said.

Ron grunted and nodded.

I gave a short, "Hey."

Ron pulled out a needle from its plastic wrapping. "Sit down."

I sat down in the chair, suddenly feeling hot and shaky. Some of the guys in my grade had tattoos and Dodge's arms were filled with them, as were most Lawless'. Jackson got his first tattoo when he was fourteen. Most of the girls I knew didn't have one, and if they did, it was a flower, a heart, or their boyfriend's initials which they tatted on their own skin with an ink pen.

Dodge grabbed a barstool from somewhere and sat down in the corner.

"I don't even know what I want," I said to Dodge.

He smirked. "Trust me?"

I wanted to say, "no" because a tattoo was permanent, but instead I said, "I don't know?"

Ron gave a half-grunt, half-laugh. "Smart kid."

"Look," Dodge said, ignoring Ron's laugh. "I already gave Ron the design. Trust me. You'll like it."

I sat back in the chair, not confident I could trust Dodge, but also knowing that I couldn't say no. It would piss Dodge off, and that wasn't good either.

I ended up nodding, unable to say the words aloud. Ron took that as the go-ahead sign.

"Where do you want it?" Ron asked me as I sat back in the chair.

Before I could answer, Dodge said, "Upper right arm."

I guess Dodge was making all the decisions today. Ron nodded and moved his chair and equipment to my right side.

"Don't forget to breathe." Ron grabbed the needle.

I nodded. "Okay." My knees danced in place. I was *actually* getting a tattoo.

The buzz of the tattoo pen filled my ears, and I felt the needle pierce my skin and . . . Black spots appeared in the corners of my vision and multiplied like cells. The buzzing stopped.

"Damn it, girl. Breathe," Ron said.

I inhaled deeply, and the black spots disappeared after a few seconds. I took a few more gulps of air until my breathing returned to normal.

"Sorry," I said between breaths.

Ron moved the gun back to my arm. "You good?"

I nodded; I was good. Ron began again, and I made myself breathe. This was not how I imagined a tattoo would feel. Each flick of the tattoo gun was a long, drawn-out burn that went far beyond the layers of skin on my arm. It was a branding on my inner self, one that Dodge watched intently. I tried to see what the tattoo was going to be, but the angle wasn't right, and I couldn't move my arm. I looked up at the indents in the ceiling, counting them to keep a queasy feeling at bay. I hoped I'd been right to trust Dodge because this tattoo would be with me forever, a scar on my soul.

Thirty minutes later, Ron turned off the gun. "Outline's done."

I moved my arm to get my first look.

Half Outlaw.

When I first started riding minibikes, I had wiped out hard in the field behind the house. My knees and elbows were a bloody mess, and I had a gash on my forehead.

I pushed the bike off me about the time that Dodge ran up. He'd been timing my speed. Tears began to fall down my cheeks, even though I pursed my lips hard enough to keep the sobs in.

"Don't you cry, Raqi," Dodge said roughly as he grabbed my bike, pulling it to a standing position.

I swallowed a salty mass. Dodge didn't like crying, but for once, I think he saw the pain I was in as I tried to stand up. My knees throbbed, and my legs trembled. Dodge put the kickstand on the bike and stooped down in front of my face.

"Look here." He paused as if thinking. Finally, he said, "You know, I'm an outlaw, right?"

I nodded.

"And outlaws don't cry. Hm?"

I shook my head. They didn't.

"You—" Dodge paused. He looked me up and down and bit the

inside of his lip. I squirmed. Dodge was taking note of how different I looked from him, from everyone he knew.

"You—" Dodge began. "You got outlaw in you, too."

"Like—" My voice was raw with clenched tears as I searched for the right word. "Like I'm—I'm half outlaw?"

Dodge nodded hard and sharp. "Yep, half outlaw."

That was the first time we'd said it. From there, it became a little joke between us, and eventually spread to some of Dodge's closer friends. We'd stopped saying it years later, and I wasn't sure why, but looking at my arm now, I was glad I had trusted Dodge.

"You good?" Ron asked, ready to fill in the outline of my new tattoo.

I nodded and looked at Dodge perched on the stool.

"Yeah, I'm good."

Hours later, my tattoo was finished. Small dots of blood erupted from unseen pores around the black ink. The tattoo reabsorbed the blood sacrifice growing darker on my arm with each metallic taste. I couldn't wait to show it to Bethie and Jackson, though I wondered what Jackson would think.

Earlier that year, I'd suspected Jackson had started helping his dad on runs. He'd been talking about becoming a Prospect, which made my stomach churn. He'd have to do bad things if he ever wanted to join the club. I wasn't sure what, but it wasn't hard to guess.

Regardless of what Jackson thought about my tattoo, Dodge was happy. I'd never seen him this aware, this awake, this alive. After the tattoo, we made our way to Bethie's house. By the time we arrived, the party had already started. The adults were clustered closer to the house or inside, while the kids my age sat under some trees near the edge of the backyard. When I found Bethie, I pulled back the bandages for her and she squealed. Suddenly exposed, the Gothic letters moved closer together, making the tattoo look more ominous than it was.

"You're such a badass now!"

My mood dampened a little when Jackson saw it. His nose and forehead scrunched in distaste. He shrugged his shoulders.

"Ain't nothing like real ink, is it boys?" he said to a few guys. They laughed and high-fived. My tattoo burned my upper arm, pressuring me to knock out Jackson for insulting it, insulting us. I put the bandage back on and punched Jackson in his side, rolled my eyes and found a seat next to Bethie.

She handed me a beer, and I quietly fumed. Five minutes later, Jackson came over and sat on the arm of my chair and tried to give me a kiss.

"No thanks, man." I pushed him away with one arm.

"Come on, Raqi," he whispered in my ear. "You know I didn't mean anything against you."

He sat up straight. "I was just saying it wasn't a club tat—couldn't ever be." He meant because I was a woman, and a brown one at that.

Jackson finished his beer and called to Max for another one.

I looked toward the house and found Dodge watching me. I thought about my tattoo and wondered if it was or wasn't "the real thing," and more importantly, if I wanted it to be or not.

26

Billy stood outside the motel with a small group of Lawless when I pulled in. As I walked over to him, the guys around him melted away.

"I don't want to do this thing tonight," I said.

Billy shrugged. "Tough luck. Got to make a living."

"Exactly," I said sarcastically. "You get caught and I'm with you, I get disbarred. No more being a lawyer for me."

Billy smirked. "Look, this ain't our first rodeo. We know how to do this. We got associates setting us up."

Using associates didn't always mean things went smoothly. Couldn't he see this was giving me heart palpitations?

I shook my head. "Billy, I can't. I've done everything else you've asked. I came on this ride to take Dodge to Kentucky so I could get my grandfather's address. This isn't part of the deal."

Billy shifted his pants and looked over my head. "This *is* part of the deal, and you've known that since you were little. This is what we do."

"But I didn't choose—"

"Don't make a damn difference."

I shook my head. "Can't do it, Billy. Don't ask me to."

Billy crossed his arms and looked down at me. "Guess you won't get your grandfather's address."

He started to turn away.

Ah, fuck. "Wait." I grabbed his arm, and he stopped. I half expected him to be smiling when he turned around. The fucker had me and he knew it. I needed that address, perhaps now more so than when we started.

"Motherfucker," I said and kicked a motorcycle near me with my boot.

"That's Greg's bike," Billy said.

"I don't give a fuck about Greg. I don't even know Greg," I snapped back. I stood with my hands on my hips, fuming and thinking. Should I go on the night ride? Risk it to get my grandfather's address?

"This is the last stop before Kentucky, Raqi. You go, and I'll give you your grandfather's address once we arrive in Arkansas. Afterwards, we go to Kentucky and scatter Dodge's ashes, and you can do whatever the hell you want," Billy said.

I looked up at Billy. "You're not lying to me, are you? You'll give me his address in Arkansas, not in Kentucky?"

Billy leaned back on a motorcycle. "I planned on giving it to you in Kentucky, but if it'll get you on your bike tonight, I'll give it to you in Arkansas. I can't make you continue with us to Kentucky, but I'm hoping you will."

I stared at Billy as he spoke. His nostrils didn't flair. That was one of his tells. Something told me he was being honest. Grieving Rides were a big to-do for him, and he took it seriously by following all the Lawless' wishes to the T. He was taking a big risk by giving me the address in Arkansas. I could skip out on the rest of the ride, and not honor Dodge's wishes.

But wasn't the risk higher for me? I had a great job and a career that I loved. I had made partner, something that was very difficult for women, especially women of color, to accomplish. Things with Trevor and I weren't . . . perfect, but I still had a boyfriend, and my own house, and Lisa, and whatever my future had in store for me. I was only thirty-one. A federal sentence could ruin all of that.

Was I going to do this? Was this worth it? Deep down in my heart, I knew it wasn't. But when an image of me hugging an old man popped into my head, my heart pushed down every argument my mind made. I needed my grandfather and everything he represented about who I was and where I came from.

"Fine," I said, "If shit goes down, I'm out. You all will be on your own and I'll—" I couldn't say it. I wouldn't ever get my grandfather's address and I'd have to live with that.

Billy chuckled. "You'd do that to your family?"

I turned away and walked to my Ironhead. My family had never protected me; I always had to do that for myself.

I had about eight hours to kill before we took off, so I visited the nearest department store and bought a couple of shirts and another pair of jeans. My clothes were starting to smell, and I wasn't going to wash them in a motel laundry room. I went back to Eddie's room and tried to call Trevor. There was no answer and leaving a message didn't seem worth it. I took a nap instead. Eddie slept in the chair, and I got the bed again.

By the time it was nine, we were all suited up and ready to go downstairs. My insides tingled, and my arms wanted to tremble, but I held them in place. God, this was irresponsible. What was I thinking? Someone tapped me on the shoulder. I jumped and turned to find Beth trying to hold back a smile.

"Calm down there, cowboy," she joked in a Southern drawl.

I leaned my head back and groaned. "Sorry, I—God, this is such a bad idea."

She shrugged, and it reminded me of when we were teenagers. "Eh, it'll be fine. Always is."

"Not always," I said, thinking of the Lawless I had represented over the years who had been busted on rides.

She lightly punched my shoulder. "Hey, can I ride with you? Jackson's acting like a bitch on her period."

Beth nodded her head over her left shoulder. I looked past her and saw Jackson crouched next to his bike, examining the tire. He stood back up and kicked his bike lightly, then pulled out a pack of cigarettes from inside his vest pocket. His movements were jerky, and I heard a curse float on the wind.

"Billy had Dad chew out Jackson over his fight with you, so he's pissed. Apparently, Billy's even rethinking whether Jackson's gonna get Dodge's route." Beth rolled her eyes. "He acts like it's not his own damn fault."

As soon as she spoke, Jackson looked at me. I could have sworn he had a busted lip, but I looked away quickly, so I couldn't be positive. I wasn't even mad at him right now. This night ride had my complete focus.

I nodded. "Yeah, sure." I shook my hands out by my sides as if I could shake out the nervousness. Beth grabbed both my shoulders.

"Raqi. Look at me," she said, leaning her forehead against mine. She smiled and squeezed my shoulders. "It's going to be fine. Say it."

"It's going to be fine," I said monotonously, not believing my words.

She stood back up and let my shoulders go. "You act as if you never went on any runs with Dodge."

I grabbed my hands and twisted them before leaning back on my bike.

"I was a kid and didn't know any better," I said. "Now, I do. My entire schooling and career have focused entirely on not breaking the law."

Beth laughed and pointed to my upper arm where my tattoo hid beneath my jacket. "Come on, girl, don't act like you don't have any outlaw left in you." My tattoo pulsed under my shirt.

As we mounted the bikes to ride off into the night in a row of chrome and rubber, I couldn't help but think maybe I still did.

Streetlights winked out of sight as we rode farther out of the city, until finally we crossed over into a black hole in East Oklahoma. Identical small towns and lone gas stations were the only bits of life, but it didn't take long for them to be snuffed out by the ever-expanding darkness of night. There weren't many cars on the road when we left Tulsa, so we took up all four lanes of the interstate. I maneuvered to the back of the line, hoping that if shit went down, I might have some sort of forewarning to escape.

Thank God for Beth because she broke up the dullness of the view. Sometimes she'd lean forward and lay her cheek on my shoulder. Other times she'd lean back. Once, I glanced over my shoulder to find her looking up at the sky.

At one point, she yelled, "Think there's aliens?"

"What?" I shouted over my shoulder.

"Aliens! Think they're out there?" she said a little closer to my ear.

"Maybe!" I shouted back.

She tapped me a few times on the back as if to say she heard me.

During the ride, I saw Lenora ahead of me. She wore a vest with turquoise studs that sparkled every few seconds before the night swallowed their light. After this ride, what would she do? By most accounts, Old Ladies who had kids were taken care of by the club. Those without kids sometimes stayed and shacked up with another Lawless, and other times they left. I couldn't quite tell what Lenora would do.

Thinking of Lenora got me thinking about Dodge's home. What would happen to it? Would I have to sell it and get rid of everything inside? Had Dodge left it to Lenora? God, I hoped he had. I didn't think I could go through the process of getting rid of all his things. Not because I was the sentimental type, but because it meant returning to my childhood and I wasn't sure I could handle any more trips down memory lane.

We stopped every few hours for gas, but we did so in quick groups. Billy and the older Lawless were at the head of the pack, so once they arrived, they started fueling up in a few lanes, and left the pump going until we'd all gone through. Later, we'd be expected to split the cost with cash. Each section of riders quickly did their business and followed suit. We were a large group, so we looked suspicious no matter what, but the quicker we got out of a gas-station parking lot, the less nervous folks were and less likely to call the cops. We didn't need that tonight.

Right after we entered Arkansas, I relaxed. I'd overheard someone at the last gas station say that Oklahoma was of more concern than

Arkansas. Oklahoma sat smack dab in the middle of the states making it the crossroads for all drugs and deals and cops who wanted to stop such traffic.

"We're good!" Beth yelled in my ear. I nodded. Thank God. We were less than an hour away, less than an hour from a bed and sleep.

I had only begun to relax, to feel immense gratitude to have made it through the night ride, when the moon turned blood red, blue stars fell from the sky, and a siren blared long and loud signaling the end of times. The words "pull over" erupted over an intercom, knocking the breath out of my chest.

The Lawless began circling their left pointer finger in the air, the hand signal to pull over and prevent the cops from pursuing Billy and four other men who had taken off at full speed with bags and bikes full of a load.

I ignored the hand signal and hit the throttle, whipping left into the opposite lane while the bikes in front of me slowed down in the road. I barely missed the back wheel of a young male rider in front of me as I sped off. *Get away, save yourself* chanted in my mind.

"Raqi!" Beth yelled as I raced through the left lane, past the Lawless, Prospects, Old Ladies, Mamas, and Sheeps, all of whom were more focused on the flashing lights of the cop behind us. Beth squeezed my waist tighter.

"This isn't what we're supposed to—" I drowned her voice out with the roar of my engine, hitting the throttle harder. There was a four-way stop ahead. If I could get there, I could turn left or right and take the back roads to Oklahoma and then Texas, or even all the way to Los Angeles.

I was not losing my life, my career. I couldn't. I wouldn't.

I zipped past the front section of riders, barely noticing Eddie who was getting off his bike, his mouth slightly open in surprise. He would be in charge since Billy had escaped ahead to Fayetteville to drop off the load. Eddie would take care of the cops, which would either mean being jailed or paying the cops to let everyone go. I was not going to stick around to find out what he managed to do.

"Raqi—Jackson!" Beth yelled in my ear.

I didn't know what she meant, and I couldn't look behind me to find out. My eyes were intent on the four-way stop, a few meters ahead. I didn't even slow down to turn a sharp left, my body and mind reverting to the daredevil racing instincts I'd had as a kid, when the motorcycle and I were one and nothing could knock me off.

Beth screamed high and shrill, burying her head in my shoulder. The roar of my Ironhead filled my ears, my brain, my limbs. As we turned, I noticed a large hulking black truck approaching the four-way fast from my left. In my mad dash to get away, I hadn't even seen its dim lights. We turned sharply with room to spare, and as I glanced up slowly, the driver—a man in his forties—and I locked eyes for a moment, before I looked away and he continued to drive forward.

I pulled the Ironhead upright and saw a clear path into the night, empty of police lights and sirens. I hit the throttle again. But the screech of tires and the harsh crash of metal on metal, followed by multiple thuds that reverberated through my Ironhead and into my body, stopped my escape.

"Jackson!" Beth screamed as she beat my shoulders with her fists. I pulled over quickly, buckling forward from the force of my brake. When I turned around, Beth was already off the bike running toward a mangled mess of smoke and metal.

The roar of my bike echoed in my ears for a few seconds, before it disappeared, and I was left with a silence that gripped my neck and squeezed. The slaps of Beth's shoes echoed on the asphalt as she ran to Jackson, sprawled under his bike, which had wedged itself under the front left tire of the black truck's wheel. His skull lay split open, and blood and brains mixed in a puddle. The Arkansas highway lapped up the unintentional sacrifice greedily, unsure when another would come.

"Jackson! God. No!" Beth wailed. When she reached her brother, she fell to the ground and tried to pull his body free from the crushing weight of the truck. The driver, who I had locked eyes with seconds ago, had stumbled out and was attempting to pull Beth away. He swayed, either from a concussion or because he was drunk, so he couldn't get a good grip on Beth. She wailed hysterically for her twin brother and slapped the driver away anytime he came near her.

I threw up over the side of my bike, then retched again, the burning bile aggravating my throat. And that's when I heard someone yell, "Eddie! You okay?"

I turned back and saw what I had not seen before. Eddie was laid out on the ground 10 feet from the truck, his bike crushing his legs. Blood covered his face, and he was feebly trying to push the bike off him with one arm, yelling out in frustration and pain. Lawless ran to his aid.

Even though I was so close, I felt far away, like I was sitting on my couch watching it on television. Beth's reddened face dissolved in salty tears as she tried to put Jackson's head back together, her hands covered in blood that looked black in the darkness. The driver had given up on trying to pull Beth away and had fallen to the ground, his hands over his face, his body rocking back and forth. The Lawless had reached Eddie and were pulling the bike off him. Eddie, my Eddie, in pain.

When I saw the cops running toward Eddie and Jackson, speaking rapidly into their radios, I didn't think but kick-started the Ironhead to life and sped away. If I looked over my shoulder, I'd see them all, my family and friends, their faces melding into accusations at the sound of my engine, telling me that if I had not run, if I had not come on this trip, if I had not been taken in by Dodge, this would not have happened.

27

"Hand me the—" Dodge held out his hand at the same time I placed a wrench into his palm. He paused, then grunted, his way of saying thanks.

We'd been working on my 1972 Ironhead for a week during every spare minute we had. It was starting to look like a real bike again.

When Dodge had brought it home, it was a metal skeleton miss-ing bones and ligaments, held together by damaged nuts and bolts and duct-tape bandages. The previous owner was some rich chump who liked the idea of riding but didn't know shit about it. After crashing it a few times over the years, his wife made him sell it for parts. How Dodge stumbled upon it before too many parts had been sold off was a mystery and a miracle.

My throat knotted with salty tears when Dodge said it was for me. We weren't the hugging duo, but I risked a small hug. Dodge waited six seconds before pulling away, a record for him.

Dodge tightened the boat tail now. Most bikes didn't have this kind of tail, and I couldn't believe that I'd soon have something so sharp to ride. The Ironhead turned to me and asked if I could take her outside now. She needed to run. We needed to run.

"Bob says they added a Bendix unit to the seventy-twos. Thinks we can get one in to replace this Tillotson carb I found," Dodge said.

"How soon?" I asked.

Dodge tightened the last bolt and stood up, shrugging. "Maybe a few weeks."

I huffed. I wanted it now. "What's the difference between the two? Do we even need it?"

Dodge set the wrench down on a workbench. "Guys came in with vapor lock with the Tillotson. Don't happen with the Bendix."

I groaned inside and then gave a clipped, "Fine." The Ironhead sagged at the news.

Dodge pursed his lips like he might smile, but before he did, his mouth relaxed and returned to its normal frown. He walked to a small cooler in the corner and pulled out two Miller Lites, then handed me one.

I tried not to show my surprise when I took it from him. Sure, I drank. Bethie and I had been drinking since we were fifteen, and that was two years ago. While Eddie let me have a few shots here and there, I had never had a beer with Dodge.

Dodge turned and sat down on an overturned bucket. He pulled out a cigarette and popped the top of his Miller Lite. I took a large swig, and the ice-cold beer made my front teeth ache. We sat there for a few moments, me trying to sip more quietly and Dodge taking a drag, then a sip, and a drag again. The silence stretched long and loud as it always did with us. I don't know why I spoke. I usually tried to remain as quiet as I could around Dodge, but my throat itched with questions.

"How did you learn to fix bikes and stuff?"

Dodge didn't reply right away. He took a longer drag and looked at me from beneath his bushy eyebrows. Dodge's knowledge about bikes had always been there, but with us working together on my bike, I wanted to know how he was so capable with the machine, like second nature. Working on bikes was the only thing he was good at. That and getting high.

After letting out a puff of smoke, he said, "Was a mechanic in 'Nam." The smoke turned into the shape of a country I recognized from my geography textbook.

I nodded and took a sip of beer. A little dribbled down my chin, and

I quickly wiped it away with the side of my arm, hoping Dodge hadn't noticed. He hadn't. He'd been looking down at his beer can.

"Bikes weren't used a lot in 'Nam, but I had to know how to fix 'em and every other engine out there."

I knew Dodge had been in Vietnam during the war, in its earlier years. A bullet to the thigh had sent him home early.

"That's where I met Billy," Dodge said.

"Didn't know that." I took another drink.

Dodge nodded his head and looked off into the distance. "After they released me, I came out here to California and stayed with Billy's brother. He had started the club years before. Billy got back about a year after I did."

I hadn't known Billy had a brother either. "What happened to Billy's brother?"

Dodge pulled out another cigarette. "Died a few months after Billy got back. Truck swiped him on the One."

"Damn," I whispered.

Dodge pointed to my Ironhead. "Same can happen to you." He took a drag of his cigarette. "These dumbasses don't give a shit about you. Gotta be aware when you're riding alone."

"I know," I said a little harshly.

Dodge knocked ash into his empty beer can, never taking his eyes off me. "Until you seen a man's brains splattered over the highway, you don't know shit."

I looked down and hunched my shoulders. Had Dodge seen that happen to Billy's brother?

I took another slurp of my beer, while Dodge continued to smoke. The vapors rose to the top of the ceiling and escaped through a hole in the corner where birds entered to create their nests in the rafters.

Dodge broke the silence with, "Be smart, okay?"

"Yeah," I replied and took the last sip of my beer.

Dodge stood up and threw his empty beer can into a trash bin nearby. He pulled up his pants on his skinny frame and took another drag of his cigarette.

"Got a club meeting tonight," Dodge said.

I stood up quickly. "But we aren't done."

"Can't do more till we get the rest of the parts in to replace the ones that fucker sold off."

I threw my can in the trash and huffed. Damn it. I didn't want to wait any longer to ride my Ironhead.

"How long again?" I asked, grabbing the end of my long ponytail, putting it in my mouth, and chewing on the ends.

"Few weeks."

I rolled my eyes, and while that would generally drive Dodge mad, he smirked.

I stilled. "What?"

He took the last drag of his cigarette. "You kind of look like your mom."

I stopped chewing on my hair. Dodge smiled a bit more, threw his cigarette on the ground, and snuffed it out with his toe. He didn't pick it up but left it in the graveyard of other decaying cigarettes that would be buried slowly under the steps of his boots for years to come. He walked past me, giving my shoulder a small squeeze, before leaving the garage. The hair from my ponytail fell from my lips as I turned around and watched Dodge walk to the house.

My fingers lightly skimmed the leather of the boat tail. I rubbed the seat for a second, wondering exactly how I looked like my mom and if I'd ever have the guts to ask Dodge more about her.

28

1990, thirty-one years old

About an hour later and a few turns left then right, I was back in Oklahoma territory and well away from the Arkansas police and the Lawless.
I made it to the main highway and found a gas station to fill up. My
hands trembled as I held the gas guzzler. Under the bright lights, I felt
like an animal cornered by predators. Anyone could see me, find me.
I was easy prey.

After filling up, I drove another twenty minutes before pulling over
at a rest stop. It was empty except for a few shaded wooden tables with
benches and a bathroom. Thankful for the solitude, I turned off my Ironhead. As I unmounted, I flinched. My body ached, and I assumed it was
from the tension of this last ride mixed with the bruises that Jackson had
inflicted days ago.

Jackson . . . He was dead. Had to be. Brains on asphalt—you don't
come back from that. I stumbled to one of the wooden tables, making
sure to grab my bag, which weighed far heavier than I remembered.

Eddie was hurt. While I didn't think it was that bad of an injury,
there was always the possibility that it was worse than what I saw. Thinking of Beth's wail and Eddie trying to push off his bike broke something
inside of me. I swung the bag on top of a table, fell forward, and caught
myself on the ledge with my hands. I half stood, half knelt on the bench.

The tears were there, right under the surface. I could feel the moisture pooling beneath my eyelids, ready to release, but they wouldn't come. I grunted and focused on my eyes, hoping that might make the tears come. When it didn't, I tried to remember Beth's face, how she had pulled hard to free Jackson's body. But my mind protected itself, releasing a metal gate that crashed down, hiding the images from me until I found the lost key.

I hit the table with my fist and yelled. It was animalistic, a roar of frustration that was long and deep, echoing through the night, scaring away any creature that lurked nearby. I could not cry, and that scared me because I should be crying, should break down because it—everything—was my fault.

I shouldn't have left the pack, shouldn't have sped away. I wasn't exactly sure what happened, but Jackson had probably followed me, and Eddie followed him and then the truck . . . The exact logistics didn't matter because if you broke it down and solved for X, I was X. I was the problem.

After a few minutes, my body began to relax and every bit of energy and tension I had drained away. I dragged my body on top of the wooden table, which sagged under all the shame and guilt I carried. I tried to lie on my back, then thought better of it and curled onto my side, placing my head on my bag. In this infantile position, I hoped the night might swallow me up and birth me out a few hundred years in the future.

I didn't want to think about how I'd caused Jackson's death or Eddie's and Beth's pain. How I had done what I told Billy I would do—survive. How I couldn't figure out if I had done the right or wrong thing. Whether it was worth getting away from the cops and the Lawless with my life, my freedom. If it was worth losing my grandfather.

I closed my eyes, and sleep came swiftly. Everyone knows, only the guilty sleep.

I woke in the morning to the sound of a car pulling up. My face felt wet. I must have been crying in my sleep. A man in a brown truck parked in front of the bathroom. He scrambled out, saw me, and nodded a sharp acknowledgment before running into the restroom.

I pushed myself up and groaned. The map of bruises on my body ached and throbbed. Sleeping on a wooden table had done nothing to help that. I settled my feet on the bench below and readjusted my body with a few cracks and stretches. Minutes later, the man ran out, started his truck, and took off. I was alone again.

Clasping my hands in front of me and placing my forearms on my knees, I leaned forward and tried to think about my next steps. I'd been right to leave last night; I'd done exactly what I told Billy I would do. I'd come so close to losing my life in Los Angeles, everything I'd worked so hard to achieve: my job, friends, respect, success, boyfriend, my home. I had kept my word, at least to myself, and my life as a lawyer with Trevor was safe . . . right? While I wasn't happy that Jackson was dead, my body ached more for Beth and her mom, even for her father who had stood up for me against Jackson. They would suffer all the pain of losing a loved one, and I was partly to blame for that.

Then there was Eddie. My Eddie. The only person who showed me the love I deserved as a kid. He'd fed me, made sure I had cash, took care of me when Dodge couldn't. He was hurt. I wanted to know he was okay, needed to know he was fine. If his injuries were worse . . . I couldn't even think about that.

But there was Billy to deal with. He would not be happy, to say the least. I'd told Billy I hadn't wanted to ride, and he hadn't listened to me. Or had I not made him listen, hadn't put my foot down hard enough?

I looked at my Ironhead, gleaming in the morning light. She stood tall, sure of herself, despite being dusty and dirty from hard days of riding. I stood up slowly, grabbed my bag, and tied it to the sissy bar.

Last night, the voice inside my head had yelled at me to get away at all costs; now it shouted at me for the foolish decision I'd just made. Every part of me screamed to run, to go back to California and leave the Lawless behind. But I couldn't. I needed to know how Eddie was, check on Beth, and stand up to Billy. I'd gone to Arkansas, and I was owed that address, regardless of what happened in the interim.

I'd handed my life to the Lawless yesterday, and it had almost been taken away. If I wanted control of my life once and for all, I needed to face the people who had shaped it most, head on.

A couple of hours later, I drove into Fayetteville, somewhat presentable thanks to a gas-station bathroom, a toothbrush, deodorant, and a hair comb. I'd used the water from the bathroom sink to tame the hair at the back of my head, but it'd only made it more apparent that I hadn't washed it in a few days. Guess it was better than nothing.

The gas attendant told me I'd likely find Eddie at Washington Regional Medical Center and gave me directions on how to get to it from the highway. It was difficult to maneuver the Ironhead toward the hospital. My body screamed that this was a bad idea, that I wouldn't be welcome—or more accurately, a lot of people would be pissed at me. But my mind won out. I hadn't wanted anyone to get hurt because of my choices, and I had to know that Eddie and Beth were okay. I wasn't a great person, but I wasn't a shit one either.

After arriving at the hospital and parking my bike, I went inside and straight to the nurse's station. A nurse with brown, curly hair looked up and whistled. "Got a shiner there, missy." Her accent reminded me of Dolly Parton's.

I paused, my hand slightly reaching for my black eye. I had tried to ignore it in the gas-station bathroom earlier. Bursts of blue erupted against a backdrop of purple on my face. It was Jackson's final masterpiece, the last thing he'd left in this world. That seemed like a fucked-up thing to leave behind, but in a way, it made sense. He was dead because of me, and I should carry the stain of that fact on my face.

I ignored her and said, "I'm looking for Eddie Roth."

The nurse bent her head and looked at a chart, flipping through a few pages.

"Yes, here." She pointed at the chart as if I could read it. "He's in

Room One-Twenty-Eight. Got him set up there until he has surgery later today."

My body turned cold. "Surgery?"

She nodded slowly as she looked at his chart. "Sorry, surgeries," she corrected. "He had one last night to stop the bleeding of his ruptured spleen, and he'll have one today to work on his leg."

"What happened to it?" I leaned over the counter.

"Shattered," she said looking up, her blue eyes bearing into mine. "His motorcycle shattered his entire left leg. I tell you, he's lucky that's all that happened. Those things are death traps—and he wasn't even wearing a helmet!"

The roof of my mouth became hot, and I felt my throat constrict and my stomach heave up and down. He was in pain because of me.

"Miss, are you all right?" She combined 'all' and 'right' together, like it was one word, and left off the *t* at the end so that it sounded like "alrigh."

I nodded, trying to take deep breaths through my nose in the hope that it would prevent me from retching up the muffin I ate at the gas station. She didn't look like she quite believed me, but instead of asking if I was okay again, she said, "Room One-Twenty-Eight is down that hall, the last one on the right."

"Thanks." I walked slowly toward his room, my feet sinking into the white- and yellow-tiled floor with each step I took.

Eddie was going to hate me. I could deal with the Lawless hating me, but not Eddie. If Dodge was my uncle, Eddie had always been more like my dad. He'd been proud of me for my schoolwork, told me to go to college, cheered me on when I raced bikes as a kid, and taught me how to throw a punch. These last thirteen years, I'd ignored him, left him like I'd left Dodge, but now that I'd been back in his life these last few days, I couldn't let him go, couldn't believe I ever had.

His room door stood slightly ajar. I tried to peek in but couldn't see anything. What if Gray or Billy was in there? I pushed it open a tad to get a better look.

"Who is it?" Eddie's voice rang out.

Shit. He'd heard me. I took a deep breath. It was now or never.

I pushed the door open and walked slowly forward. Eddie laid on a hospital bed with the right side of his face a tapestry of broken skin and lines of congealed blood. His left leg rested in a sling, waiting for the next surgery, while his left arm sported a tie-dye painting of blue and black bruises.

He smiled. "You're okay."

And that's when I lost it. The tears that couldn't come last night came rushing out after seeing Eddie's smile imposed on his damaged body.

"Fuck," I said, the tears flowing freely down my face. They pooled together on the tile floor until they created a salty sea. With every small movement I made, waves crashed against my feet and ankles. I put my right hand to my mouth to stifle a sob and my shoulders shook. "God," I said though another sob. "I did—" I sobbed again. "This. To—" I wiped more tears away from my vision, trying to catch my breath. "You."

"You didn't," Eddie said.

"But I did—I'm so sorry." I moved closer.

I stood next to his bed, and he smiled. How could he be smiling right now? The tears were starting to slow down a bit, and the salty sea that soaked my jeans around my knees became choppy. He held out his left hand, and I grabbed it.

"If I hadn't taken off when I heard the siren, you wouldn't be here, Jackson wouldn't be—" I stopped. I couldn't say dead, but I didn't have to. Eddie's eyes said it for me.

He squeezed my hand and looked up at the ceiling.

"He shouldn't have gone after you. He knew better." He looked back at me. "But the kid never used his head around you."

I rubbed tears that pooled under my nose. "God, if I'd known—"

"Known what? That some rookie cop was going to show up and try to be a hero, even after we'd secured the route? That there'd be a truck there and Jackson would hit it? You couldn't have known, Raqi."

I shook my head, "I know. But if I hadn't been so scared, at least you wouldn't have gotten hurt."

Eddie smiled. "That was my own fault. Went after Jackson and hit some gravel on the road and wiped out. Probably lucky on my part."

There was a chair behind me. I let go of Eddie's hand and pulled the chair closer to me so I could sit.

"But still, if I hadn't—"

"Raqi," he said my name quietly but with force. "You told Billy what you were going to do, and you did it."

I opened my mouth to protest again.

"Raqi," he said firmly. I closed my mouth. He reached for my hand and squeezed it again, and we sat there for a few moments in silence.

Finally, I asked, "So, did everyone get arrested or—?"

Eddie shook his head. "No. The rookie was so freaked out after the crash that he called an ambulance and let everyone go. Billy sent most folks back to Oklahoma. A handful are here at the Rock Inn to take care of Jackson's body and finish Dodge's ride. I'm stuck here for a week, at least."

Eddie shifted on the bed and winced in pain. He grunted as he repositioned his hanging leg. I stood up, my hands going out to help, but I wasn't sure what to do. He put his right hand up as if to say he was okay, then settled and exhaled deeply. I sat back down and looked at my boots coated in dirt.

"Raq," Eddie said, and I looked up.

"It's okay."

"What is?"

"To want to know who your grandfather is. To want to get away from the Lawless—"

"I don't—"

"You do," he said. "I don't blame you. Shit, I couldn't believe you showed up for the ride, even though I knew the only reason you came was for your grandfather's address. It's okay that you stayed away, wanted to get away from us, this life."

My heart hurt hearing the words. "I didn't want to get away from all of you. Not you. Not Beth."

Eddie looked at his leg in the sling. He sounded far away when he said, "Sometimes you got to cut everyone off. Sometimes it's better that way."

I didn't think Eddie was talking about me. It was quiet for a few beats. The silence was too much for me, so I tried to lighten the mood. "They have you on some good pain killers or what?"

Eddie turned his damaged face toward mine, clearly not amused. He ignored my joke and said, "I'm serious, Raq. This life ain't for you, and you don't have to be a part of it. Not for me, Billy, Beth, Dodge. Get free of us for good. You deserve it."

The tears started flowing again. "Fuck," I said and rolled my eyes. "Why are you so good to me? Why am I crying?"

Eddie chuckled.

I wiped my eyes again and shook my head. "Before this ride, I thought I was done with the Lawless, free from it all, but I didn't realize how much I missed you and Beth and how—"

I didn't want to say it, but I was rambling with tears, and if I didn't say it now, I never would. "I feel like you are all a part of me, but I don't belong, and I can't escape you guys no matter what."

Eddie sighed. "It's hard to get away from your past, but you gotta try, Raqi. Dodge didn't want this—"

"You!"

I flinched. Shit. Billy.

I jumped up from my chair. Billy took up the whole doorway, his body vibrating in anger, the tension clear from the throbbing veins of his forearms.

"I told you—" I began.

Eddie said, "Billy, she didn't—"

But Billy didn't hear. He stomped into the room and right up to me. I stepped back a few paces, unable to speak.

"It was under control until you took off." He pushed his finger into my chest. The force cracked my sternum and sent shards of bone into my heart. "Now Jackson's dead, and Eddie's fucked to high heaven. May not be able to walk after this."

I turned to Eddie quickly, my mouth open in shock, the shards of bone burrowing deeper.

Eddie shook his head. "I'm going to be fine," he said, the words barely audible over Billy's yelling.

"And you disappeared. The hell were you thinking? Now I—"

As I watched Billy scream and throw his hands in the air, I suddenly felt calm, like I did in court, when all the noise melded into a low hum which allowed all my thoughts to come together. Everything I needed to say and do was floating right under my skin, and it would only take three deep breaths for it to appear.

One.

"Gotta pay off—"

Two.

"You betrayed—"

Three.

"How could you—"

His words faded until I couldn't hear anything at all. No sound came from Billy's mouth as he waved his arms in the air, puffed out his chest, and spit as he spoke. Without the sound, I could see it. See everything so clearly for the first time in my life.

"Are you done?" I spoke quietly and stood straighter. I stopped the shards of bone from going any deeper into my heart.

"What?" Billy yelled again.

Just then, a nurse poked her head in, her eyebrows furrowed in annoyance. Before she could tell us to lower our voices, I spoke, "Sorry about the disturbance. We'll keep it down."

She opened her mouth to say something else, but Billy whipped his head around and whatever she saw made her leave the room immediately and close the door behind.

Billy turned back to me and opened his mouth.

"No more," I said before he could get anything out.

"You got the nerve—"

"I said *no more.*" The last two words held a threat. Billy's mouth opened and closed. I had the offense now, and I had to take it.

"I didn't want to come on this ride, but I did it for the address—not for Dodge," I said calmly and evenly. "I told you I didn't want to do a night ride, and I told you that if anything went down, I would be out."

I narrowed my eyes. "Something went down." I sighed. "While I never wanted Jackson to die"—God, that felt bad to say aloud—"and didn't want anyone to get hurt . . ." My heart constricted. I'd always carry around the guilt of hurting Eddie. "I couldn't risk my life or my career for the club, so I took off. Even my grandfather's address wasn't worth that."

Billy had his hands on his hips, and I could tell it was taking everything he had to not yell. He was a raging wild boar, and if I didn't speak calmly, he might charge.

"I had to do it for me, Billy."

Billy crossed him arms. "You almost cost me a lot more last night, Raqi," he said through clenched teeth.

I crossed my arms, too. "Almost," I said. "And you almost cost me—" I stopped and shook my head. "No, you know what. I almost cost me the life I've built by agreeing to ride along. That's on me, not you, and I won't apologize for leaving. I did what I had to do—for my life."

Billy's eyebrow rose in surprise, like he couldn't quite believe that I was taking responsibility for it. I couldn't either, but I was right. I shouldn't have gone, shouldn't have been seduced by the false idea that it would all work out, or that obtaining my grandfather's address would change my life. There was no guarantee that it would fix me, bring me closer to my identity, or make me feel loved. I knew better, but I'd given in. I couldn't make that mistake again.

Billy wouldn't let it go though. "Your life." He scoffed. "This is your life, your family. Dodge died without you." His hand turned into a fist, and he shook it. "You should have been there for him."

"That's not true," Eddie said. It wasn't loud or aggressive, but it got Billy to shut up.

"What's not true?" I asked.

"You didn't need to be there for Dodge. He was okay with you being gone. Told me so a month before he passed."

I stumbled, the words knocking me a few steps back. "Wait, what? Then why am I here?"

Eddie shrugged. "I swear it, Raqi. He said he couldn't remember what went down the last time he saw you, but he knew it had to be pretty bad."

I touched my throat and swallowed.

Eddie continued, "Dodge said it was probably for the best that you weren't around anymore. He always figured you'd move on from us, that it made sense."

"How?" Billy demanded.

"Said he'd left home when he could, too, and never looked back," Eddie replied. "Made it sound like it was family tradition. And . . ."

"What?" I asked.

Eddie shook his head and looked down. "He said you weren't like us, Raqi."

A lump formed in my throat. Had Dodge meant that in a good or bad way?

"Bullshit. He wouldn't say that," Billy said.

Eddie held up his hands. "Swear to God. I ain't ever seen Dodge that serious, or calm for that matter."

I looked at Billy as if he might be able to verify what Eddie said. If that was the case, why was I on this ride? Why had Dodge planned this trip? Billy rubbed his mustache with his hand and looked away. If I didn't know him any better, I might say he was trying to hold something in. Tears, maybe. But Billy was a Lawless and when he turned back to me, his eyes were hard and dry.

"Fine. Dodge didn't need you. You're free of us, that's what you want, isn't it? Go back to California."

Billy was pushing me away now. Two seconds ago, he had wanted to tan my hide and treat me like part of the club, hold me responsible. Now he was freeing me, pushing me to the door. I could leave and not look back. Something about the way Billy wouldn't look me in the eyes, how angry he was at hearing the news about Dodge, it clicked for me. These men were far more complicated than what they showed on the surface.

Decades ago, Billy would have released his anger upon me. I'd seen him do it to people he loved, but he didn't do that now. Maybe these old dogs could learn new tricks, and maybe my presence in their life had had something to do with that.

I didn't think but rushed the big bear of a man and wrapped my arms around his torso. It was the first hug I'd ever given him. He flinched, then stiffened before wrapping his arms around me. I breathed in the decades-old cigarette smoke in his vest and burned my rage and love into his body, hoping that it might do something for him when I was gone.

Leaving the Lawless hadn't only affected Dodge and Beth, but also Billy and Eddie and maybe even the Lawless as a whole. Billy and his wife had never had kids, and when I looked back to my childhood, I remembered Billy's wife handing me bags of clothes and schools supplies every August and a handful of Christmas presents surrounding the TV that sat on the living room floor each year. "To: Raqi" had been written on the tags in different handwriting. There was always a blank space after the word "From." I never asked where the presents came from, but I knew in my heart Dodge hadn't bought the dolls, the toys, the games I'd been gifted.

Then there were the times that Billy yelled at Dodge when he had been too high to function. I recalled him once shouting at Dodge, "Get your shit together," when he took me to a bar at one in the morning. Dodge was so shitfaced that night that he swerved between lanes on the drive there and fell to the ground when he tried to sit on a bar stool. After berating Dodge, Billy had marched over to me and asked harshly if I wanted some chicken fingers from the bar back. I nodded, slightly scared by the intensity in his voice, his large stature. I would have said yes to anything he asked, because as a kid, I realized he was special, important, and yet, I never realized that maybe he saw me the same way.

They say it takes a village to raise a kid . . . I'd had a motorcycle club, and each member had contributed to my upbringing, probably in ways I would never know or fully understand. As I hugged Billy, I felt the rigidity of his muscles relax, proving that even ice kings have some vulnerabilities.

I let go of Billy and pulled back. I could swear his eyes glistened.

"Thank you," I said. My throat constricted, and I fought against more tears. Billy put his hands on his hips and nodded once, while he looked at the floor trying to pull his face together.

"I—uh," I paused, trying to figure out what to say. "Thank you," I turned and looked at Eddie, too. "For everything you ever did for me."

Eddie smiled. I turned to Billy, who fumbled for a cigarette in his pocket.

"Despite how it looks, I don't have my shit together," I said. I thought of Trevor, my lack of any real relationships beyond Lisa and my career. "And while I have a lot of love for you guys, I need a clean break from the Lawless—for good. Get my life on the right track."

I turned away quickly, unable to look Billy in the eyes, and walked over to Eddie and grabbed his hand. He squeezed it tight, and I bent down to kiss him on an unbroken spot of his shiny bald head. Letting go of his hand felt like a rear tire blow out. I wobbled on my own.

I squeezed Billy's upper shoulder when I walked past him and out the door. The cord between me and the men behind me stretched to its breaking point until finally it snapped.

I wasn't two steps out when Billy called out to me. I stopped and turned around. He walked up slowly, grabbing his wallet from his back pocket, and pulled out a piece of paper. He handed it to me.

The faint scent of burning tobacco appeared when I opened the piece of paper. An address written in Dodge's handwriting. A flood of emotion washed through me. I bit the inside of my cheek to stop myself from crying. When I looked up at Billy again, our eyes locked. There was so much I wanted to say to him, but when you grow up in the club, you learn there's no reason to say it.

So instead, I choked out, "Thanks."

His eyes held mine for a second and then he replied, "Anytime."

29

When I left the hospital, I sat on my bike for a few minutes looking at my grandfather's address. I let out a loud "Yes!" and laughed for a few seconds. A nurse who had been walking by me hurried inside.

"Sorry," I said to her retreating form.

The address was in Wichita Falls, Texas, where I'd lived before my parents had died and I was sent to Dodge. I stared at the paper some more then stuffed it into my pocket. I hopped on my bike and went in search of a nice hotel. It didn't take long to find one. After getting on the highway, I found a cluster of them seven minutes away. Unfortunately, the first—and fanciest—one didn't have any rooms available, so I made my way to its neighbor where I had more luck.

After parking my bike in a garage—no way in hell I'd let the valet do that—I went to my hotel room. It was not like the motels we'd stayed at along the way. Mold didn't grow on the ceiling, and the comforter and furniture were free of stains. The warm brown furniture looked new, as did the fluffy maroon bedspread, a large box television set, work desk in the corner, and a bathroom with a large soaking bath and a separate shower.

I'd decided to recharge before visiting my grandfather. My body ached, and I needed some time to deal with everything that had happened—Jackson dying, my split with the Lawless, my grandfather, Bethie . . .

Besides, I could afford it.

After throwing my bag onto a luggage rack, I stripped off all my clothes and put on a robe that hung in the closet. Then I called for laundry and room service—grilled chicken in a lemon sauce with a side salad and roasted potatoes. My body craved something green and healthy; no more burgers or sandwiches.

The food would take twenty-five minutes to arrive, so I used that time to jump in the shower. The hot stream of water caressed the bruises on my body, while the perfumed shampoo and soap rinsed away a grimy and greasy layer of hate, shame, guilt, and pain that had burrowed into my skin and hair. The water around my feet ran black before escaping into the drain.

Thoughts of the past week barraged me. Juana the Bone Lady, Mr. Sand, Charles, Lee and Linh, the crash . . . It was all so much in such a little time. The soap could wash away the dirt of the road, but it couldn't take away all the questions I still had about Dodge, about myself, my past, and my future. With short hair, it didn't take long to shower, so I stood under the hot water a little bit longer trying to make sense of everything I'd been through.

After I dried off and put my robe on, I looked in the bathroom mirror. The bruise around my eye looked bad, especially in the harsh bathroom light. With makeup, I could probably make it look less so. My wet, short hair looked darker than normal, as did my face, sun-kissed from all the riding we'd done. This woman in the mirror looked . . . different. Tired, for sure, and aged by the mental and physical hoops she jumped through this last week. My reflection smiled awkwardly, like it wasn't sure if it wanted to or not. She stared into my eyes and introduced herself with a soft "hey," and I reached up and touched her hand in reply.

When the food arrived, I grabbed the plate, hopped on the bed, and turned on the TV. After I'd stuffed my stomach, I picked up the information packet about the hotel and skimmed the amenities. A spa . . . why not? My shoulders and back were sore from gripping the handlebars.

The spa had an opening in thirty minutes, so I brushed my teeth and dried my hair with the blow dryer in the bathroom before making my way down.

My massage therapist's name was Ana Hernandez. She had shiny black hair with intermittent strands of silver woven into a long braid that rested on her shoulder. Her eyebrows were dark, and though she had more yellow undertones in her skin than I had in mine, she was Mexican, too. The wrinkles around her lips and at the corner of her eyes made me think she was close to the age my mother would have been if she were still alive.

Ana introduced herself and led me to the massage room, asking if I had any problem areas.

"Everywhere," I replied.

Ana left the room for a few moments, and I crawled under the covers of the massage table. When she returned, she pulled the blanket up to my shoulders and straightened it out. Ana turned away to prepare the massage oils but continued speaking.

"My daughter has skin like yours. Her father may be white, but she's darker than me." Ana chuckled. "Y'all are probably around the same age."

Her daughter was Mixed, too. I didn't know how to respond, but I managed a muffled, "Oh."

Ana walked toward me until I spied her white tennis shoes through the hole of the face rest. She cupped her hands below my nose. "Take a few breaths in. This is lavender; it'll help you relax."

I did as she asked, the smell overpowering my senses, sending a tingling down my spine. Her hands moved away, and a second later, I felt the sheet that covered my back being pulled down, so she'd be able to massage my entire back.

"You know what I find funny? All these celebrities and women around her go to tanning salons to get my daughter's skin color, but it never comes out right."

I chuckled. I'd witnessed the same in LA.

She began rubbing my shoulders with oiled hands and then down the length of both sides of my back.

"It doesn't seem right to me." Ana sighed. "They want to look like

my daughter, but I wonder if they ever think what it's like to be her."
She paused. "Or even me."

Ana grew quiet as she continued to massage my back. I wasn't sure
if it was her words or what I'd been through in the past few days, but I
started to cry. The pillowed face rest around my face soaked up the silent
tears, becoming damper by the minute.

How Ana noticed I was crying, I wasn't sure, but she spoke softly,
"Está bien, mija. Let it out. I got you."

The knots in my back and shoulders that Ana worked on were
as tough to release as it was difficult for me to understand what had
happened this last week, the people I'd met, the things I'd learned. Ana
worked on a lifetime's worth of tension, confusion, fear, heartache, and
pain, born from a childhood of lost parents and tumultuous times with
Dodge and the Lawless. It was painful and torturous, and I suffered
silently, too afraid to move, to have it end before it was finished. I'd
carried around so much that it had sat in my bones and burrowed into
my DNA, making me tough and cynical. A simple massage wasn't going
to cleanse me of my past; only time, acceptance, and a lot of therapy
could help me do that. But at least I was ready to start.

30

1974, fifteen years old

"Raqi!" Dodge yelled.

I stopped polishing Dodge's bike for a moment. "Coming!" I placed the rag on the garage counter and walked to the house. Dodge stood on the porch, his hair freshly cut. That could only mean one thing . . .

"Who?" I asked as I walked up, fearing it might be Eddie. Hell, I'd be sad even if it was Gray, who rarely talked to me.

Dodge rubbed the back of his head. "Don. Got shot by a cop a few nights ago in Nevada. His ashes arrived today."

The tightness around my chest eased. I knew Don, but we hadn't had much interaction. His daughter, Elizabeth, was a year younger than Bethie and me. She had tried to push her way into our friendship, but eventually got tired of how Bethie and I excluded her and found other friends. Now I felt like shit for how I treated her.

"We're taking the ride tomorrow. Coming?" Dodge looked at his boots when he asked.

"Yeah, definitely."

As I got dressed for the Grieving Ride the next evening, I felt the heaviness of it for the first time. Most Lawless didn't bring their kids along for rides, so it always made me feel special that Dodge let me join. But this ride felt different. I knew Elizabeth. She was a sweet, shy girl. I wouldn't call her smart, but she wasn't dumb either. When I walked by her in school, she always said, "Hi." This must be killing her.

I rode on the back of Dodge's bike. Even though it was illegal to ride underage, he sometimes let me ride his back-up bike to the store or to Eddie's house. For big things like this, I couldn't ride alone.

We arrived at Elizabeth's house around 4:00 p.m. The front yard was full of Lawless and their families, kind of like our barbecues, but less raucous, more serious. I hopped off the bike and told Dodge I needed to use the bathroom, but really, I wanted to find Elizabeth. I walked inside the house, past Elizabeth's mom who cried in the living room with a group of women patting her back and making soothing noises. Her short hair reached to the end of her ears and looked unevenly cut. Since I hadn't seen Elizabeth outside, I figured she was in her bedroom.

The doors were shut, except one. It was slightly ajar. Elizabeth sat on her bed, looking straight ahead at nothing. Her hair had been cut short like her mom's, but her thick curls made her hair pouf out. She sniffled when she breathed, and her eyes were red. I wrestled with myself to go in and tell her I was sorry or give her a hug, or something. But I didn't. A few moments went by, and I cowardly slipped back outside. I sat on the ground near Dodge's bike. I'd seen him talking with other members and I knew better than to interrupt.

When my parents had died, I'd pushed thoughts of them deep into my body, but now they crept out of that box from within, grabbing for bone, sinew, and ligament until they reached the surface. What had their funeral been like? Had I cried? I recalled a few blurred faces that day and a tree near a grave. Were they buried under a tree? Why couldn't I remember any of this? And why did thinking about them now make me want to cry? I squeezed my legs and rested my head on my knees while an empty hollow feeling filled my chest cavity. Why hadn't I thought about them over the years? I wondered if that meant something was wrong with me.

An hour later, we got on our bikes.

Dodge turned around to look at me. "What's with you?"

I shrugged and looked away. Dodge wanted to say something more, but instead he looked forward and followed the others out. Elizabeth's mom rode with Billy in the front, and Elizabeth rode with Bob E. right behind them. The rest of the Lawless packed the highway as we followed behind. We went south on the 15, then west, before a short ride north on the 5.

Billy led us off the interstate, through Cardiff and onto the PCH which hugs the California coastline. Shades of orange and red smeared across the sky and reflected on the choppy blue ocean. We pulled into a small parking lot near a beach, our motorcycles filling half of the two rows in the lot.

We followed the others to a set of stairs that took us to the beach. It was quieter now, with murmurs and low chatter among the Lawless men. Smoke from the cigarettes that stuck out of every man's mouth wafted between us, before floating into the heavens, taking with it our fears of death and loss. We must have been a sight to see. Black-leather- and jean-clad men with similar short haircuts and arms covered in tattoos, following a crying woman with a bad haircut who held her daughter close to her right side. And me, a brown gangly girl somewhere in the middle.

The group stopped near the edge of the ocean and Billy, Elizabeth's mom, and Elizabeth faced us. We gathered closer to hear over the soft roar of the sea. The fiery sun moved near the horizon, producing dabs of purple and pink in the sky.

Billy held a silver box in his hand. "Don was our brother."

Elizabeth's mom sobbed loudly, so Billy raised his voice to continue: "He was a good husband, a father, and a man. He served his country and did his job well, without complaint. Took care of his family and was proud to be a part of a brotherhood."

Billy paused. Elizabeth's mom held Elizabeth's head to her chest.

"Don requested that we come here to scatter his ashes in the ocean."

Another sob from Elizabeth's mom.

"He said it was where he spent the happiest evening with his family when Elizabeth was first born, watching the sunset."

Billy paused for effect. I crossed my arms and felt the hollowness in my chest constrict.

"Our brother may no longer be here, but we'll remember him. We'll take care of his family in honor of him. We are the Lawless, and we don't abandon our own."

Billy walked with Elizabeth's mom and Elizabeth to the shore. He opened the box and held it out to them. They each grabbed a fist of ash, and, together, waded into the water and let the burnt fragments fly softly from their hands and land on the waves that ebbed and flowed. Tears fell down their faces gathering memories of joy with husband and father before falling into the sea.

Elizabeth's mom's cries increased, and Elizabeth took on the role of caretaker as she guided her mom to the steps of the parking lot. I couldn't help but notice she wasn't crying. It made her seem taller and older than me.

Now it was our turn. The Lawless formed a line with Eddie in the front. He took a pinch of ash and let it dribble from his fingers into the ocean. A few threw offerings of unsmoked cigarettes into the water. The white sticks turned into minnows in the cauldron of ash, sea water, and tears.

When I walked up to grab some ash, I felt Billy's gaze in front and Dodge's from behind. I looked up at Billy, the tallest man I'd ever met, and then quickly away. His eyes always broke through the brick tower that protected me and went straight to thoughts I didn't want to share. Sometimes, when Dodge was real messed up, and Billy saw me, he'd give me ten or twenty bucks or buy me a McDonald's burger. He'd always say, "Take it," real hard, like he thought I might not.

As I let the ash fall from my hands into the ocean, I wished good things for Elizabeth and her mom. The white minnows lapped up my offering and nipped at my legs. Billy said they'd be taken care of, and I hoped that was true. I walked back to the stairs, following the line of Lawless, with Dodge at my back.

I wondered what would happen if Dodge died. As I mounted the stairs, I realized I had no one else in the world. Dodge was it, and if he died tomorrow, how would the Lawless take care of me? When we got to the parking lot, I looked behind me at Dodge who smoked another cigarette. He was it. This mean, skinny guy who looked nothing like me or what I remembered of my mom.

We quietly stood by our bikes, facing the sunset, waiting for Billy. Elizabeth's mom's sobs were the only sound among the group, but they didn't take away from the beauty of watching the bursts of red, orange, and pink that hung over the horizon, slowly transitioning into a midnight blue. The smoke from the Lawless' cigarettes floated toward the sea as a blanket of fog in search of someplace new.

I didn't realize that I'd done it, but I scooted next to Dodge as we leaned on his bike. Our arms touched. He looked down at me and I looked up, and for a second, I saw that Dodge was thinking what I was thinking.

We were all we had.

31

While I slept in the cozy hotel bed, my dreams twisted the events of the last week into something that made sense, or almost. I was so close to figuring it out, like a puzzle that needed a few more pieces to be complete. Unfortunately, I knew where to find the pieces, and it wasn't a place I wanted to go.

Before I checked out of my hotel, I used the phone in my room to make a call. As the phone rang once, then twice, a feeling of dread settled on my shoulders. I leaned my head against the headboard and closed my eyes.

"Hello?"

"Hey, Trev," I said weakly.

His breathing was his only reply.

"I know you're mad at me and you have every right to be," I said.

There was a huff on the other side of the phone. "Raqi, I think we should talk when you get home." His voice sounded far too in control.

My stomach flipped, and I felt queasy. Deep down, I knew that what me and Trevor had was not a healthy relationship. I'd depended on him because I had no one else. I pretended that our relationship was normal, ignoring the cracks that had formed over time. This ride brought those tiny cracks together, forming one large, jagged crack that I couldn't ignore. I hadn't been open, hadn't dived into our relationship. Hell, it hurt for me to even say the L-word most of the time, but I did it to make him happy. It wasn't fair to Trevor. Or me. Our relationship had held me together all these years like duct tape, but even duct tape loses its grip eventually.

"I know." I sighed.

"When will you return?"

I wasn't sure, but I said, "Soon. It's almost over."

His grunted in acknowledgment, and we sat there for a couple beats in silence.

"Trevor—"

"Okay, see you then." He hung up before I could say goodbye.

I placed the phone back on the receiver. Great. That'd gone about as well as I'd expected. Trevor would probably break up with me upon my return. Hell, he would probably move out before I got home.

I punched in the numbers for a second call that I hoped would be a little easier. When Lisa answered the phone and realized it was me, she went straight into business mode explaining everything I'd missed. God, she was the best. She'd already pushed back all my appointments, had filed a case I had sitting on my desk, and told me she would reschedule my tattoo removal appointment for the end of the month. My arm throbbed in rebellion at that last one.

"So," Lisa asked. "How's the trip?"

"Uh . . ." I didn't know what to say. *My ex-boyfriend died, and I met a ton of people who told me all these weird things about my uncle* couldn't be summed up in a short phone call. That would take many nights with many glasses of wine. I opted for, "Worth it. I have my grandfather's address."

"What? Why is this the first time I'm hearing about this?"

I chuckled.

"Which grandfather?" she asked.

"My dad's. My Mexican side."

"Damn, Raq." She whistled softly. "That's amazing. I—I don't know what to say."

"Me neither."

"You're going to see him, right?"

I smiled. "Yes, tomorrow."

"Good. You deserve that. Take your time and don't hurry back."

I planned to. I was going to have to ride my Ironhead to Los Angeles and that would take some days on the road anyway. Who knows? Maybe I'd even stop by to see some people on the way back. I wanted to milk Charlie dry of every detail about my mother and have some of Linh's egg rolls. I wasn't sure about Mr. Sand or Juana. My visits with them weren't entirely positive to say the least. Plus, I didn't want to prove Juana right—that I might need some help to move on. I'd rather find that in a therapist, not from a bone woman.

"David might not like it, but he'll survive," Lisa added.

I groaned. "He's going to go ballistic."

She chuckled. "It's your grandfather, honey. Who cares how David feels?"

"Thank you, Lisa. For everything."

"Always," she said.

I sighed. "Transfer me to David I guess."

She chuckled. "You sure?"

I groaned. "No, but I hear responsibility is part of being an adult."

She laughed and the line clicked over.

David sounded more tired than pissed. I promised him overtime when I returned and that I'd bring in four new clients in two months. He sighed and said it was fine.

"You haven't taken a day off in the last three years. Because of you, I've been able to focus more on the kids now that they're getting older," he said. "We're good."

I smiled. "Thanks, David."

"Where the hell are you anyways?" he asked at the end of the call.

"Arkansas."

"So, hell?"

I chuckled. "Basically."

We hung up and I felt a little bit better about going home. At least, I would still have my job.

After checking out of my hotel and asking directions from the front-desk person, I hit the highway bound for the Rock Inn. When I arrived, I discovered the universe was on my side. Lenora walked out of the diner across the street. I left my bike in front of the motel and met her at the edge of the parking lot. She quickened her pace as soon as she recognized me.

"Raqi! Billy said you left and weren't finishing the ride." Lenora smiled, and I noticed for the first time how her incisors were browning near the gum line. "Thank God you're back and we can finish this ride like Dodge wanted."

I crossed my arms and her smile faltered. "Lenora," I said calmly.

She smiled, but when I didn't return the smile, she knew something was wrong. Lenora looked around her like a mouse caught in a corner, searching for a way out.

"What?" she said.

"It was you, wasn't it?"

"What was me?"

I shook my head. "The ride, Lenora. This was your plan, not Dodge's."

She shook her head too fast, loosening more wisps of curly hair from behind her ears. "No, it was Dodge's idea."

I stepped closer and she stepped back. "Dodge wouldn't have done this—" I began.

"He did—"

"A simple ride into the desert would have been fine for him—"

"No, you didn't know him anymore—"

"But this ride is more manipulative. Was meant to try to get me to see he changed—"

"He had changed!" Her voice rose, and I knew I hit a nerve.

They say dreams help your mind to sort out things it can't seem to put together in your waking state, and that's exactly what mine had done last night. After talking with Billy and hearing what Eddie had said, maybe even because of a good night's sleep away from the Lawless, I knew definitively that this Grieving Ride had not been Dodge's idea.

"So, what did you do?" Lawless wrote up their wills and handed them to Billy. I'd bet a hundred bucks Lenora had somehow changed it. "Stole his will? Changed it yourself? Told Billy to use my grandfather's address as leverage?"

Lenora's eyes narrowed and the wrinkles around them hardened like armor ready for battle. "Of course not. I wouldn't—"

"Cut the crap, Lenora." My voice rose slightly. "Eddie told me that Dodge had let me go—"

"He hadn't!"

"So, it makes no sense for him to put this together." I poked her in the chest with my finger. "Admit it." I poked her again. "Dodge." Poke. "Didn't." Poke. "Want." Poke. "This." Poke.

"He did!" She yelled. "He just didn't know it!"

There it was. I'd gotten her to crack and confess, like I'd done plenty of times in court.

"I couldn't let him give up on you—" she began.

I hit her with a quick, "Why?" The faster you kept them talking, the more likely they'd hit you with honest answers.

She huffed as if she was out of breath. "Because—"

I stepped forward again. "This is my life you fucked with, Lenora. Why did you do it?"

"Because—"

"Say it!"

"I was afraid if he gave up on you, he might start using again."

I stopped. That wasn't what I expected.

"It was getting you back that drove him to go to meetings, got him clean. And if he didn't need you anymore . . ." Her face crumpled, her shoulders sagged, and tears began to pool at the corner of her eyes.

I shook my head. "That doesn't make sense. How would crafting this Grieving Ride help him get me back when he was alive? He had to be dead for me to go on it!"

Lenora was crying now; her black mascara ran down the crevices of her face in slow trickles. It made her look older and weathered.

She sniffled. "We wrote it together one night. I thought it might help him to see all the good ways he had changed, all the people who could tell you that he was different—a better man."

"So, you and Dodge put everyone I met on this ride on the list? All the people he'd become nicer to? And used my grandfather's address to get me to come?"

"Dodge always planned to tell you about your grandfather," she said. "He wanted to tell you in person, but you wouldn't speak to him. Billy knew about your grandfather. It was his idea to use the address to get you on the ride. I swear."

"And then what?"

She wiped her eyes, spreading black mascara across her face. "Dodge told me to throw our plan away, but I didn't. I gave it to Billy. It was a backup plan in case he never connected with you. You had to see he had changed, Raqi, even if he was de—dead."

Lenora began sobbing again, covering her face with her hands.

What we did in fear. I'd come on this ride for fear of standing up to Billy and losing out on a chance to meet new family. I'd kept myself closed off from Trevor, for fear that he wouldn't understand my past, something that I hadn't ever examined myself. Lenora made this all happen because she was scared that she would lose the love of her life. We were all fucked up.

The anger I thought I'd have at getting her to confess wasn't there. Without this ride, I wouldn't have stood up to Billy, apologized to Bethie, or even realized that Trevor and I shouldn't be together. Bethie. I turned to the motel, hoping I'd see her, but all the doors were shut, and no one stood outside.

Lenora's crying intensified and she hunched over.

"God, Lenora, stop. Stop. It's fine," I said, patting her twice on the back.

"I'm so—"

Damn, this was starting to make me feel like shit. "Lenora, it's fine," I said touching her shoulder. She looked up at me, her face a wrecked mess of black mascara and reddened cheeks.

"What?"

"I said it's fine."

"You mean it?"

I grinded my teeth. If I thought about it logically, no, it was not fine. Because of her, I'd been dragged on this trip, my career and relationship put into bad positions, but goddamn it, if this trip hadn't given me some truth, changed my life even.

"Yes, but shit, if Billy found out what you did . . ." I trailed off because I wasn't quite sure what he'd do but I knew it wouldn't be good. Eddie had been hurt on this trip, and Jackson died. If we'd done whatever Dodge wanted to do, none of this would have happened.

Lenora sobered up quickly and looked around the parking lot to make sure no one was around. "Don't tell him, Raqi. I can't—we need to finish this ride, for Dodge."

I shook my head. "I'm not going with you, Lenora," and as I said it, I felt a twinge between my chest and stomach, that in-between space where all my feeling stayed.

"But we still need to scatter his ashes. You need to do this for Dodge."

I sighed and ran my hand through my hair. "Dodge is dead, Lenora." The weight of those words exhaled from my body. "Me scattering his ashes isn't going to change that."

If Dodge were alive, I wondered if I would have stood up to him, hashed out our shit eventually, maybe even gotten on better terms. If this trip taught me anything, it was that he may not have been the same man I once knew.

"Scatter his ashes wherever you want," I said. "I'm—"

Lenora's eyes flickered to my left and opened wider. I turned around. There was Beth. She was walking toward my bike from the gas station next door, but she hadn't caught sight of us yet. Her head was bent down, and she fumbled with something—a packet of cigarettes. She was trying to take off the plastic wrapping.

I walked toward her not thinking about what I was doing.

"Raqi, no!" Lenora grabbed my arm. "That's not a good idea. She's pretty tore up."

I pulled my arm away and kept watching Beth. She still hadn't noticed us.

Lenora spoke in hushed tones. "Her and her daddy have to stay here a week before they can take his ashes home."

I had to speak to her. I knew it would be hard, but I couldn't abandon Bethie again. Not the way I'd done it the first time, and especially not now that Jackson was gone. I owed her that much.

I turned to Lenora and spoke quickly. "Take Dodge's house. Everything in it is yours." I wasn't sure if Dodge had an actual will that turned over his property to anyone, but my guess was he didn't. I'd probably have to do some paperwork, but it would be worth it. Lenora searched my face to see if my words were some cruel joke. She'd screwed everyone over and now she was getting her late boyfriend's house? God, I'd gone weak.

"Bye, Lenora," I said, nodding once.

"Wait, Raqi! Don't you want anything to remember him by?"

I looked at the tattoo on my upper arm and back at Lenora, shaking my head before walking away. Dodge was a part of me, and I didn't need anything else to remind me of that.

I walked quickly to Bethie, hoping to intercept her in the motel parking lot. She tore the plastic wrapping off the cigarette packet just as she passed my bike. Her head was still down, so she didn't see me approach. She was opening the packet when she tripped, which sent cigarettes flying onto the asphalt.

Beth fell forward, landing on her hands and knees, and didn't move. Her greasy hair kissed the gravel. I rushed over, thought for a moment about helping her up, but then thought better of it. Instead, I gathered the cigarettes and placed them in the packet. When I'd grabbed the last one, I looked up. Beth watched me between the fan of hair around her head.

I stood up quickly. Beth stood up more slowly, methodically. Her eyes were red and puffy, and the skin was peeling around them like she'd rubbed it raw trying to wipe the tears away. Her mouth was set in a firm line. Beth looked frailer than usual. All the excitement and love that had filled her disappeared when Jackson died, leaving behind a flaky shell that might crack with a single touch.

I wasn't sure what to say, so I held out the cigarette pack. She took it, slowly. Her silence was torture.

"Bethie, I'm—" I began and stopped. Her head cocked to the side, and she waited.

"I'm so sorry, I shouldn't have sped off like that," I said. Beth opened the packet of cigarettes.

"And I know you may never forgive me, but I never wanted Jac—"

She flinched at his name, then pulled out a cigarette and rolled it between her thumb and forefinger.

"—him to—" I didn't want to say *die*. What was better? *Passed away*? Nothing sounded right, so I stopped talking.

Beth looked down at the cigarette, her face blank. I wasn't even sure she had heard me, but I had to say something. She would either attack me, ignore me, or hate me, and I could handle all three if I at least tried to make things right. I could have left and skipped this, pretended I never saw her, but I couldn't have lived with myself if I'd abandoned her again.

"I'm sorry, Bethie. It was my fault. I'm so sor—"

She held out a cigarette to me, cutting off my words. I looked at the cigarette and then back at her. Her face had not changed, her mouth still sat in a firm line, so thin her lips almost disappeared. I hadn't smoked in almost ten years, but that didn't stop me from taking the cigarette. She pulled one out, too, and a lighter from her back pocket. She lit her cigarette and then handed me the blue lighter. I lit mine and handed it back. The cigarette tasted like my teen years and burned slowly like my childhood. A tingling feeling crept through my body, and I realized I had missed this.

She wasn't looking at me any longer. Her gaze moved from the paved parking lot to the motel, occasionally to the sky, anywhere but me. I felt the silence press down on us as the smoke from our cigarettes rose in the warm Arkansas air. I knew that if I broke the silence, she'd never forgive me.

We stood in the parking lot of the motel taking our time. Cars came into the lot, people passed from the diner on their way back to the motel, others stood by their motel doors smoking their own cigarettes. Lenora watched from hers, Billy from his, and a ghostly figure with pale blond hair studied us as he stood next to a mangled bike. Birds chirped, cars honked far away, and still we smoked. There was no talking, no meeting of the eyes, just two women standing together, not quite facing but not quite looking away either.

As the minutes ticked by, I thought about what would happen when we were done. Bethie would return to her motel room, perhaps where her father drank away his sorrows. I would leave, hop on my bike and speed away as Billy watched me from the second floor of the motel.

I inhaled the cigarette between my lips, the smoke burned down into the depths of my branded soul before it rose back up to be released into the sky. My smoke mixed with Beth's, and I watched as it replayed the memories we had together—the midnight beers, the lipsticks we stole, the movies we watched, the childish fights we had, how we danced to our favorite bands. Each fresh exhale of smoke played a memory for a few seconds before it floated slowly away and was replaced by another below. My heart ached to return to those days, when Beth was Bethie and we were ignorantly happy with what little we had, because at least we had each other.

Even though I could feel Beth's sadness across the short expanse, I was thankful that she had let me stand with her. Maybe she needed my presence as much as I needed hers. I was about to take off on a new journey, to meet a side of me I'd never known. From now on, I'd be on my own, free from the Lawless for good, and I'd have to find out exactly who I was without them in my life.

My cigarette was down to the last available puff. I looked at Bethie and she looked at me. We inhaled one last time, long and hard, held it for a second, then blew out all the betrayal, anger, and pain we had for one another. We threw the charred cigarette stubs onto the ground where they were swallowed by the parking lot instantly. She turned to me and whispered, "I'm fucking glad you're here."

32

Sure enough, it took two weeks for Bob to get the Bendix unit. When it arrived, I pushed Dodge to install it in the Ironhead immediately. He was prepping to go on a ride for Billy the next day and didn't have a lot of time to spare, but I didn't care. I needed my Ironhead done now. My body ached to take her out, to show her off, to have her to myself.

After he finished, I hit the road as quickly as I could. I rode on backcountry roads at a speed faster than light, leaving behind a deep, unbroken ravine in the road the size of the width of my tires. I slowed down when I made my way into Escondido and couldn't help but beam as I rode through the streets of the city and caught men staring at the glistening chrome when we sat at stop lights. I tried to play it cool, but my excited energy fueled my bike, leaving behind burnt tires and puffs of smoke that smelled like true and unbridled independence. A few times, I even hit the throttle hard and took off quickly so my engine revved, my tires squealed, and admirers honked from nearby cars.

I drove by the Landing my second hour of riding. I figured most of the Lawless would be there. They knew how long I had waited for my bike to be finished and many of them inquired about its status day after day. Eddie saw me first, and hooted three times before yelling, "Looking good, Raq!" The others cheered and held up beers. A few even banged their glasses on the wooden fence post that made up the outdoor patio fence. Dodge wasn't in sight.

Billy raised his glass before taking a sip. It was that gesture that made me stand up and throw my fist in the air. The Lawless' cheers sent a burst of energy into my Ironhead, and we sped away hard, fast, and free.

After that, I went by Scott's, a drive-in burger joint where most of the kids from my school hung out. Bethie had told me she would be there. I tried to keep my face composed, not quite smiling but not quite stoic. It was the right level of smirk that would match the cool, sleek bike that was all mine.

As I rode by, the sound of my Ironhead's engine turned heads. Brent, Anthony, Jackson, and Mark sat at a picnic table smoking and sharing fries with Bethie, Cindy, Jordan, and Crystal. I saw Brent nudge Jackson and point at me. Anthony's and Mark's jaws dropped. Their dads were Lawless, so they knew bikes and they knew I was sitting on a badass piece of metal.

Jennifer, Crystal, and Cindy didn't look very happy that the boys' attention had turned from them, but Bethie stood up on the picnic table and threw her hands in the air. "Woo!" She yelled. "That's my best friend. Looking hot, girl!" I blew her a kiss that floated across the distance and landed on her cheek.

I rode my Ironhead for another hour, stopping once to get gas and grab some tacos. I bought a pack of beer at the gas station from a club Sheep named Susan and held it between my legs as I drove to my favorite lookout point, a spot where everyone went to hookup on Friday nights. It was a Thursday, so I knew it'd be empty. Upon arriving, I saw that I'd been right. I had it all to myself. I parked at the far end, climbed off the bike with my six-pack and walked to the edge of the cliff and sat down. The sky was already turning orange and pink. Soon it'd be dark.

I hadn't been there for more than thirty minutes when I heard a motor behind me. It was Jackson and Bethie on Jackson's bike. I smiled. Jackson pulled up beside my Ironhead and Bethie jumped off before he'd even stopped. I grabbed a beer and handed her one, which she popped right away, guzzling for a few seconds before sitting down.

Jackson stayed on his bike and pulled out a cigarette. I looked over my shoulder at him. He winked. I turned away quickly, hoping Bethie hadn't seen. We had made out a few times, but I hadn't told Bethie yet. The first time, he kissed me in the middle of the night when we both got up to go to the bathroom. He hadn't even asked but pushed me up against the door and pulled my face to his by grabbing the back of my neck. He was shirtless and wore a red pair of boxers. After five seconds, I pushed him away and said "asshole," before walking into the bathroom and shutting the door. When I emerged a few minutes later, he wasn't there.

The second time, he found me after school. I had stayed behind to do some extra credit for Bio, and when I walked out of the class he stood by a janitor's closet.

"Hey, asshole," I'd said, staring him directly in the eyes.

"Hey, loser," he'd replied, before opening the janitor's door, grabbing my hand, and pulling me in the closet. I'd let him feel beneath my shirt that time.

Bethie smiled now, then burped loud and hard. I laughed and tried not to think about Jackson's eyes bearing into my back.

"Took forever to convince the dickhead to bring me." She nodded behind her. "I figured you'd end up here eventually."

I squeezed her hand and let go, grabbing another beer and taking a drink.

"Haven't been here for long." I looked out at the fiery sky and sighed.

"So, drinking and hanging then?" Bethie asked.

I nodded. "Yeah, and thinking."

Bethie took another drink, slurping loudly. "About what?"

I had been thinking about what happened before I'd left Dodge's that evening. He was wiping his greasy hands on a bandanna while I enthusiastically pushed the bike out of the garage and onto the pavement.

I had turned to Dodge and said, "Going to take her out for a few hours. I'll be back later."

He nodded and pulled out a cigarette. "Probably be at the Landing later."

I swung my leg over and kick-started the machine to life. My Iron-head growled low in her belly and nuzzled my legs, thankful we'd revived her from death. I wasn't speaking to Dodge, but more to myself when I said, "I can take this baby all over the world and never come back."

And as soon as I said it, Dodge replied so evenly and lucidly that I was surprised I heard it over the engine, "Wouldn't blame you if you did."

Wouldn't blame you if you did. The words echoed in my ears, softly at first, but gained volume the longer and longer I rode. The echoing stopped when Bethie and Jackson had arrived, but now the stars, which had slowly started to appear, spelled out the words across the darken-ing sky.

I didn't know why Dodge had said it and if he meant it, but I couldn't tell Bethie that. I looked over my shoulder at Jackson and back at her, admiring how her blond, wispy hair floated in the breeze.

So instead, I said, "I was thinking about freedom."

33

1990, thirty-one years old

The road to Texas would have been long and God-awfully boring if I didn't have a billion thoughts running through my head. I was on my way to see my grandfather. My skin tingled, and bursts of electric energy entered my hands, revvin' my Ironhead to go faster.

A tiny part of me felt guilty. I'd just left my best friend who was waiting for her brother's ashes to be released from the mortuary, while I went off to meet family I never knew existed. After hugging Beth for a few minutes, I promised her I'd stay in touch. She nodded and kissed my cheek. "I hope so," she said, tears pooling in her eyes.

Almost six hours later and a few stops for gas, I came upon the Red River. Once I'd crossed it, I quickly pulled over, causing a car behind me to honk its horn. I didn't care though. I put the bike kickstand up and trudged down a small hillside thick with greenery until I got to the bottom.

The river wasn't as swift and flowing as it'd been in my dream a week ago. Drought, I assumed, had made it a small river with muddy embankments on either side. The river sat lifeless like a drying puddle of mud. I doubted that where I stood was where my parents and I had spent the day so long ago. There must be some other pull off area where people could walk down and hang out by the river.

My sweat-soaked shirt stuck to my stomach, and the high energy that I'd had for most of the trip sobered up inside me. I was here. This was the only place I could remember being with my parents before they died. I never had the chance to mourn their death. The moment I entered Dodge's home, I went into survival mode, and any thoughts of my parents had turned cold and practical. Even though I was excited to meet my grandfather, I hadn't thought about how twenty-seven years of repressed feelings might arise when I set foot in Wichita Falls again.

I picked up a large stone near my foot and threw it into what was left of the Red River. The stone hit the still body of water and sent ripples out, giving it the momentum needed to burst forward with a new flood of life.

Wichita Falls wasn't much to look at. A haze of gray painted the roads and buildings, built decades ago. Traffic was minimal on the highway. I passed building after building and even a set of cascading, dirt-colored waterfalls which I assumed the city was named after. It didn't take long to realize there was nothing in my memory bank of my time in Wichita Falls.

I stopped at the first gas station I saw off the highway and showed the clerk the address.

"Know where this is?" I asked.

He was an older Black gentleman with gray hair and a warm smile. "I think that's off Seymour Highway." He grabbed a map off the wall. "Let's see here."

We spent a few minutes looking for 528 Beverly Drive, and sure enough, it was off Seymour Highway.

"Not too far," he said.

I nodded and bought the map for a buck. It showed Wichita Falls, North Texas, and parts of Oklahoma.

"Thanks," I said as I ran out the door. He waved to me.

I pulled into the parking lot of a blue-and-white diner with a large neon sign that read "Hector's." The parking lot was empty. I jumped off the bike and ran up to the door. It closed at 3:00 p.m. and wouldn't reopen until 7:00 a.m.

I hit the glass door lightly with my open palm. "Damn."

Stepping back, I looked at the sign. Was my grandfather Hector? I'd have to wait until the next day to find out. I kicked the gravel and returned to my bike.

I followed Seymour Highway back to I-44. I'd seen a motel next to the highway. It wasn't upscale like the hotel in Fayetteville, but I needed a bed, and I didn't feel like searching for another one. Besides, it was 7:00 p.m. and the sun would set soon.

After checking in and putting my bag in the room, which wasn't that bad, considering, I got on my bike and followed the directions that the front-desk attendant had given me to a restaurant called Bar-L. He'd looked at my bike through the glass window and back at me and said, "You'll fit in. Plus, the ribs and the reds are the best in town." I wasn't sure what he meant about me fitting in or what a "red" was, but I looked forward to finding out.

I drove through downtown Wichita Falls, which looked more like a graveyard of medium-sized towers and blocky buildings with old signs that hadn't been turned on in years. Upon arriving at Bar-L, the sun had lowered, casting a soft light on the brick building that had a trapezoidal-like sign that read, "Bar-L Drive Inn Lounge."

An older white woman manned a brick smoker on the side of the building. The smell of barbecue made my mouth salivate. Mine wasn't the only bike in the lot. A white man and a woman sat on their bikes under an awning with beer mugs in their hand. Two Mexican men sat on the edge of a pickup's flatbed sipping on golden ales. I saw a waitress hand a driver a beer in a frozen mug. A drive-in where you could drink? I'd never heard of such a thing.

There weren't any parking spots under the awnings. I parked my bike in the parking lot and walked toward what I thought was the main entrance, passing by the man and woman who leaned against their bikes with mugs filled with a murky, red-colored drink.

The woman was about sixty with blond hair pulled back in a ponytail under a red bandanna. Her husband had gray hair, a goatee, and a black bandanna. Even though he wore a leather vest, it didn't have any patches. These were not club folk.

"First timer?" the woman asked.

I nodded. "Yeah, I was told I'd find good ribs here."

She looked at my bike and then back at me. "Probably better if you go inside and eat. Go on in right there." I smiled and said thanks. Her husband held up his mug in acknowledgment.

Bar-L was dark inside with soft yellow lighting from hanging lamps. A few tables were filled with patrons chowing down on their food. Two men sat on the stools at the bar talking with one another.

"Sit where you like," the bartender called out.

There was a doorway on the other side of the main room, so I walked through and into another room with Polynesian wallpaper, worn-out booths that lined the wall, a pool table in the center, and a small hall that led to the bathrooms. The leaves of the Polynesian wallpaper swayed in a breeze I could not see.

I found an empty booth and slid in. A white waitress no older than forty walked up. She had on a pair of jeans under a small apron, a red shirt with black lettering that said, "Go Coyotes," and white tennis shoes.

"Hey, honey, what will it be?" She pulled out a notepad, not once looking up at me.

I looked around for a menu. "Um, a beer?"

"Make it red?"

"What's a 'red'?"

She looked up confused for a second. "Oh!" She chuckled. "You've never been here before. I swore you were one of our regulars."

I shook my head no.

"A red is short for Red Draw. It's tomato juice with beer. Kind of a Wichita Falls specialty."

I liked Bloody Marys, which had tomato juice, so I figured a Red Draw couldn't be too far off in taste.

"Sure, a Red Draw."

She smiled and wrote it on her pad.

"And I heard the ribs are good?"

She nodded. "The best in town. Want an order?"

"Yep."

"A side? We got potato salad, onion rings, fries, beans—"

"I'll go with the onion rings."

She quickly scribbled the rest of my order on her notepad, then tossed it in her apron.

"Passing through or visiting family?"

"Kind of both. I, uh—" I wasn't sure why I was being so chatty with the waitress. Something inside me wanted to share my good news with someone. "I was born here but haven't been back since I was four."

"Oh, my goodness!" she exclaimed. "I'm sure some things have changed since then. Let me go put this order in and I'll bring you a Red Draw in a sec."

I nodded in thanks.

As I waited for my beer, I looked around. The people in this restaurant may have known my parents, met them once, crossed by them on the street. My parents could have sat at this booth.

I'd never thought of my parents much over the years. It had hurt to think about them, even felt pointless to try to remember them. They were gone and I was alone. Trevor had asked about them, what they were like, and the memories of our time together. For once, I couldn't share much with him even if I wanted to. Their faces had faded into blank, gray spaces, the things we did together were . . . gone. I had nothing, no recollection of my time with them before Dodge, except that one memory of us at the Red River.

"Here you go." The waitress returned and set down a tall, frosted mug filled with a red liquid.

"Thanks," I said. She didn't immediately leave, and I realized she was waiting for me to try it. It felt weird to drink in front of someone, but not more awkward than having to eat in front of Linh in Oklahoma City. Tangy tomato mixed with the beer to create something crisp and sort of refreshing. It wasn't anything like a Bloody Mary—there didn't seem to be any spices—but it was good, nonetheless.

"Pretty good, huh?"

I nodded. "Yeah, not bad at all."

She winked and walked away. I sipped on the Red Draw, and with each sip my taste buds got more and more used to it. Moments passed and my mood sunk a bit lower. I'd thought arriving here would be all about joy and happiness in meeting my grandfather, but here I was, suffering from the knots and twists borne from the passing of my parents, a loss of identity, and a life never lived. Such feelings had long been buried under Dodge and Lawless shit. This was the first moment in my life where I'd ever had the space to think about my mom and dad.

If my time with the Lawless this week had taught me anything, it was that I couldn't run from my past and the bad things that had happened. I had to hit my parents' death head on. Dodge hadn't done that, and you didn't need to be a child psychologist to see how his parents' abandonment had created knots and twists inside him, too. He'd turned to booze and drugs to numb the pain, and I'd built a brick tower to keep everything in, which ultimately kept everyone out.

Maybe I was more like Dodge than I wanted to believe, but I wasn't going to stay that way for long. As I downed the Red Draw and finished off the ribs, I promised myself that I would do whatever it took to build a new life. And if that meant I had to dive into repressed feelings and traumatic memories, then so be it. I'd already been through hell and back—what was one more stroll through?

34

My hands visibly shook as I walked up to Hector's the next morning. I know this because when I grabbed the handle of the front door, my right hand clearly vibrated with . . . excitement? Fear? A bell sounded when I opened the door.

A Mexican man behind the counter looked up. "Morning." He seemed too young to be my grandfather, but I wasn't sure.

I looked around the tiny diner-like restaurant. A woman and a man sat in the corner with coffee mugs and newspapers open. Another customer waited at the front, probably for a to-go order. I walked to the cash register where the man stood.

"Uh . . ." I began, not quite sure what to say. The piece of paper only had an address. I pulled it out of my pocket, held it between my fingers, and felt the weight of all the hope I'd placed on it.

"For here or to-go?"

"I—uh, I'm actually looking for somebody." I showed him the piece of paper. "This address—it's here, right?"

The man leaned forward and squinted. "Yep, that's my place. I'm Hector."

I smiled nervously. "Hi. Um, so I'm looking for my—uh—grandfather."

His eyebrow rose. "Your grandfather?"

I nodded. "Yeah, but I don't know his name. I was only provided this address and I'm not sure what else to do." Panic seized my heart. What if this wasn't the right place? What if my grandfather wasn't here? What would I do then?

Hector looked at the address then back at me, his eyes lingering a moment on my leather jacket. He looked outside.

"Is that motorcycle yours?"

That was an odd question. "Yes, it's mine."

Something clicked; it showed on his face. "Dionisio Gonzalez. That's who you're looking for."

"Dionisio?" The name tangled in my mouth, and I had to say it slowly to get it right.

Hector nodded. "Yes, he'll be here soon. Used to work for me but retired recently. Sit, sit, until he comes. I'll get you a coffee."

I smiled nervously. "Okay, thank you." I sat at a table and angled myself toward the front door. Hector came out with a pot of coffee and a mug.

"Don't worry," Hector said. "He'll be here. Always is, every morning."

"Thanks."

"Want a breakfast burrito?"

Might as well. I hadn't eaten yet because I had been too nervous when I woke up this morning. At least it'd give me something to do while I waited. "Sure, thanks." Hector smiled and walked off.

My foot tapped incessantly, and I drank the coffee far too fast. I was meeting my grandfather. He was really coming. Dionisio Gonzalez. That was my grandfather's name. I'd been Raqi Warren my whole life. Raquel Gonzalez may have survived her parents, but she'd lost her name, her identity at only four years old. I couldn't help but think of the short life she had led and the life she could have lived.

I had eaten half of the burrito by the time an older Mexican man appeared through the glass of the front door. I put the burrito down and wiped my face with a napkin. The older man didn't see me yet, but when he opened the door, stepped in, and caught sight of me, he paused.

His black hair was peppered with white, and he wore a striped shirt and a pair of slacks over his thin frame. He pulled an oxygen tank behind him and wore gold-rimmed glasses. We stared at each other, until his mouth opened slightly, and he covered it with his hand, saying "Oh."

I stood up, feeling wobbly and hot.

"Dionisio—" Hector said from the cashier. Dionisio looked to Hector who said something in Spanish. Dionisio looked back at me.

"La hija de Tomás?" he said. Tomás. That was my father's name.

"He asked if you're Tomás's daughter," Hector said.

I nodded and smiled, then nodded some more.

Dionisio—my grandfather—raised his hand up. It shook as it reached out to me. And then tears came to his eyes, and I knew I couldn't hold my own tears back. I rushed over to him and stopped, not sure what to do.

"Oh, oh." He put his hands on my face to make sure it was me. I smiled and laughed through tears, and he smiled with yellowed teeth and hugged me. I melted into the warmest pair of arms I'd ever known. The warmth seeped through my skin, healing jagged scars that covered the soft flesh inside me.

We pulled back from each other. I was concerned he was going to fall over, so I moved us to sit down. He smiled, then suddenly succumbed to a coughing fit. My grandfather grabbed his oxygen mask, turned the tank on, and inhaled three times before setting it down again.

He breathed in and out calmly before asking, "Raquel?" He rolled the 'r' in my name.

I nodded, "Yes, Raquel. Raqi."

"Raqi," he repeated, then placed his hand on my cheek for a second. I liked how he said my name. He laughed, took off his glasses, and wiped his tears away. I took the moment to wipe mine with the back of my hand. Hector walked up with another mug of coffee. He smiled and spoke with Dionisio in Spanish. Dionisio replied gesturing toward me with a smile.

Hector turned to me. "You don't speak Spanish?"

I shook my head, mad at myself for being too scared to minor in Spanish at UCLA. I had so many questions, and now my insecurity had gotten in the way of my ability to communicate with my grandfather.

"No problem. I'll get my son to help," he said. "Junior!"

A teenager appeared behind the counter. He had his father's nose.

"Come help Dionisio speak with his granddaughter."

Junior came around the counter to us, while Hector returned behind it. Before sitting down, Junior touched my grandfather on the arm and my grandfather tapped his hand a few times. My grandfather reached for my hand. I gave it over a little hesitantly. He wrapped his knobby hands around mine and held them for a second before patting them and letting go.

"He doesn't speak English," Junior said. I had figured. I looked at my grandfather, not quite sure where to start.

"So . . . ?" Junior asked. I looked at him a little closer. He was young, like nineteen or so, and as impatient as most people are his age.

I searched for the first question. So many hit me at once. "I guess, um, how did he find me? Why didn't I know about him before?"

Junior turned to my grandfather and translated in Spanish. My grandfather looked down as he spoke slowly. He raised one hand and moved it about in a circle. When he was done, he reached for my hand and squeezed a few times.

"He says that when your parents died—sorry—he and your grandmother tried to get Social Services to send you to them in Mexico," Junior said.

"My grandmother?" I asked.

My grandfather answered Junior but looked down at the table when he did and sighed heavily after he was done.

Junior looked uncomfortable repeating it. "She died about eight years ago, before he came here. Cancer."

"I'm sorry," I said to my grandfather. He smiled weakly and nodded. "Continue," I told Junior.

"Social Services said that since you were a US citizen, it would be too messy to try to get Mexico to allow you to stay with your grandparents, so it was easier to let your uncle raise you."

I shook my head and muttered, "Yeah, easier."

"Your grandparents started the process for their green cards. They planned on coming here to find you, but your grandmother got sick, and she couldn't be moved so . . ." Junior paused and squirmed in his seat. "He came as soon as your grandmother passed."

My grandfather reached into his pocket and spoke in Spanish. He took out a leather wallet and pulled out a sepia picture of a young woman and a man, smiling without showing any teeth.

"He says that's your grandmother and him," Junior said. I held the picture in my hands and felt my heart break at the thought of another family member I'd never meet. The woman, my grandmother, winked at me before kissing her husband on the cheek.

"She's beautiful," I said, and Junior repeated it to my grandfather. He smiled and handed me another picture from his wallet. It was a baby girl in a red velvety dress sitting on a white pillow, giving the camera a toothless smile.

"Is this me?" I asked my grandfather.

He nodded and turned it over. There was my name on the back and the date. I was a year old. The slanted handwriting had been done in a black ink pen that hadn't quite dried before someone touched it. They left behind half of an inky fingerprint. I touched it and felt the softness of a finger. My mother's or father's?

My grandfather said something, and Junior replied in English, "He wants you to know they never forgot about you."

My eyes watered, and I worked hard to maintain my composure, wiping them as quickly as I could. My grandfather noticed and patted my cheek. A few tears fell onto his hands and seeped into his skin, leaving behind a light, tear-shaped stain on his weathered hands.

I sniffled. "So, um, he came here after my grandmother died—and then what?"

Junior asked my grandfather. It took a bit longer for Junior to reply, but when he did, he said, "Señor Gonzalez says that he came to Wichita Falls because that was the last place you were. He figured he might be able to reach out to Social Services from here. It was hard at first because he had to find a job and a place to live . . ."

Junior paused and listened to my grandfather for a moment. "My dad gave him a job and he got a small apartment. After a few months, he tried to find the right people to talk to. He had a lot of trouble since he didn't know English and people kept sending him to see other people," he continued. "He finally found the woman that was on your case, but she wouldn't speak to him unless she had proof that he was your grandfather.

"He then had to petition the Mexican government to send a copy of your father's birth certificate. That took some time.

"Finally, he had the paperwork and the lady told him your uncle lived in California. They tried calling the number they had on file, but it didn't work. They had an address, though. Mr. Gonzalez didn't think that would work either, but he sent a letter anyways because he didn't have any other options."

My grandfather stopped speaking and took a drink of his coffee. I looked at my untouched coffee. A letter appeared on the surface of the brown liquid before falling deeper into the mug and landing in the rickety black mailbox at the end of Dodge's driveway.

After placing his cup down, my grandfather continued.

Junior translated, "He never received a response. He didn't know if the letter arrived, if the address was wrong, your uncle had moved, or if you didn't want to have anything to do with him."

I interrupted, "If I had known, I would have called right away." Junior translated, and my grandfather nodded and spoke again.

"He believes you," Junior said. "He wasn't sure what to do next, so time passed as he tried to figure out his next move. Then one day a skinny, white man showed up here on a motorcycle saying he's your uncle."

"Dodge?"

Junior nodded. "Yeah, I remember that day. We don't get many people like that here and he stood out."

"What happened?" I asked.

Junior's account included both his and my grandfather's words.

"He asked my dad who Señor Gonzalez was, so we went to get him from the kitchen. When Señor Gonzalez came out, your uncle started pointing at him and saying things like 'You don't get to come here asking for her' and all this stuff. My dad tried to explain that Dionisio didn't know English, but your uncle didn't seem to hear."

Sounded like Dodge.

My grandfather patted Junior, so Junior would listen to him again. Junior cocked his head to the side as my grandfather spoke. "He said Dodge was scared."

"Scared?"

My grandfather chuckled after Junior translated.

"He says your uncle was scared he would lose you."

I was already out of Dodge's life by then. According to Billy, Dodge had tried calling me, but I wouldn't pick up.

"After he calmed down, your grandfather took him to a table. I thought your uncle might cry he looked so upset." Junior paused. "I ain't ever seen a man cry but he looked close."

Dodge crying? No way. And yet, I couldn't help but smile slightly.

"Señor Gonzalez brought him something to eat and then sat down. My dad went over, too, and translated. Your uncle said he couldn't get a hold of you."

I did the math. I was living in that small, white duplex in San Pedro, working like a dog for my firm, since I had just started. Anytime I moved, I never gave my number or address out, but somehow, some-way, the Lawless eventually found me. The club had multiple chapters in SoCal and the Southwest, so eventually someone saw me or heard of a girl named Raqi. I couldn't tell if Dodge had lied to my grandfather or if he had been telling the truth.

"He visited over the years," Junior said.

"Dodge came back?"

Junior nodded. "Yeah, not a lot but a couple times a year to see your grandfather. They'd talk if there was someone to translate and we weren't too busy. Sometimes they'd sit and eat, not even speak."

I looked at a table in the corner and saw Dodge, twitchy and smelling like smoke, sitting with my grandfather who exuded calm and pure sweetness. It seemed unreal, the two men sitting together, but I had to admit that Dodge had changed, a little at least, and maybe my grand-father gave him something that I wasn't able to give him the last few years.

"Someone called up here about a week ago to say your uncle had died. Said that you might come here soon," Junior said. "He's come every day to wait for you."

I nodded slowly, taking in all that I had learned. There was so much I wanted to know—like stuff about my dad. What was he like? How did he and my mom meet? My grandfather could potentially give me my past.

I held out my hand to my grandfather, and he took it, smiling.

"Thanks," I said to Junior. He nodded, his cheeks reddening a bit.

"I have so many questions," I said. "About my father, my family. I don't remember much from when I was a kid. I don't know anything." Junior translated, and my grandfather replied.

"He says you should stay with him tonight. He has some photo albums—"

"Really?"

"Yeah, he wants you to see them."

I nodded. "Okay, if he doesn't mind."

Junior chuckled. "Kay usually picks him up an hour after she drops him off."

"Who's Kay?" I asked.

"His neighbor who drives him around," Junior said. "She should be back here in about thirty minutes. I need to go back to work, but I'll grab Señor Gonzalez something to eat."

"Great, thanks."

Junior went to the back. My grandfather and I couldn't speak, but we didn't seem to need to. We took our time studying every freckle, wrinkle, and shape of each other's face, stopping on occasion to smile or take a sip of coffee.

When the man and woman who had been eating in the corner left, they stopped to say hello to my grandfather. He said something excit-edly in Spanish and the man and woman opened their mouths in awe.

"You're his granddaughter?" the woman asked.

I nodded. She reached out and shook my hand. "So nice to meet you." They waved and said a few more things in Spanish to my grandfather before leaving.

Thirty minutes later, Kay arrived promptly in a maroon pinto. I followed my grandfather out the door and saw that the drab gray city of Wichita Falls had turned colorful and bright. An elderly white woman sat in the driver's seat of the pinto. When she saw me, her mouth opened wide and she hastily got out of the car, or as fast as a woman her age can go. She stood well over six feet tall and wore a loose top with flowers that bloomed, withered, died, and bloomed again. Her red pants matched her fingernails, and her white cowboy boots were a reminder that I was in Texas.

"Oh, my! Is this who I think it is?"

"Raquel, Raquel," my grandfather repeated.

She grabbed her own face with her long bony fingers. It was an exaggerated gesture, but I had a feeling that this was exactly the type of woman she was.

"Boy howdy." She wrapped me in a hug. The top of my head barely came to her shoulder. She let go of me and grabbed my hand and shook it hard.

"I'm Kay."

"Raqi."

She let go of my hand and put her hands together, her bright red nail polish glinting in the morning light. "Dionisio"—she said each letter of his name in a Texas drawl—"is so happy you're here. He's been waiting for you!"

I smiled. My grandfather waved his hand at Kay and pointed to the car. He shuffled to the passenger side.

"You'll be following us?" Kay asked.

I nodded and pointed to my bike. "Yep."

Her eyes widened and she smiled mischievously. "A rebel. Vroom-vroom!"

I chuckled. She was funny.

Kay drove slowly on the highway, which didn't make it easy to follow. I wanted to speed so fast until my breath was taken away because that's how I felt. Elated, flying, over the moon, all those cheesy clichés people talk about. I'd met my grandfather.

The thought of Dodge keeping him from me was a bit of a thorn in my side, but there was nothing I could do. The happiness that overwhelmed me when seeing my grandfather for the first time was far more important than any bad feelings I had toward Dodge. All the shit he did throughout my life didn't matter anymore. Besides, he'd finally done something right by giving my grandfather's address to Billy, and Billy had done something right by giving it to me. Dodge could have ignored it, thrown the address away, but he gave me a lifeline to my past, to my future, and I was grateful to him for that.

Eventually, we left the highway, made some turns, and found ourselves slowing down in front of a house. Kay parked her pinto in the street, and I parked my bike behind her. My grandfather got out slowly, as did Kay.

The red brick house with gray siding had a gorgeous green lawn and a large shady oak tree on the right side of the yard. Hedges grew along the front and the vines of a rose bush crept between two white windows.

"Is this your house?" I asked Kay.

"Not mine," said Kay. "Or Dionisio's. He guided me here."

"How do you two communicate?"

She smiled. "He knows a little bit of English, but I'm learning Spanish. Can you believe it? Eighty-nine and learning a new language. Got some tapes at the library."

My grandfather walked slowly over to me without his oxygen tank. He put his arm around my shoulders, resting his hand where my Half Outlaw tattoo hid under my shirt. I put my arm around his waist. I'd just met him, but this felt right, like we'd been close my whole life.

"Why are we here?" I asked.

He squeezed my shoulder and smiled. "Tu casa."

Casa. I knew that word. It meant house. I looked back at the house and then at my grandfather. He poked me in the heart with his free hand and repeated, "Tu casa."

Kay stood next to me with her hands on her hips, squinting against the sun.

"I think this is your family's old house, sweetie," she said.

My grandfather nodded.

The house was everything I could have hoped for in a family home. Though it had been a long time, the house recognized me and welcomed me home with a few memories of the past. My dad stood on the roof hanging Christmas lights while my mother—holding me on her hip—guided him from below. I ran barefoot on chubby toddler legs in the front yard while my dad washed the car, and my mom trimmed the hedges. The garage door opened, and I pedaled out on a tiny tricycle. My parents followed behind taking pictures.

The visions changed. Suddenly, I saw a life that I could have lived, if only my parents hadn't died. I broke my arm when I was nine trying to climb the tree in the front yard. At twelve, I stood in the front lawn posing with my lunchbox and backpack on the first day of school while Mom and Dad took pictures. My dad drove my first car into the driveway and my mom yelled, "Surprise!" when she dropped her hands that covered my eyes. Inside, we watched movies together and ate dinners at the dinner table. I had a lime-green bedroom suite and pictures of friends and family on my walls.

My grandfather squeezed me toward him and the spell broke. I had not grown up here with my parents but had been shipped hundreds of miles away to be raised by my uncle. The only thing I had taken from this childhood home were a handful of red bricks that I had used to create a fortified tower to protect me from more pain and loss.

I'd grown up without the comforts that the house in front of me held, without my parents, my grandparents, sometimes without food and new clothes. That's not to say I didn't have some good childhood memories or a family who didn't love me. Sometimes they loved me too much. They never gave up on trying to win me back even when they weren't quite sure they wanted me in the first place.

I couldn't change my past, and even though a tiny part inside of me would have loved to have had a life with my parents, none of that mattered, because I was here with my grandfather now.

Five minutes later, Kay and my grandfather got in their car, and I kick-started my Ironhead to life. I left my tower of bricks behind in a pile on the ground in front of my childhood home. I didn't need them anymore. Before we turned the corner at the end of the street, I glanced back and saw a thin, white man with black hair and a bushy beard gathering the bricks in his arms to return them to their rightful place.

35

Two weeks later
1990, thirty-one years old

I rapped on the door twice and was about to knock a third time, when Juana answered.

"About time you showed up." She stuck her head out of the door frame and looked up. "You almost missed it."

"Missed what?" I looked over my shoulder but didn't see anything besides a darkening sky empty of a moon.

Juana nodded her head to the side of the house. "Go to the back. I'll be there in a sec, and we'll get started." She closed the door, and I walked the same path I'd taken not that long ago.

For the last two weeks, I'd been spending time with my grandfather. I convinced David to let Lisa manage my workload while I oversaw everything over the phone. I even bought a cell phone just so I wouldn't have to use my grandfather's phone for long-distance calls. Not only was I going to give Lisa a bonus when I returned, but a job too. David agreed that if she could handle my clients, she'd have a job at our firm when she passed the bar in a few months. I had no doubt she would succeed.

Everything seemed to be working out for me. Sure, things hadn't gone down great with the Lawless, and Trevor and I were completely over, but I had my grandfather and a future that was full of hope and promise. That should have been enough, but it wasn't. Even though I could breathe for the first time in twenty-seven years, something was off. I couldn't sleep, food didn't taste right, and I kept catching sight of a skinny, white man with a bushy beard turning a corner just ahead of me. When I caught up, he was never there. Even in the little time we'd known each other, my grandfather knew I wasn't okay. He made me attend Mass, which was an odd experience for someone who had never been to church. I guess he thought God might do something for me, but the whole experience was confusing and boring to say the least. It wasn't until after the service was complete that I realized why he'd brought me there.

He approached an older woman from the congregation, and after they kissed on the cheeks, he said something to her in Spanish. She looked at me and then back at him, an odd look on her face before replying to him in Spanish. My grandfather nodded his head and then shook her hand.

I was so confused by what was going on until the woman turned to me and said, "Your grandfather says you need a cleansing, but I can't do it. You've got the smell of La Loba on you. Like the musty smell of bones and dirt. It's suffocating. Only she can help."

She pursed her lips and walked away.

Later, I used Kay's Spanish dictionary and discovered that 'La Loba,' meant 'female wolf.' The woman had mentioned the smell of bones and dirt. It sounded all-too-eerily like Juana. I had to know more.

After my grandfather told me where I could find Virginia, the woman from church, I rode to her house one morning. She invited me in, and we sat at her dining room table with coffees in hand. I told her what happened with Juana and what Lenora had told me about her. She listened carefully, not once laughing or smirking. It was a surreal story, so I wouldn't have blamed her if she did. When I was done, she set down her coffee.

"Like I thought, La Loba. Some people call her La Huesera, the Bone Woman, but it's all the same. They say she can sing the full skeletons of wolves back to life and that some of these wolves can transform into women."

"But why?" I couldn't believe I had asked such a question. A month ago, I'd have laughed and said "fuck off" to the person who told me such a tale. But something had changed inside me since the ride, and I had an inkling that I needed to take Juana's advice to return and experience what Dodge had experienced.

"Who knows why La Loba sings their souls into existence? It's what she does. Or at least one of the things she can do." She took a sip of her coffee again. "If she takes a liking to you, she may sing *your* soul song."

"What does that mean?"

Virginia smiled. "She helps you see what she sees—your past and the present at the same time. It's one way to heal a soul that's fragmented and lost."

Shit. Was that what had happened to Dodge? Virginia watched me closely.

"How do you know all this?" I asked.

Virginia sat back. "I'm a curandera, a healer. I can heal a tummy ache, help a woman give birth, cleanse babies of mal de ojo, but my abilities are limited. There are those who know how to do so much more." She smiled. "La Loba has taken an interest in you. I suggest you don't leave her waiting."

That's why I was here, at Juana's, doing something almost too ridiculous for me to believe. I trudged to the back of the house. The bones that had covered the ground on my first visit were still missing. No other bones had taken their place.

"Now," Juana said. I jumped at the sound of her voice. She walked in front of me. "We have a new moon in the sky. It'll help you let go of it all."

I shifted between my feet. "What does that even mean? How do I do that?"

Juana smiled. "Relax. I have the perfect song for you."

She stepped forward, and I fought not to step back. Her face was mere inches from mine and her breath smelled like wet dirt on a rainy day. Warm brown eyes bore into my soul, and I suddenly realized that I had misjudged Juana's age. She wasn't in her forties or fifties, not even in her sixties. This woman was ancient, born in a time when trees and creatures ruled the world.

Her index finger aimed for my forehead.

"Will this hurt?" I whispered.

"You can't heal without the pain." She lightly touched the tip of her finger to my forehead, and I was pushed with the force of a giant hand backward into the air. Juana crowed and raised her hands, just as I hit the ground and fell through layers of dirt. My body came out on the other side and slammed onto a slab of stone on the floor of a cave littered in bones.

I didn't have time to worry about the pain in my back because Juana appeared above me, her head haloed by a circular opening at the top of the cave. She raised her hands up and sang. The words were a language I did not know, but the tune was as familiar as my hand. It had been woven into my being, and as Juana sang, I realized she was unraveling a song from within me.

The song was my life, and it started at the exact moment that Ms. Cook left me at Dodge's. Juana sang my past and present life into being but not in any chronological order. I relived the night that Billy called with news of Dodge's death, my anger at Dodge's lifeless body on the toilet, arriving at Dodge's home for the Grieving Ride, fighting with child Jackson after he called me a slur, meeting Juana for the first time, racing at the Ritchie field, meeting Mr. Sand, Bethie getting an abortion, my talk with Charles, building my bike with Dodge, crying with my grandfather, and on it went.

I saw my life in a way that I had not seen it before. I picked up on subtle tones in Billy's voice, the strain in Trevor's face as he tried to appease me, felt the cracking of my heart when I walked away from Dodge forever. Presented in this way, everything started to make sense.

As soon as I saw myself arrive at Juana's home hours before, the song changed, bringing forth a new type of pain. The flesh around my ribs and leg bones disappeared, joints pulled apart, ligaments snapped, and organs melted onto the rock that I laid upon. The pain was too much for screams or cries, so I laid silently as Juana sung me undone in a matter of minutes.

Suddenly, the song slowed down, the tone turned soft and warm, and it reached out to put me back together again. Above Juana, a woman's head appeared over the ledge of the cave. It was the woman I met the first time I visited. She smiled as she watched Juana's song make me new.

Next to her, the head of another woman appeared, and next to her another, and another, until women of all ages, body types, and skin tones circled the cave mouth. Though I couldn't understand Juana's song, I knew it was almost done because I felt the last bits of flesh creeping over my bones. I realized now what Dodge had gone through for me—even when he knew I wasn't coming back. To be complete in the present, you must confront the past.

I blinked, and the women above Juana's head disappeared, replaced by wolves who turned their mouths to the night sky. They ended my soul song with a howl that brought forth the light of day and new beginnings.

Acknowledgments

The idea for *Half Outlaw* came about in 2014 from a conversation with my uncle Donny, who turned to me and said, "I'm an outlaw. You know that makes you half outlaw." The words echoed in my ears, and I knew there was something in that phrase that I had to explore, especially as it related to my Mixed identity.

The Mixed identity is historically complicated. There have been points in colonial history where we were born of violence and rape. And even if our parents had consenting loving unions, at times in the eyes of the government, we were considered illegal. Our existence and experiences were (somewhat) validated with the *Loving v. Virginia* ruling in 1967, but change takes time. We exist in a place that's in between, and we often have to navigate that with families and societies that don't understand what that really means. Perhaps that's why the world pressures us to choose one side or the other rather than lets us exist as we are.

It wasn't until late 2017, a year after one of the most divisive elections in our country, that I wrote the first draft of *Half Outlaw*. I used to say that I wrote this book in anger, but five years later, I can say that I wrote this book in pain. I sought to better understand the dynamics of love, hate, privilege, and power in the family structure, particularly how it relates to Mixed people and especially those who are half white. Through Raqi's story, I discovered some answers I sought, and more importantly, I found some peace.

Mixed people, be we multiethnic, multiracial, or both, are one of the fastest-growing populations, and in my engagement with others like me, I have found we have similar experiences. When I am with another Mixed person, I feel at home. My main wish is that this book resonates with others who identify as Mixed, biracial, multiracial, multiethnic, etc. After reading Raqi's story, I hope they feel seen.

It is likely that you know someone who is Mixed; you may even be related to them now or in the future. Perhaps this story can offer some insight into the experiences of your Mixed friends and family members, and you can take that newfound knowledge and empathy, and build better relationships.

No book has ever been written without the help of others. Since I became an author in 2018, I've been filled with gratitude for the love and support that my parents, brother, and sister have provided me—from word-of-mouth marketing to story feedback and sitting front row at readings and conferences. Thank you Pops, Mom, Erik, and Tiff. I love y'all.

I must acknowledge Dr. Clarissa Pinkola Estés and her book *Women Who Run with the Wolves*. The character named Juana, or the "Bone Woman," was inspired by the book's first chapter which features the retelling of the Southwestern myth of La Loba. Your exploration of the Wild Woman archetype was a source of encouragement as I developed Juana—and in some senses, my main character, Raqi.

Between 2017 and 2018, I received wonderful feedback from a critique group called the Writer's Block. Thank you for being the first set of eyes. To Rachelle Morrison, I am so grateful that I was able to share this story with another multiracial woman and receive helpful notes during the editing process. A big thanks to Lori Bentley-Law for sharing your insightful knowledge of motorcycles and the experience of women riders. With your help, I was able to build Raqi's world more accurately.

Toni Kirkpatrick—I am so lucky that you were assigned to be my editor. Your edits were thoughtful and your connection to the main character's identity made for an editing experience that I never dreamed I would have. To Mary, my literary agent, thank you for helping me to shape the plot, always being upfront with me, and championing Raqi's story. I'm glad you're in my corner.

Thanks to my uncle Donny for calling me "half outlaw." It inspired a story that I needed to tell.

To my core and extended family: Our family is a complex one, as most families are, and I have not always understood you or liked your decisions, words, or actions. Sometimes these dynamics have angered, saddened, and ashamed me, but I cannot deny that I have always felt immensely loved and supported by you in all that I do. I hope you read this story and understand that I love you, too.

And lastly, to the little Mixed brown girl that built a brick tower around herself to feel in control and protect her soul, heart, and mind, rest easy knowing that I've taken the tower apart brick-by-brick and it sits in a pile somewhere far in the past.